For Love of a Vampire

by
Eileen Sheehan

This book is a work of fiction. Characters, names, places and incidents are either the product of the author's imagination or are used fictitiously, and any resemblance to any actual persons, living or dead, events, or locales is entirely coincidental.

This book is dedicated to all you incurable romantics
who enjoy mixing fantasy with reality.

CHAPTER ONE

"Jane Wells! Where are you?"

I covered my ears with my hands. The old crone's screeching was enough to make me want to rip them from my head. Mildred Elliot's squalling voice grated on my nerves like nails against a blackboard. I'd told her so on more than one frustrated occasion. It had little impact on the old woman, other than reinforcing her viewpoint that I was a bit "odd in the head". Mildred hadn't a clue what a blackboard was. They weren't invented yet. That came years later, around the turn of the nineteenth century, when a headmaster in Scotland named James Pilans got it into his head to frame a piece of slate for the school's use. The screeching old crone I was fervently dodging happened to be located in England in the year seventeen-forty-five.

I didn't belong in that time or place. I was a covert transient from the twenty-first century. I'd traveled back in time for one purpose only. To change the future for the one I loved.

I was never very good at planning things out. I'm more of a grab the seat of my pants and go kind of girl. Patience has also never been one of my strongest virtues. Historically, this grab and go habit always worked for me. Somehow, I managed to achieve my goals. This time I wasn't so sure. Had I jumped the gun without adequate preparation?

I'd arrived outside the village of Colchester, England almost seven weeks earlier. The first thing I did was steal what had to be the scratchiest, most abrasive bodice, skirt, and gown in existence. I'm not a thief by nature. It's just that, since I'd jumped back in time without considering what I was going to wear I needed to do something. Jeans, a tee shirt, and

1

a hoodie weren't the proper attire for someone trying to blend in. I spotted the apparel drying on a bush behind a little farm cottage not far from the cave where I'd teleported into the eighteenth century and grabbed what I could. As luck would have it, the owner and I were close in size. Over time, I managed to acquire a few more necessities for my needs.

"Jane!" the old crone screamed out so loud I was sure she was going to go hoarse, "Where are you, gal? The washing will not tend to itself!"

I held my breath as I waited for her to finish her bellowing.

"Fie... the wench will be the death of me," she muttered.

I felt a little guilty about referring to Mildred Gould to an old crone, even if she did look the part with her piercing black eyes and hawk-like, wart infested nose. If she was in the twentieth century she could have easily gotten the part of the Wicked Witch of the West in the Wizard of Oz film. The makeup department wouldn't have had to do a thing, except paint her green. She'd shown me a bit of kindness and deserved a little more consideration and compassion from me. After all, there were no plastic surgeons around to help the poor woman out.

Mildred and her oversized husband, Carl, owned a busy little inn on the edge of town on the main road of travel. They were not a bad sort, as persons of the times went. They lived a life comfortable enough to keep them above the pits of poverty, but not sufficient enough for them to rub elbows with the upper class in any way other than catering to their needs on the occasions a lord or lady saw fit to patronize their little establishment. The innkeepers belonged to a branch of society destined to be labeled the 'middle class.'

Mildred was good enough to take me in and give me a roof over my head, a uniform, and food. I was fed a decent portion of gruel in the morning to start my day. In the evening, I was provided with a sparse portion of hard crusted bread with the tiniest bit of butter, bland potatoes boiled in oxtail broth with an occasional piece of meat stuck to them, and weak ale. In exchange for these I worked, and worked, and worked some more. I was left with about two shillings at the end of the month, when all was said and done. I continually had to remind myself that in a time when generosity and kindness were not at optimum -with no governmental social services to fall back on- I was lucky to have stumbled upon the inn almost immediately after arriving. Talk about serendipity! As unprepared as I was for survival, I might have been forced to go into a workhouse.

So, why was I hiding from good old Mildred?

I'd stolen again.

I'd just finished hiding a crisp white falling band and a pair of beautifully embroidered mules amongst my other stolen goods and I needed time to compose myself.

I'd made good use of time, since teleporting from the future, to acclimate to their ways and culture. I spent every waking moment studying the language, style of dress, politics, mode of living, et cetera. Working at an inn located on a heavily traveled road gave me the opportunity to witness a variety of life. I saw travelers from varied social stations enter and stay in the humble place of food and rest.

I was grateful for the linguistic lessons I took to enhance my acting skills. I was able to pick up the dialect of both the tavern workers and the elite who occasionally passed through. Since I still hadn't worked out how I was going to pull off my mission, I needed to be prepared to pass as a person of whatever social standing proved beneficial for me to be successful. Feeling confident in the versatility of my linguistic skills, it was time to move on to the next stage of my mission. I had to do what I could to change the course of history for Duncan. This was my one and only chance. If I was unsuccessful, he would be doomed to a life he despised... a life that saddened him to the core... the life of a vampire.

****

I first met Duncan Colliers at the neighborhood bar located just below my apartment in Queens. I hooked up with my friends, Doug, Chuck, and Linda, at Patty's Pub every Thursday night for our ritual of a few drinks and a few games of billiards. It was ten thirty and I was leaning against the wall and casually rolling a cue stick between my palms while I waited for my turn at the table. I was in-between acting jobs, but my friends had to work the next day. We were just about to call it a night when I felt Duncan enter. His presence was so strong and commanding, there was no way I couldn't feel it. I don't know if everyone felt him; probably not, but since I'm a little bit psychic and extremely sensitive there was no getting his arrival past me.

Just as I knew there was something uniquely different about him, he recognized a difference in me. He said I stood out from the rest of the room and was like a beacon of light in the gloom of his existence. Who knew such a corny comment could send shivers of delight up and down my spine like it did? I watched him out of the corner of my eye while my friends and I finished the game and said our good-byes. I pretended to leave with my friends. After we parted ways, I waited in the foyer of my building until I was sure they wouldn't see me before heading back into the bar. I brazenly sat on the stool next to him. I knew the bartender, Julie, so it was easy to find an excuse to justify my presence. He never let on, but I'm pretty sure he saw through my charade.

I didn't have to wait long before he struck up a conversation with me. We talked until Julie made last call. He asked me to meet him the following night. I agreed. The next night he asked me to meet him the night after that. I agreed again. Then the following night we agreed to get together the next night... and so on.

Never once did he mention he was a vampire.

Never once did I see signs of him being a vampire.

Never once would I have even considered he would be a vampire.

First of all, I didn't believe vampires really existed. Secondly, from what I'd read in books and seen in films, vampires were quite grotesque with long nails, red lips, and piercing yellow eyes. Duncan's hands were extremely well manicured, his lips were normal in color, his eyes were a delicious sea foam blue and his hair was the color of sun kissed wheat. He stood half a foot taller than my five-foot-five inches and moved with the grace, beauty, and self-confidence that radiated wealth and good breeding. Everything about him spoke of 'rich kid from the right side of the European tracks'; nothing more.

We'd been together for a few months before I learned of his true nature. It wasn't as if he'd intended to show me. He confessed sometime later that he'd feared showing me his true self because he worried I'd walk away if he did. That was a natural fear. I'd probably feel the same if the situation was reversed. In fact, it was in a way. He may have been keeping his vampire identity a secret from me, but I was doing pretty much the same thing. Not that I was a vampire; because I wasn't. I was a psychic, and a sensitive who dabbled in magic; real magic, not that of an illusionist. Could I have been called a witch? I wouldn't have called myself that. I practiced no rituals and belonged to no covens. I simply had abilities to feel and sense things. I occasionally saw and spoke to spirits -although the ability wasn't something I had a lot of control over- and I possessed a strong curiosity and interest in alchemy.

One night, after visiting my favorite occult book store, I was followed by a small group of freaky looking characters. There were five or six of them. From what I could tell, they were all boys, but I could be wrong. They wore their hair in a green, orange, and blue punk spike. I assumed it was some sort of gang symbol; like them all having the same tattoo or something. They sported leather studded jackets and body piercings of indescribable locations and amounts. This was in stark contrast to my designer jeans, navy wool pee-coat with a matching beret -that was pinned just right on my fashionably braided long, honey blonde hair-, pear studded earrings, and Movado watch. I was wearing green and tan pumps and carried a green and tan Liz Claiborne crossover bag to match. They actually had the audacity to taunt me for being weird because I'd bought a few things at a spooky occult store. Imagine that? I did my best to ignore them while I picked up my pace. Unfortunately, they were itching for a confrontation. Since I'd never considered myself a fighter or the least bit brave, I did the only thing I could think to do.

I ran.

Right into a dead end alley.

Before I knew what was happening, I was on the ground with those punks ransacking my Liz Claiborne shoulder bag, pulling at the pockets of my pee-coat, and tossing the contents of my shopping bag back and forth between each other. In my struggles to be free and salvage what I could, I'd managed to obtain a few cuts and bruises. Unfortunately, due to poor blood coagulation, I bled a lot more than one would have expected wounds of that nature to bleed. Needless to say, even though my wounds weren't really bad, my type "A positive" blood was all over the place.

What happened next I can only say was so farfetched, had I not known better, I would have thought I was dreaming. There was a loud swooshing sound. I heard it clearly above the cackling of the haughty attackers as they reveled in their torment of me. Either they didn't hear it or they just didn't care because they kept on doing their utmost best to rob me of all I had to offer; my dignity included. A loud anguished cry brought the entire scene to a standstill while everyone focused on the source. As my assailants slowly backed away from me, I witnessed a sight that burned so deep in my memory I'm sure I'll carry it with me forever. Two vampires stood over me. Their mouths dripped with the blood of several of my tormentors who now lay in a heap on the ground nearby.

It's strange what goes on in one's mind when facing

death. I'd always been told my life would flash before my eyes chronologically. That didn't happen. Perhaps it was because in some crazy way I didn't think what happened to my attackers would happen to me or perhaps it was because I'd been misinformed. I couldn't say. There was certainly no walking down memory lane. Instead of reviewing my almost nineteen years of life, I studied the faces of my soon to be slaughterers. I stared deep into their eyes, while noticing the kaleidoscope glow that shot light from their pupils like one of those mini flashlights on key chains. I felt their rage permeate my surroundings. One vampire was male and one female, but both radiated equally angry power. Had I not seen them and only been privy to their energy, I would have been hard pressed to decipher gender.

Their faces were distorted. It wasn't just their anger causing it. Their bones were... how do I put it? Off. They looked animalistic. These were like the faces you'd expect to see on the silver screen. Exactly!

I looked beyond the distorted bone structure of the female and decided she was a beautiful woman when she was in human state. She must have felt my energy piercing through her vampire veil because she stopped advancing and stared at me, as if bewildered.

The male, on the other hand, kept on coming. I could smell his foul breath as he closed in on me. His halitosis was so horrific, I gasped for air. I cringed at the long, pointed nails on his hands when he reached to grab my shoulders. They resembled claws. Even while he was lifting me effortlessly to my feet, I couldn't help confirming that the nails matched the vampire stories as well. It was hard to tell how his lips compared - since they were dripping of blood and were overshadowed by elongated fang-like teeth at the moment-, but his eyes actually flashed some sort of red spark from them. It wasn't quite like a strobe light, but more like a neon light gone bad.

As crazy as it sounds, I'd yet to fear for my life.

My feet were several inches off the ground when I

heard, as well as felt, the swoosh of someone else arriving. It was an energy I recognized, but I couldn't place it in my chaotic state. I twisted my head as best I could to look for the familiar. Through the entire ordeal, I'd stayed relatively numb. Now, I was finally shocked! There, only feet away from me, stood Duncan... my Duncan... or a version of him, anyway. His face was not as distorted in the animalistic manner as my captors, but it certainly wasn't the handsome face I'd made love to over the last few months. Long canines projected from his beautiful set of brilliant white choppers. His normally rosy cheeks were sunken and hollow. His sea foam blue eyes were so dark they could have been mistaken for black.

I gasped -more with surprise than with fear- while I watched him tear the heads off my assailants with rapid speed and incredible ease. It brought to mind my brother's slaughter of my dolls when we were kids.

I fell to the ground along with my headless attacker and quickly pried myself from its lifeless vice grip. I stayed breathless and motionless while I watched Duncan look around with disgust before he scooped me into his arms. He half-ran, half-flew across roof tops to my apartment building, with me in his arms as if I weighed no more than a feather. He quickly found the doorway from the roof to the stair well and continued until he deposited me on my living room sofa. Without a word, or allowing time for me to gather my wits to comprehend the reality of what was happening, he disappeared.

For whatever reason –probably shock- I decided to play Scarlet O'Hara and deal with what happened another day. I immediately went to bed. Believe it or not, I slept like a baby that night. One would have never guessed I'd been through such an ordeal. It wasn't until the following morning, when I turned on the news and saw the report of the dead bodies of the punks who'd tried to mug me, that reality struck and I collapsed from the trauma of it all.

CHAPTER TWO

I came to my senses by evening and called Duncan's cell phone. No answer. So, I tried his house phone. Again, no answer. This went on for days. Thinking me disgusted and frightened by his true identity, he'd gone into hiding. It took almost two weeks for him to resurface.

I used this time of separation from my lover to study and research as much as I could about vampires. I ran across a statement that stuck in my head and just kept playing over and over. God makes and loves all things and all creatures. It's man who decides what's evil and what's not. It was so true. Sure, the vampires that attacked me and my group of muggers were bad, but so were the muggers. There are good and bad in all species. I knew in my heart of hearts that Duncan was good. If the truth was to be known; even if he was bad, it was too late. I'd already fallen in love with him.

I felt Duncan standing in the hall before he gathered the courage up to tap quietly on my door. He'd expected me to scream and refuse to open the door. Instead I'd surprised him with my wild abandoned welcome. I swung the door open and flew into his arms; kissing him wildly. In turn, he surprised me by trembling from the sheer joy of my acceptance of him. It was a powerful reunion.

We spent the next few days making love and baring the deepest secrets about ourselves. I learned Duncan was turned just days before his wedding was to take place in the year seventeen-forty-five. He'd never encountered supernatural creatures such as vampires, so he never thought to take heed of the stories or precautions while traveling certain roads alone at night. There were rumors that Lady Vivian Everhoust -the season's most eligible debutant who was madly in love with

Lord Duncan and made no secret of it- dabbled in witchcraft. When she realized Lord Duncan planned on going through with the union with another woman, she assured him that his black heart would be devoured by one even blacker and he would live eternity in darkness and remorse. Duncan considered her words the idle threat of a thwarted woman and paid it very little mind.

He never saw it coming.

After his change, he faked his death and moved away. He confessed that, although he spent his time traveling and experiencing the world, the sadness of leaving that he carried with him over the centuries had, little by little, chiseled away at his heart. Lady Vivian had gotten her revenge.

He and his future bride were sweethearts since childhood. The marriage bands were read early in their life and were to be fulfilled when she turned eighteen and Duncan was twenty-five. He told me the sadness only began to lift when he met me. He couldn't or wouldn't tell me why; just that when he met me, he found hope for his future. What type of hope? He didn't say. Just hope.

I believed him.

I shared my own secrets. I told how I'd kept my abilities close to my chest for fear of being ostracized by my fellow man. Even though times were progressing, I still found myself uncomfortable admitting my true nature. Look what happened on the street with those punks simply because I'd made a purchase at an occult shop. Surely that was sufficient evidence to support my hesitancy.

Duncan agreed.

Intrigued by my abilities and skills, Duncan pressed as much information from me as he could. He'd met plenty of people with my "talents" over the centuries and was certain he could find someone to help me perfect them. It was such a twist to have support for my skills and actual encouragement to use and enhance them. I hadn't really thought about working with them -nor was it really important to me to do so- but, if learning more about the arts of alchemy was part of the being with Duncan package, then I was willing to give it a shot.

He introduced me to an ancient witch named Isabelle. When I say ancient, I really do mean ancient. Isabelle was almost as old as Duncan; yet, she looked not a day over forty. How did she accomplish this? That was part of my lesson plan.

I could hardly wait.

Once I'd moved through the jealousy of discovering that Isabelle and Duncan were once an item, I was able to relax and actually enjoy her company, tutelage, and eventual friendship. She confided that I was the first person Duncan ever asked her to instruct. It pleased her. I pleased her. Apparently, she didn't harbor my insecurities. I couldn't detect a jealous bone in her body from the moment we met.

Her lack of jealousy bothered me enough to spend longer than usual in front of a mirror scrutinizing my looks. Isabelle had porcelain skin, an oval face with a Vivian Leigh chin, dark dancing eyes, and thick black hair that traveled down her back like a sensual waterfall. We couldn't have been more opposite. Whenever my jealous monster raised his ugly head and insecurities reigned supreme, I reminded myself that without her magic she'd be a hag; or a skeleton, since she would have been long dead by now.

As the wisdom of the ages poured forth from my mentor, our friendship grew naturally. It soon became clear that we had a lot more than Duncan in common. Isabelle was impressed with the education I'd given myself. It may have been limited, but it was thorough. She used this education as a platform to build upon. It wasn't long before I was casting spells and transforming materials.

It took the better part of a year of intense study for Isabelle to announce she felt I was ready to learn to teleport. We started small at first. I'd move a pencil or a book from one side of the room to the other. Eventually I graduated to bigger items and greater distances.

During this time, I moved in with Duncan and gave up the waitress job I worked to support myself while I pursued a career in acting. This allowed me to focus completely on my studies with Isabelle. It was Isabelle's idea, but Duncan agreed whole-heartedly. He took delight in watching me develop from a bud to a flower. It was a corny phrase, I know, but I liked it.

Actually, finding out his true age and era of birth did wonders for us both. It allowed us to relax with each other. Duncan was no longer forced to monitor his style of speech and often slipped back into an antiquated pattern of speaking. For the first time in years, he was able to be himself; with no fear of judgment or chaos. With a natural curiosity and desire to perfect my dialect for my future career in acting, I delighted at every opportunity to mimic him and query him on words and their meanings. We were an ideal couple. He felt it, I felt it, and much to my surprise and delight, Isabelle voiced it.

Now that I was learning from Isabelle, the fear of Duncan outliving me no longer cast a shadow on our relationship. What did, was his sadness for being a creature of the night. Being a sensitive can be difficult at times. Some days I could hardly bear the sorrow that I picked up from him. It was almost crippling. I discussed this with Isabelle and we came up with a solution. Isabelle would anchor me to the present while I went back in time and stopped Duncan from being turned into a vampire. Then, I would bring him back to the future with me where Isabelle would work her magic on him to prevent him from aging. After which, we would live happily ever after.

What a great idea!

We approached Duncan with our great idea. He surprised me by opposing it. Apparently, he was far more informed on the rewards, perils, and pitfalls of magic than we gave him credit for. He was fully aware of the risk both Isabelle and I were taking by sending me back in time. He would have no part of it.

"It warms my heart that you love me enough to want to do this for me," he said to us both, "but I cannot let you go through with it." He took Isabelle's hands in his. "It is my understanding that you must do more than simply anchor Jane. She is not yet developed enough to do this on her own. You will have to use much of your own magic in order to make this happen. I am correct with this, am I not?"

Isabelle looked away while I gasped. This was a bit of information she'd neglected to share with me.

"Is this true?" I asked quietly.

"Yes, it is," she whispered, "but I have no doubt you will be able to succeed, dear Jane. It is worth the risk to me." She looked Duncan in the eyes, "I have loved you for so long, but my love has never given you the joy I see in your eyes and feel in your heart whenever you are near Jane. If we can find a way to remove this blackness that burdens your heart and make you whole again to live and love, I want to try. To see you happy... truly happy... would bring me the greatest pleasure. If you ever cared for me, you won't deny me this."

"What will happen to you? What risk are we talking about?" I demanded, more than asked.

It was all fine and dandy that Isabelle chose this moment to act out some scene of a romance novel and sacrifice herself for her love, but if it meant her life... well, I wasn't that selfless. I'd grown attached and a little dependent on Isabelle as a friend and a tutor. I wasn't all that eager to give her up.

"She risks losing her magic," Duncan stated flatly. His eyes never left Isabelle's.

"I won't," Isabelle protested.

"How can you be so sure?" I interjected. "If you lose your magic, what happens then?"

I already knew the answer, but I still needed to hear someone say it. It was Duncan who did the honors.

"She turns to dust," he said flatly.

"But, it's your era. You were born then, how could you turn to dust?" I asked with confusion. "Is your magic at risk if you help me from here?" I demanded, "Be truthful."

She nodded slowly.

"I did not simply travel through time to get here. I used magic to live through time. Because of this, my cells have matured and would remember that I should be long dead if the magic that keeps them alive leaves me," she said sadly. "It would be risky for me to teleport back to the time when I was born. My cells might reject the magic of the future. I would have to help you from here. If you run into trouble and I have to stretch across time with my magic, it is possible I would have to use too much of it without being able to replenish it."

"In which case she would turn to dust," Duncan interjected.

"Oh, hell no!" I bellowed. "Duncan, I love you. You know I do. I feel really bad about your sorrow about being a vampire. I want to help you. I do. But... I can't risk killing Isabelle in order to do it."

"Nor can I," he stated passionately.

For a brief moment I forgot I'd worked through my jealousy over those two having been a onetime couple as I watched them look into each other's eyes and basically reminisce of days gone by. My psychic abilities were working overtime. I was able to witness what they shared in my mind's eye. They'd been together in an era far more romantic than the times we lived in now. The romance and chivalry was wonderful. I felt cheated. It seemed so unfair that I'd never be privy to experiencing a life of privilege and romance of this magnitude.

I struggled to subdue the green-eyed monster that threatened to creep up on me. Duncan loved me body and soul. There was no mistaking it. He had a history with Isabelle. He loved her, true, but in a way far different than he loved me. She was no threat. Furthermore, she was my friend. For what seemed like the hundredth time, I mentally chastised myself for my insecurities.

"Is that the only danger?" I blurted out, forcing them to return to the here and now".

"No," Isabelle sighed. "There is more. When you work

against nature and time, like we desire to do, there is always danger."

"Tell me," I said as steadily as I could.

"She did tell you there's a chance you could get stuck there, did she not?" Duncan asked.

CHAPTER THREE

Isabelle's warnings were significant, but not enough to change my mind; even if Duncan was able to change hers. It took some time before Duncan managed to convince Isabelle that our plan was a bad idea. By the time he did, I'd already learned enough to do it on my own, if need be.

Once my mind was made up, I took the time to study enough on the sly until I was able to work a spell to teleport myself through time without risking Isabelle by using her as my anchor. When no one suspected what I was up to, I did just that.

I'd cast a spell to travel back in time far enough in advance of the attack on Duncan to allow time to find him, meet him, gain his trust, and then return to the future with him before the fateful attack could take place. I was to return no later than the day before the attack. I hadn't the skills to elongate my visit. If we missed the opening of the portal of time, I wasn't sure I'd be able to work a new spell while in the past. If I'd been teleporting to the future, I wouldn't have been as concerned. Going back several centuries before my birth put a different slant on things.

Now, here I was, crouched behind an out building hiding from screeching Mildred while I looked for a way to sneak off with my little trunk of mainstays and the coin I stole from the recesses of a traveling gentry's receptacle. I hadn't taken all he had and, since I'd heard no mention of it, I doubted he discovered its absence before returning home and unpacking. I felt bad for the servants who unpacked him. Surely they would get the blame, but what was I to do? I couldn't function without it. I also had in my possession a small traveler's trunk with a new kirtle, a gown of velvet, a gown of silk, a spare chemise, traveler's shoes, house shoes, a cape, and other accessories. I'd snuck each article, bit by bit, from rooms of gentry staying at the inn over my weeks of working there. I wasn't sure what role the gentry I'd stolen from played in society, but the embroidered fabric seemed of quality velvet, wool, silk, and linen and the cut fashionable enough for me to believe them of a reasonable status.

I managed to hide the little traveler's trunk in the recesses of the older, less used stable under an enormous pile of hay until things cooled down. The last thing I needed was to be attached to theft. Prison wasn't on my agenda.

Oh, Duncan, my love. The things I do for you!

I needed to leave, but I also needed to time it just right. I could feel Duncan's energy all around me. The time was close for me to connect with him. I could feel it. I just couldn't hone in on it.

If only Mildred would stop her screeching and let me think. There was no hope for that. I heaved a sigh and hoisted myself from the squatting position I'd curled up in behind a coop. My feet felt like lead as I forced myself to return to duties I certainly wouldn't miss when I was finally free of them. At least I would be left alone to think while doing the laundry.

Their methods of washing and hygiene had a lot to be desired. The caustic soaps and boiling water practically tore the flesh from my slender fingers. A messenger notified Mildred of a small party of aristocracy that would be stopping for the night. The inn was in a frenzy preparing for the guests. I had no idea who they were, but they were important enough to warrant the cleanest sheets in the county and a meal of roast chicken, rosemary potatoes, apple pie and Brussel sprouts, while the rest of the guests made due with mutton stew. When I heard Carl ordering a barrel of his finest wine to be brought up from the cellars, my curiosity was peaked.

My duties didn't include serving the guests. This made it necessary for me to be creative in finding ways to monitor them. Normally, I would stay in the shadows and study their language and mannerisms. I'd managed to find a spot that only Kitty, the scullery maid, knew about. There were times when she'd squeeze in next to me, but most of the time she was too busy making sure food didn't burn or performing one of the grueling tasks the cook forced upon her. During these times, Mildred and Carl were so busy skittering around to make sure their guests were fat and happy, my whereabouts was never a curiosity.

The party was rather large for the little inn, but somehow Mildred and Carl found rooms to accommodate them. This resulted in extra chores and duties for the staff, me included. I was so busy making up rooms that I completely missed the pomp and circumstance when the first of the party arrived. I was informed by other members of staff that there were five men and two women of almost royal status. Apparently, they were to be guests at the inn for an anticipated few days while they awaited the arrival of the Earl of Winterspring and yet another small party, who was delayed in London. Once he caught up with them, they would travel on to his estate.

It was not uncommon for guests to await the lord of a manor in his home, but this particular party was anticipating the arrival of a young woman who was promised in marriage to the earl's son. They had not seen each other in months, during which time the earl renovated one wing of the particular property of their destination as a gift to his son's bride-to-be. He wanted to be by her side when first she laid eyes upon her future home.

Finally, after weeks of toil and monotony, I was privy to the chivalrous romanticism I attributed to these historic times; among the fortunate at least. I couldn't help being a little envious of this bride-to-be when I considered the overtures taken to make her feel at home and happy in her new family. I couldn't imagine a father of my time going through such a process to please his daughter-in-law.

The extra work load thrust upon me was taking its toll. I was eager for the earl to arrive and whisk his party of elite away. He was expected to arrive at any time and it was none too soon for me. I was exhausted. I doubted there was one inch of my body that didn't ache right down to the marrow of my bones. People were less rushed in that day and time, but the lower class toiled and labored significantly more than someone of the twentieth-century. I wasn't prepared for it; mentally or physically.

I was at the washing station tending to the never ending pile of linens when I heard the commotion coming from the kitchen. Cook was in an uproar. When the earl sent his man ahead to notify the inn of his pending arrival, he'd actually put in a menu request. From what I'd witnessed during my time there, special requests for dinner were only granted to the elite. It was one thing for Cook to kill a chicken or two, but an absolute different thing altogether for cook to send servants wily-nilly to market in search of ingredients rarely kept in the inn's humble kitchen. Whoever the earl was, he was an important man in these parts. I decided it was time to find out a little more about him. Perhaps he could be a lead to finding Duncan.

"Ho there," I called to the buxom tavern maid, Sally, as she waddled past toward the milk house, "I bid you what happens?"

"No time to chat, luv. His lordship is nearly here," she said with a huff.

"What lordship?" I called out as I watched her waddle by at a speed that was far too quick to be normal for a larger than average body that was proportioned as awkwardly as hers was.

Sally stopped for a moment and stared at me, as if seeing me for the first time. Her oversized green eyes almost bulged away from her round, rosy cheeked face as the disbelief of what I was implying hit her.

"Truly, you know not of the earl?" she asked incredulously.

"None," I said as I shook my head.

"How can that be? Where be you from?" She asked as she spied me closely.

My explanation to Mildred upon my arrival was scant and brief, yet believable. It was the story that Isabelle and I started to work on when we conjured up the idea of my traveling back in time. Unfortunately, once Duncan swayed Isabelle's thoughts on the matter, the storyline went unfinished and I'd had to improvise. Even so, telling Mildred that I was of foreign elite accounted for my odd pattern of speech. Claiming that my family's ship perished at sea explained why I was left to find my own way. I had no family in England and all of my money was washed away with the ship. It was agreed between us that I would work for my keep while I sent word to my homeland of my tragedy and awaited rescue. Now that sufficient time had passed, it was not only Mildred who was expecting a fine carriage to pull up and whisk me away like some fairy princess. It appeared the staff was starting to question my story as well.

It was definitely time to leave.

"You know I come not from here. Why would I know this earl?" I snapped, hoping my aggression would halt any further questioning from her.

There was a long moment of deafening silence between us. My nerves jumped to attention as the adrenaline needed to flee one's pursuer surfaced. I felt trapped. What would I do if the tavern maid saw through me? If my memory served me correctly, they were still performing witch hunts. If anyone caught wind that I'd traveled from the future -let alone that I knew a certain amount of alchemy- they'd hang me for sure... or worse; burn me. I could feel the bile creeping up my esophagus from my wrenching stomach. I swallowed it down; while doing my best to look calm, cool, and oh so tough.

It worked!

"'His lordship," she said, emphasizing her words dramatically, "is only the richest man in these parts. He owns half the county side."

I knew I was pressing my luck on several accounts. One, was that, because of Sally's lowly station, it was probable she wouldn't be able to answer me. Two, was because I was risking showing just a little too much interest in the richest man in the county.

I asked anyway, "Truly? Pray does he know the Earl of Winterspring?"

The look of disdain she slapped at me was enough to knock me over. Had I not been holding onto a sheet I'd just draped over the line, I very well might have sat down on the muddy ground.

"You jest, surely," she screeched incredulously.

I shook my head.

"Ach!" she eked out as she waved her hand in the air as if to dismiss me and started toward the milk house.

"Pray, tell me!" I called after her.

As foolish as I felt I just couldn't give up.

"He is the Earl of Winterspring," she howled over her shoulder, never giving me a second look.

With that, I did sit down.

Duncan's father was coming! What should I do? I wasn't ready. I still had no plan. It wouldn't do for him to find me scrubbing laundry at an inn. From all I'd learned about the classes of eighteenth century England, I'd be lucky to get him to spit in my direction, let alone let me get close enough to do what needed to be done.

"Why are you dawdling about, gal?" Mildred wailed from the back door of the tavern. "There is no time for day dreaming'. The earl is to arrive any minute now. Come on, get cracking. I need you inside to help out."

"I am doing my best, mum," I called out. "Twill only take a bit longer."

"See that it does," Mildred grumbled.

She watched me briefly with her hands on her hips, as if to make it a point she was in no mood for slackers, and then moved back into the inn. I plunged back into the chore of dealing with boiling lye water.

The romantic setting I'd witnessed while watching Duncan and Isabelle reminisce was nowhere to be found in the Colchester I was experiencing. The nobility and gentry were a minority. The chores I drudged through each day were only a fraction of the chores the average resident did on a daily basis just for survival. I learned that most of the income in the small villages in the county went to pay taxes and the crops available to the villagers were barely enough to sustain them. It was a sad, sad scene. If UNICEF and the Peace Corps were around, they'd be kept busy.

CHAPTER FOUR

I thought of Duncan. I was actually going to meet him... or the him he was... is... The situation was complicated, even for me.

Duncan. I wondered what he was doing in the future. Was he searching for me? Had he even noticed I was gone? One of the things I learned from Isabelle was that there is no such thing as linear time. Man fabricated it to support the reality he chose to experience when he was placed on the planet. Many creatures other than men -such as vampires- are aware of this to some extent and can in many ways bend time. This meant that, if a person knew the way to break the barriers that split the illusion of time into linear sectors, it was possible to go back and forth with only a matter of seconds being realized by those you left behind. Therefore, even though my reality was experiencing weeks of my absence from the twenty first century, those I left behind only experienced a few minutes of time; a day or two at the most. If my calculations were correct, I would be in the future with a human Duncan at my side before anyone noticed I'd left.

I questioned both Isabelle and Duncan on why, if a vampire was able to manipulate time, Duncan simply didn't return and change the outcome of his encounter with the vampire that attacked him. Or, better yet, change his day so the encounter never occurred.

"Because, my dear Jane," Isabelle replied patiently, "Duncan is not magical and that is the time in which he was born. If he returned, he would have no knowledge of what is to occur in the future. He would simply fall into life and play it out all over again."

"Is that why you can't return with me?" I asked.

"Not exactly," she replied, "That is also my era. I was actually born but a few years prior to Duncan's encounter with the vampire. Unfortunately, my magic would disappear if I returned fully back to my true time of birth. I would retain the knowledge and wisdom, but not the ability. Duncan was a vampire for several decades before I reached magical maturity. This is also why my cells wouldn't be able to retain the magic that keeps me alive. I didn't even know what magic was then."

"What about me? I wasn't even born then. What happens to my magic if I go back in time?" I asked with concern. I'd only just started to tap into the edges of what I knew I was capable of doing with magic. I had no desire to have those skills stripped from me.

"Nothing will happen to you because it was not your time of birth," she explained. "If I chose to go back to Roman times, I would be fine because it was not my time of birth. It must be your time of birth in the body you presently occupy for this to occur. Otherwise, you will remain the same. This... today... is your true era. Because of this, you will retain the knowledge of all time recorded up until this moment. You are the only one who can return to assist our dear Duncan... the only one."

"If this is true, then I don't understand why there would be a risk for me to go back," I stated.

"The risk is that you could get stuck, my love," Duncan said. "What would happen if you were not successful in meeting me and swaying my future? What if your journey drew too heavily on Isabelle's magic and she perished? What if I was still turned vampire after all your efforts and something happened to prevent you reaching the portal in time to return to me? These are all possibilities and risks I am not willing to take."

"Okay. For argument's sake," I said firmly as I looked directly at Isabelle, "let's say I didn't pull on your magic and you lived," then I turned to Duncan and continued, "and I succeed in preventing you from becoming a vampire, but I didn't make it to the portal on time and got stuck." I looked back at Isabelle, "Couldn't you just work your magic and keep me alive?"

Isabelle shook her head slowly.

"If it were only so easy, my child. Sadly, I could not," she said softly.

"Why?" I demanded.

"I cannot keep someone alive who is yet to be born for an extended period of time," she sighed, "You will be on borrowed time provided by magic when you enter the past. If you do not make it to the portal when it is time, you will cease to exist shortly thereafter. Everything I have learned tells me such."

"There's no way for me to stay alive?" I asked with concern. I wanted to help Duncan with all my heart, but the information being shared with me was chipping at my confidence.

"You could become a vampire," Duncan said with a sarcastic chuckle.

Although I barely comprehended the complexity of it all, and my confidence was waivered just a smidgeon, I was still determined to give it a try. I had to try; for Duncan's sake, if not my own. His sadness could be overwhelming for an empath.

My musings were brought to an abrupt halt at the sound of trotting horses on the inn's cobblestone drive. I dropped the sheet I'd been washing back into the water and rushed to the side of the building to get a look at the new arrivals.

I saw eight horses. All were average size and various shades of brown, except for one. It not only stood out from the rest with its muscular mass and its dapple grey coloring, but its saddle and bridle indicated its rider was of position and power.

Duncan!

I looked at the man astride the majestic beast and my heart fell to my knees in disappointment. It was not my Duncan. That man leading this small group of men was definitely related to Duncan, but much older. If memory served me, the wheat colored locks, high ruddy cheekbones, and broad shoulders of the man I was looking at was Duncan's father. He truly did resemble the small portrait Duncan showed me during one of our intense conversations where we exposed our most secret selves to each other.

Just as I leaned with my cheek against the cold stone building and fought the mounting disappointment while my mind raced to figure out what I'd do next he spotted me. Out of all the servants and hustle and bustle that was happening, he somehow singled me out of the crowd and locked eyes with me.

My heart threatened to pound its imprint in my throat as waves of energy permeated the air from him to me. I dug into the recesses of my memory, but I couldn't recall Duncan ever mentioning his father being supernatural or gifted. Clearly he was something other than your ordinary human being. What was even clearer was the fact that he realized I was as well.

This was a disaster.

I raced to the back of the inn and didn't stop until I'd reached the milk house. Planting myself inside the recesses of its dark, cool walls, I molded my body with the rough stone while I caught my breath and tried to think. What if he mentioned me to Mildred?

I regretted assuming that Duncan's life was a normal one prior to his vampire encounter. Obviously I was wrong. I longed to be able to sit down with my vampire lover and ask him just exactly what type of dysfunctional upbringing he experienced, but, of course, that wasn't going to happen. I would have to work through this on my own.

I needed to observe Lord Colliers a little more closely before I could work out my next plan of action. This meant keeping out of his sight while he was in residence.

That was not such an easy thing to accomplish. It

26

seemed at every turn there was a chore for me to do that caused me to be in the vicinity of the Earl of Winterspring. I started to wonder if he planned it that way in an effort to get me alone. Why he didn't just ask for me to be sent to him, I didn't know. A man of that stature surely could have done so without question. I was just glad he didn't. Perhaps it was the cloaking spell I'd attempted out of sheer desperation. It hadn't hidden me from him like I'd hoped, but it at least kept him at bay to some degree.

I managed to tuck myself away in my favorite observation spot so I could observe the earl and his guests at dinner. If I hadn't had that experience with him upon his arrival I would have never guessed the man wasn't a normal earl dining with his guests.

I was almost noticed by him when Sally unexpectedly slid in behind me and startled me by whispering harshly in my ear that Mildred was looking for me. I covered my mouth in dismay at my sloppiness while I plastered my body as far into the shadows as I could to avoid his inquisitive stare. His eyes were the same striking sea foam blue as Duncan's, but there was something different about them. Even though Duncan had lived for hundreds of years and seen who knows what during that time frame, his father possessed the eyes that showed they'd seen more than one should ever see in a life time. There was also another major difference between the eyes of father and son. Duncan's eyes were kind, with a hint of sadness tucked in; while the earl's eyes portrayed a mistrust and hardness. From the way his guest swooned and interacted with him, I'm not sure they detected that trait in him, but I sure did. I was hard pressed to stay put and not flee as he looked in my direction. Fortunately, wisdom overcame urge and I was able to stay statue-like in the shadows and avoid his visual detection; even if he knew inherently that I was there.

When I was sure the earl's attention was called elsewhere, I slithered out of my hiding place and sought out Mildred. It was abnormal to be needed at this time of the day, but, since the earl's arrival, nothing had been normal. I caught up with Mildred at the stable. She was in the middle of scolding the stable boy about wasting precious hay for bedding. I stood back and waited while she directed him in a more economical method before I cleared my throat to make my presence known.

Mildred turned to me and scowled.

"Where have you been, gal?" she asked briskly. "Do you think I have all day to lag around waiting on your precious person to see fit to grace me?"

"Mum, you search for me?" I replied timidly.

I was still wary and uncomfortable about speaking to and interacting with these people. The least little slip up could change the outcome of my mission. The less I spoke, the better.

Mildred looked me up and down before puffing an enormous amount of wind past her thin lips.

"Your presence has been requested by himself," she said with a pout. "You have made an impression; although 'tis jargogle how you managed; what with all the chores you are supposed to be keeping up with!"

"Truly, I know not," I replied with horror.

This was a disaster! How was I supposed to present myself to the earl as a member of gentry if I was to play servant girl to him at the inn? Mildred stared at me with piercing eyes so long and hard that I was tempted to run away and not look back. If I could get somewhere safe and lay low for a bit, I'd be able to contrive some type of strategy. Clearly this one wasn't working.

"I ne'r took you for the kind of miss to be giving away your favors," Mildred drawled sarcastically.

"I... I... no," I gasped in horror, "no, I ne'r!"

"Well, if you ain't giving away any favors, and you have been doing chores, such as you tell me, then what is the reason? Why does his lordship call for you?" Mildred demanded as she rested her hands on her broad hips.

"I do not know," I replied quickly. I tried to think. "We

exchanged looks when first he arrived," I said -more to myself than to Mildred.

"They were some looks!" she exclaimed.

I shrugged my shoulders in reply. What was there to say? It was times like this that I really missed the twenty-first century. Getting used to the way they did things proved more daunting that I'd expected or been prepared for.

First and foremost, the hygiene was atrocious. I'd gained a new respect for cologne. Not only were the clothes hot, scratchy, and cumbersome, but they made my five foot-four inch, one hundred and ten-pound body look short and fat! Food was yet another anomaly. The stuff they tossed my way was bland, tough, and just plain unappealing. If the type of treatment I got was what a noble orphan from a foreign country received, I was just grateful I hadn't posed as a peasant girl in need of a livelihood.

"I do not know the reason he summons and I desire not to know," I said stiffly. "I await word from my family to soon be homeward bound. I cannot imagine why this ludibrious is placed on me while I toil for my keep in anticipation."

I knew I was treading on tender ground, but I wanted to get the focus off the earl and this was the only way I could think of doing it at the time. I braced myself for her reaction.

"Ludibrious you say? Well, well, excuse me your majesty for inconveniencing your ungrateful ass. I was remiss in misplacing the silver plate the world placed before you on," Mildred practically hissed. "I could have just let you sit on the roadside waiting for this high flouting family that is taking its sweet happy time in rescuing your pampered ass."

"They take longer than expected," I said with a sigh, while ignoring her crass remarks. "Uncle travels and perhaps 'tis harder to track him down than I anticipated."

I hoped my lie sounded plausible. I knew I was really pushing things by staying. It was time to move on to phase two of my mission. The problem was that I still hadn't come up with a plan for phase two. I needed time alone to think.

CHAPTER FIVE

The arrival of the earl's groom brought his request back to the forefront. I had no choice but to comply with the summons. I smoothed my hair under my cap as best I could and wiped my hands in the folds of my apron. It may seem silly, but I was meeting Duncan's father and my natural desire was to make a good impression. Why? I couldn't say. It just was.

My mind whirled as I followed the young man up the wooden stairs of the tavern to the Earl's room at the end of the hall. I'd never been on this floor of the inn and couldn't help feeding my curiosity a bit. The walls were covered with flocked paper and appeared smooth and well kept. As we progressed down the hall with its well tread-upon floor boards, I noticed the doors grew further and further apart; indicating that the rooms they led to were slightly larger and intended for their more important guests. This made sense, since the noise of the tavern was also quite muted this far back in the building.

The groom had barely tapped his knuckles against the polished oak door when it swung opened. The earl's valet bowed and motioned me to enter. I passed by him hesitantly while I scoped the room for the earl. I found him sitting in the shadows on the opposite side of the room. He was so near the thick tapestry draperies; he could have easily been lost in them, had he chosen to be.

I stood motionless while the valet stepped quietly out into the hallway and carefully closed the door behind him.

We were alone.

I don't know exactly how much time passed in silence. It was probably less than what it felt like, but it was long enough for panic to start spreading through me. My legs threatened to turn to rubber and collapse at any moment while my arms felt like they'd been filled with lead. Not only couldn't I move them, but their weight was bound to pull my torso to the floor with swiftness when my legs finally gave out.

That was exactly what was about to happen when he spoke and stopped the pro-cess with three little words, "Good evening m' lady."

I stood frozen, unable to make sense of his statement. My panic was immediately transmuted to curiosity. After an even longer interval of silence, during which I managed to re-gain control of my facilities, he spoke again.

"I fretted you were lost to us forever. 'Tis splendid you found your way back," he continued.

If there was ever a time when I could admit to being stuck on stupid, this was it. I had absolutely no idea what he talked about and no idea how to respond. So, I just stood there like an idiot and stared at this shadowy figure that obviously had me confused with someone else. I forced myself to relax enough to find my tongue.

"Might I know with whom I speak?" I asked stiffly, while I searched my mind for an idea of how to correctly handle this situation.

This mistake in identity could actually work in my favor.

"Of course," he said as he stepped slowly into the light.

My heart caught in my throat as I stared at the man who could have easily been Duncan's older brother. With the ex-ception of a stronger jaw line, graying temples that blended in with his light hair, and lines that spoke of his years on earth, they had amazingly similar features. His height was very close to Duncan's. If I stood them back to back, I think I'd be hard pressed to measure a half inch difference in Duncan's favor. Their body type was so similar they could have easily ex-changed clothing. What caught my breath in my throat were the eyes. They were the same, piercing sea foam blue eyes that captured my heart and changed my life.

I suddenly felt very dizzy.

"Are you unwell?" he asked as he rushed forward to steady me.

I felt a twinge that could only be compared to a light electrical shock run up my arm as he held my elbow to steady me. It created an odd mixture of unsettling comfort.

He felt familiar; comfortable.

Yet, being near him also felt scary, and possibly a little dangerous.

Confusion mingled with frustration and fear as I pierced through to the recesses of my mind to somehow pull up the reason why I'd have this mixture of emotions and feelings when I'd only just met this man. He obviously felt he knew me and I was apparently held in high regard. This leverage could be used to get me close enough to Duncan to pull off what I'd come to do.

It was imperative that I said and did the right thing. This was not an opportunity to waste. I might not get another.

I grabbed my head and allowed my legs to go limp.

"Come, my dear," he said with genuine concern as he guided me to a nearby silver and aubergine dauphine chair.

I allowed him to lead me as I scrambled for a plan.

"Your time travels have clearly taken more out of you than anticipated," he said softly.

Okay. I wasn't expecting that. My body froze for a second before I collected my wits and went along with it. Apparently the plan was working itself out without my brain get-ting involved.

"I believe so," I replied weakly.

"I hate that you returned as this," he said as he swept his arms over my person. "I regret my duties prevented me from receiving you sooner. There was jargogle of times and places. Please forgive me."

"Fret not," I replied with a weakness that wasn't com-pletely false. The sudden change of events had literally knocked me off balance. "I require but a bit of rest."

"Of course. Let us get you home where you belong. I

have no doubt you long to burn those rags and soak in a sooth-ing lavender bath. I shall send ahead to inform Elizabeth to be prepared," he said as he walked toward the door.

I listened while he gave his valet, Jonathan, instructions on preparations for our leaving and did my best to release the tension that threatened to become a permanent condition in my muscles. I wondered how long it would take before I was actually in that lavender bath. I could already feel the water swirling around my tired bones and aching muscles.

When he returned, I grabbed both his hands in mine.

Startled, he gasped and knelt before me.

"What is it?" he asked gently.

"I beg your assistance with a difficulty that has arisen," I said softly. I allowed my eyes to brave his mesmerizing orbs. I felt that the sincerity of contact was needed in order to pull off my ruse, "I have lost much of my recollection. 'Tis coming to me in bits and piec-es, but I fear I shant know all I should know and people shall question me."

He chuckled.

"Our house will ne'r think a thing of it," he assured me. They are well aware of your mission and, although they might be surprised of such a side effect after several successful trips already completed without such a side effect, they shall re-main loyally silent." He massaged his chin while he thought, "It might not do to have you enter society until you have regained your memory. The house guests and staff are one thing... so-ciety.... hmm, 'twould be best to take precautions. I hope you agree."

Wow, that was way too easy. I had no idea who this lady he mistook me for was, but I wanted to thank her profusely for the opening she gave me into Duncan's home and life. With any luck, I'd be heading back to the future with my mortal honey by my side within the week. Things were looking up.

CHAPTER SIX

The inn was surprisingly close to Duncan's family estate. I soon found myself immersed in a deep copper tub filled with soothing lavender scented water, while the heat of the fireplace sent warm waves over my exposed flesh.

I was in heaven.

I'd learned from various covert conversations that the woman they mistook me for was Margaret-Jane Bush. I found this interesting since my given name was also Margaret–Jane and I'd shortened it to Jane. She'd shortened hers to Margaret.

It was remarkable enough that we shared a name, but the fact that we looked the same topped the scales of uncanny.

I found a small portrait of Lady Margaret and was amazed by the resemblance. It could have easily been me who'd sat for the artist. Not only did we look alike, but I soon discovered we wore the same size when Elizabeth helped me dress for dinner. I marveled over the fit of the yellow dress with orange underlay. The delicate embroidered flowers trailed down its front, encouraging the eye to admire the matching embroidered slippers. It would have been considered garish in my lifetime, yet quite in style there. After the baroque style wig was fitted to my head, I looked at myself as best I could in the thick, hazy mirror and smiled. I looked and felt like the lady they'd labeled me to be.

I can't tell you how many times I wanted to ask about the label of "lady", but each time I hesitated. Although I was being accepted as an amnesiac whose memory was slowly returning, I didn't know how far I could carry the ruse. Instead, I kept my eyes and ears opened for verbal and visual clues that seemed to be everywhere.

Although this was Duncan's home, I got the impression

Lady Margaret spent a tremendous amount of time there. This was good. It meant she knew Duncan and my concerns of how to get close to him were over.

I was greeted by Lord Collier as I descended the broad, curved staircase to join him for dinner. He'd brought the party from the inn with him and I could hear them conversing merrily in the dining room as we approached. No one paid us much notice as he led me to my seat next to his. I caught a bit of conversation here or there as we made our way up the twenty-six-foot mahogany table, but, in truth, I was so in awe of the massive table with its exquisite table settings and the elegantly decorated room that could probably fit my entire apartment in that I paid them as little attention as they paid me. Clearly the earl was a man of wealth and he wasn't afraid to show it.

As I settled into my seat, he called the table to attention.

"My distinguished guests, please welcome Lady Margaret back to our table," he said in a calm, steady voice while he smiled and nodded toward me. "Lady Margaret has experience trying times and has suffered amnesia as a result. Of course 'twill not last. While it exists, we shall do our best to assist her with recall at every opportunity." He raised his glass and continued to smile while he looked at each and every one of his dinner guests. "Now, a toast to our beloved, Lady Margaret."

I raised my glass in reply to their toast and savored the sweet fruity wine as it slid down my throat. It was the first drink of quality I'd had since I'd arrived. My entire body responded with a warm 'thank-you'. I was just about to dive into the tomato onion bisque one of the servants spooned into my bowl when my attention was captured by a small raucous at the other end of the exceedingly long table.

"I do not give a damn who she is or how dear my uncle thinks her," bellowed a high pitched female voice. "She was wrong for the mission and you know it. 'Twas I who should have gone. Damn you, Samuel, you know 'twas I who should have gone, but would you speak on my behalf? No! Damn you to hell!"

I followed the words to the end of the table until my eyes settled on the hostile face of the petite beauty who spat them at her nearby dinner companion. Even with her pinched up anger, her almond shaped, sapphire blue eyes sparkled against high cheek bones that framed a perfect aristocratic nose. Her lips were pursed in anger, but I could tell they were well formed and probably a bit pouty when relaxed. Her eyebrows hinted of dark hair beneath her elaborate wig. She would have been all the rage in theater. Since I'd struggled against beauties just like this one for every part I managed to scrape up, I resented her on principle alone and the hairs went up on the back of my neck.

"Is there a problem?" I asked with more authority in my voice than I felt.

"Ignore her, m 'lady," said the man to my left, "Lady Lilith cannot move past her rejection for making the journey."

"Truly?" I asked.

"She believes in her appointment based on her ancestors' higher noble status. She is the first to break that chain and she cannot bear it," he offered.

"'Tis understandable," I replied.

"'Tis not true, Marcus, and you know it!" Lilly screeched, "I was the best selection. You all know I was," she spat as she glowered at the earl with obvious resentment. "I warned you about her. I shant have returned empty handed."

I had no idea what she meant, but it was clear Lady Margaret failed her mission. What was she supposed to come back with? Better yet, where had Lady Margaret-Jane Chapman gone?

It didn't take long for me to discover the answers.

As the conversation progressed to a heated discussion that bordered on arguing, it came out that Margaret went into the future to bring back the earl's son, Duncan. Apparently, Duncan had succumbed to the wiles of a sorceress and when he finally came to his senses and tried to free himself from her clutches, she cast a spell that sent him whirling into the future. Since Duncan hadn't mentioned this to me, I listened closely and tried to make sense of the story.

"You look confused," Lilith hissed at me. "Did you conveniently lose memory of Lord Duncan?"

"That will do," roared the earl, "I shall have no more of this at my table!"

"Why do you protect her?" Lilith whined as she made to stand up and leave.

"You shall remain seated, Lady Lilith, and we shall dine as do civilized people. I shall allow no more criticism spoken at this table. Is that understood?" The earl bellowed while slamming the palm of his hand on the table for emphasis.

I'd attended some pretty uncomfortable dinner parties in my day, but never had I been the focus of the drama. I tried to sooth my nerves by reminding myself that it was Margaret and not me who was really in the spotlight, but it didn't seem to help much. I wanted to be anywhere than at that table. It took every ounce of strength I had to remain seated and participate in the table talk that went on around me.

I'm really glad I did.

Apparently Lady Margaret was the bride-to-be that the sorceress managed to keep from marrying Lord Duncan. Margaret, like me, was magical. In fact, everyone at the table dabbled in magic in one way or another. Margaret just happened to have a little more skill at it than the rest; with the exception of Lady Lilith Collier who claimed to be her equal. I assumed that the sense of familiarity I had when I first set eyes on Lord Collier was my recognition of his magic. Since the only other magical person I'd been exposed to was Isabelle, it seemed a logical assumption.

I also learned that Lady Margaret's parents were deceased and she'd been living with Lord Duncan's family for some time now. This explained the earl's possessiveness over his future daughter-in-law. Apparently her ladyship was already like a daughter to him. I made a mental note to be extra careful in his company. If anyone would realize I was an imposter, it made sense that it would be him.

Lady Lilith was another one to watch out for. It wasn't just because she was an adept magical being who had a bone to pick with Margaret, but because it turned out she was Duncan's cousin three times removed who'd also been raised by the earl. Apparently had her nose bent out of shape when Lady Margaret-Jane Chapman came into the household and usurped her territory.

"How many times are you going to let her return empty handed before you understand she is not for the task?" Lilith screeched at her dining companions, ignoring her uncle's command.

I looked at the earl cautiously and watched his face turn various shades of scarlet. Was he going to have a heart attack? I'd seen a man in central park having one once and he looked almost identical to the earl right now. This was a little scary.

"She shall go until she succeeds and that is all I wish to speak on the matter," he said between gritted teeth.

"But..." Lilith started to argue again,

"No! I mean true Lilith. One more word from you on this subject and you shall be banished to your room until I see fit to allow you in our company again. Am I understood?" he roared.

"Clearly," she spat as she resumed her seat and picked up her spoon.

Dinner was exceptional. The inn still utilized the two prong fork, so you can imagine my delight when I discovered an iron three pronged fork at my setting to assist me with consuming the roast boar and pheasant. Although large and cumbersome in comparison to the eating utensils of the future, they were beautifully made and surprisingly efficient to use. Unlike the inn that often used and reused stale bread -to the point you were wise to inspect it for maggots before you consumed it- to act as a trencher, the table sported beautiful wooden trenchers for eating and pewter platters and with onyx goblets for drinking. I was extremely grateful he reserved the silver dishware for super special occasions, since I knew the silver would seep into my food and cause toxicity.

I don't know how they managed to create such artful cuisine in what I would consider a primitive kitchen set up, but the cooks somehow managed to produce food that rivaled the best chefs and bakers in Manhattan. Since I could barely boil water and abhorred the sight of dead animals, I can't even explain how happy I was when I got passed over for kitchen helper at the inn and placed on laundry duty instead.

As the conversation around the table relaxed, I listened intently to see what else I could learn about Lady Margaret and her life at the estate. When I heard them speak of Lady Vivian Everhoust at the far end of the table, I stopped eating and focused as best I could on what was being said. To my relief, others at the table joined into the conversation and soon the entire dinner party was discussing Lady Vivian and her evil ways. It was clear she was not a popular figure amongst the group.

From what I could gather, they thought Vivian teleported Duncan into a different time and place and they kept sending Margaret off in search of him. Once she found him, she planned on reversing the spell and bringing him home. It was clear they had no idea Duncan was vampire.

"I wish I remembered where to I'd ventured in search of Lord Duncan," I whispered to the earl. "Perhaps then some information would return to me."

"Our seers tell us Duncan is in the future. We sent you there," he replied quietly before popping a boiled potato in his mouth.

"How do you know? I mean, the seers... how do they know?" I asked timidly.

I hoped I wasn't being too obvious.

"Dear child, do you remember nothing?" the earl asked

in surprise.

I shook my head.

"Dear, dear," he reached over and patted my hand, "never mind. 'Twas a challenge to send you that far into time. Truthfully, I knew not if you would survive the trip. A feat of such magnitude has ne'r been tried before. 'Twas only with the assistance of Lady Vivian's grimoire that we managed a'tall. She has retrieved it since then, of course," he shrugged.

"When?" I asked.

"When what my dear?" he said absent mindedly as he cut his meat into small and manageable bite size pieces.

"When did she retrieve it?" I persisted.

He stopped eating and thought for a moment.

"Shortly after you teleported," he replied as he continued to attack his venison with gusto. "No matter... We recorded what we needed before that happened. You never risked being stuck in the future."

"Did she know the Lady Margaret... I mean... did she know of my absence? Did she have details?" I asked anxiously.

The earl thought for a minute.

"I ne'r considered it. Hmm. Had she been aware you traveled through time in search of my son, she would likely cast a spell to make you forget. Verily, if she did know about your journey, I am surprised you returned a'tall," he said thoughtfully. "The ways of Lady Vivian are wicked," he shook his head in distaste, "I should be amazed she let you live."

It broke my heart to realize the odds that Vivian hadn't let Margaret live were pretty high. My emotions were roaming everywhere. I felt sad that Lady Margaret-Jane Chapman had been the victim of the evil Lady Vivian Everhoust, but I also felt sad and confused to discover that I was a dead ringer for Margaret. Lord Duncan and Lady Margaret were childhood sweethearts and had almost made it to the wedding alter before he became the recipient of a vampire attack. More than once he'd held me close and sworn his undying love for me, but was it really me? Who did he see when he looked at me? Was I just a fantastic find to replace the love that was stolen from him? I wasn't sure and the possibility of it broke my heart.

It suddenly hit me full force in the chest and over-shadowed all of the other traumatic news of the evening. I'd learned Duncan was gone. This meant that he'd already been attacked and gone into hiding. I'd miscalculated my timing. I'd taken the risk and endured the hardships that followed for nothing.

The earl must have mistaken the mist in my eyes as a reaction to his comment about how surprised he was that I'd returned because he immediate rang for Elizabeth to take me to my room to lay down, declaring to the dinner party that I'd had a terrible ordeal and needed rest more than I needed food. He had no idea how right he was. Besides, their meals were far larger and more complex than the microwavable ones I was used in the future or the sparse portions I'd been given at the inn and I was beyond full. I can't imagine how they managed to fit it all into their small waist stomachers. I'm sure if I ate too many meals of that proportion I'd double in size in no time.

I waited restlessly for Elizabeth to complete my toilet and leave. I wanted... no, I needed to be alone with my thoughts. What had I done wrong with my calculations? How long had Duncan been missing? Why hadn't Duncan told me I was the image of Margaret? What was his reason for keeping such a significant thing quiet? I thought we were completely open and honest with each other. I know I had been. I thought back on how I'd bared my soul to him; thinking all along he was doing the same. Now, I discover he hadn't. What else had he kept from me? Did I even really know him?

The realization that I'd risked my life to go back in time for a man who was not even there and who wasn't who or what I thought he was shattered me to the core.

I blew out the candle and wept.

CHAPTER SEVEN

Having been a sufferer of acute claustrophobia for as long as I can remember, I find the black of night frighteningly confining. Since there were no night lights to ease my discomfort and it was far too dangerous -not to mention wasteful- to keep a candle going while sleeping, I had to force myself to acclimate to the darkness. I managed, but I certainly couldn't claim to be comfortable in it. That was when I missed Duncan the most. He always made me feel so safe.

The following morning didn't bring me much comfort, other than the light of day.

Duncan. My heart sank at the thought of him. I needed to know how he truly felt about me, but how? He was in the twenty-first century going through his day without any inkling that I'd ignored his wishes and traveled back in time.

To the wrong time!

Worst yet, I'd done it without the aid of Isabelle. Now that I'd learned more about the fine Lady Margaret-Jane Chapman, I didn't know whether I should be angry or hurt. What I did know was that I felt very foolish and taken in.

I moved to the miniature portrait of her on the far wall of the room and looked at her closely. My heart felt like it was made of inflexible lead as it struggled to function. Margaret and I could have been twins. Could this be the reason Duncan was with me? Since he'd neglected to share the fact that I could be his one-time fiancé's doppelganger with me, I had no choice than to think it true. If he couldn't have his precious Lady Margaret, then he'd have the next best thing. Me. I wanted to wring his deceitful neck at the thought of it.

The urge to throw something was too great to ignore. I looked around the sparsely furnished room and soon thought better of it. If I'd learned nothing at all during my time here, I'd learned that material goods didn't come as easily to people in the eighteenth century as they did in the twenty-first. Even the poorest of poor of the future lived better than most in the past. There was no Macy's or Target to shop for clothing and home staples. Every item of clothing was painfully made by the hand of some half-starved worker and every piece of furniture or decoration the same. Even if the embroidery was done by a noble woman, it took months -not hours- to create. The room may have been sparsely furnished in accordance to my standards, but what was in it was of fine quality and made with the utmost care. There was nothing in this room that I had the heart to destroy. I wouldn't have been able to live with myself from the guilt of it.

I decided to take a walk instead.

The sensation of walking the garden was an eerie sort of comfortable. Somewhere in the back of my mind I knew where I was going, yet I'd never been there before. It was an unexplainable "odd" that I vowed I'd focus on at another time. Right then, I needed all my attention placed on the situation at hand. I'd been duped by a spoiled aristocratic vampire and may have foolishly sealed my fate if I didn't keep my head on my shoulders and find my way back to the portal that would return me to the twenty-first century on time.

First things first, I calculated how much time I had left. This wasn't as easy as I would have thought, since I owned no watch or calendar. I'd hidden my belongings in a cave when I arrived. They included a battery operated watch. I'd made note of the position of the sun when I arrived in the event my watch stopped working or was discovered and taken. Once I determined the day that I needed to return to my point of entry, I figured the worst case scenario would be that I would have to get there early and wait until the sun was once again in that same position.

My mind was so preoccupied with making my plans to return home that I didn't notice the disagreeable Lady Lilith until I'd practically stumbled into her.

If I had any doubt about how she felt about me -or should I say Lady Margaret- the look of pure hatred on her face made it painfully clear.

"Why do you hate me so?" I blurted out without even so much as a greeting.

Her eyebrows rose in surprise while her thin lips curled in a small semblance of a smile.

"I see your trip was not a total loss. You have returned with a bit of back bone," she said with a sassy tone.

"Why so?" I asked.

Although I'd been pulling off the language quite admirably since my arrival, now that I was no longer focused on saving Duncan and was focused on returning back home instead, I found the effort tedious and distasteful. I longed to speak normally, but wasn't foolish enough do it.

"You ask why? Well, my little amnesiac, I shall tell you why," she practically hissed. "You stole Lord Duncan from me and you know it. Until now, you at least had the decency to avoid me because of it. That's why. I should have been married to him right now. I have the power to subdue Lady Vivian's wickedness. I have proved it on more than one occasion. I do not understand why Lord Duncan had to fall in love with little Lady Margaret-Jane who cannot compare with me in the world of magic. You know it, even if the others do not." She looked me up and down with a sour smirk and continued, "Frankly, you fail to compare with me in looks as well. I have no doubt you worked a spell on him to get him from me. When I find him, I shall undo that spell and we shall see then who he truly loves."

I actually felt a little sorry for the slighted cousin standing before me. We had more in common than she realized. I knew in my heart that I wasn't the love of Duncan's life either. Margaret was. I wasn't Margaret. I was Jane. The thought of sharing this information with her flitted through my mind, but I dismissed it. I still didn't know who was who and who stood in what corner. Until I did, it was better to keep my secret to myself. I couldn't have anyone, or anything, prevent me from getting back home.

"I no longer wish to marry Lord Duncan. If you can find him, you can have him," I exclaimed with exasperation as I stormed away.

I thought she might follow me after that last statement, but when I glanced over my shoulder I saw she was frozen in place with a shocked look on her face. I smiled with satisfaction as I made my way to the stables.

I wasn't the best of riders, but I could hold my own. Since it was clear I'd find no peace walking the grounds, a ride was in order. I also needed to check the cave for my belongings. Now seemed as good a time as any.

I was given Lady Margaret's sorrel. The groom assured me a baby could ride it. I hoped he was right as we meandered off toward the cave. I say meander because the hoofed sloth keenly recognized that I wasn't his mistress. It made note of my lack of riding skills and took full advantage of the fact. No matter how hard I kicked, poked, or begged, we had one speed and one speed only; slow. Since I was being forced to ride side saddle -which only added to my riding distress- I decided that, as long as we were going in the right direction, I wouldn't worry about it.

I found myself going over the chain of events that led me to this moment. The table talk at dinner echoed in my mind. Lady Margaret-Jane, who was she really? Although she seemed revered by the majority of the people seated at dinner the night before, clearly the view wasn't universal. Conversing with Lilith proved that. I found myself wondering what happened to her. Did she make it to the future? Was she still alive?

My conversation with the earl haunted me. Was it really that dangerous to go into the future? What would happen to me when I stepped through the portal to return? Would I survive the transition? I'd made it back in time with little mishap. Was it different going ahead in time?

I was so engrossed in thought that, before I knew it, I was at the opening of the cave. I dismounted and tied my horse to the nearest tree. Considering the enthusiasm for moving it didn't display during my ride there, I doubted it would go anywhere if not tied, but it was better safe than sorry. I still hadn't gotten used to the type of footwear they wore and I had no desire to try walking five miles in the heeled riding boots I was wearing.

After making sure I was alone, I pulled the brush I'd shoved into the opening of the cave away and crawled into the cramped hollow. I was barely able to fit my body into it curled up, but I still classified it as a cave. I felt around for the wide crack that I'd stuffed my things into and found them still there. They were a little damp, but that was to be expected, considering the length of time they'd been shoved into the earthen crack. I shuddered at the thought of wearing them back, but knew they needed to return with me as well in order for the spell to work correctly. The last thing I wanted was to leave a part of me behind, even if it was something as simple as my belongings. Any connection would give someone with magical knowledge the power to pull me back. From what I'd gathered at dinner the night before, there were quite a few people in that category.

I returned the brush to the cave's opening and wiped as much soil as I could from my riding habit with my hands. I was thankful that the quality of the wool my costume was made of was exquisite and surprisingly stain resistant. It took very little effort to clean off any signs of my crawling around in the cave.

Moments later I was mounted on my horse and heading back to the estate. It wouldn't do to be gone so long that they would start looking for me. While the ride to the cave took seemingly hours, getting home felt like it was only a matter of minutes. It was. Once my horse realized the direction we were headed, it had a sudden burst of life and we moved like the wind. Fortunately, I managed to gain control of my balance and stopped flopping around on the saddle like a rag doll by the time we reached the stables, so I wasn't too embarrassed when the groom who that waited to assist me witnessed my return.

I relinquished my mount and walked as steadily as I could as I made the long trek back to the main house. The estate was enormous. I couldn't imagine how many millions of dollars it would sell for in the twenty-first century if it managed to survive being sectioned off by developers. Although I agreed that no one needed this much land, I had to admit I was enjoying the grandness of it all and would probably miss it once I was back in the bustle and chaos of modern day Manhattan.

Without warning, a slight tingling ran up my spine. I stopped for a moment and looked around. It felt like there were eyes on me everywhere, but I saw only people engrossed in their task at hand. No one seemed to be staring in the way I felt they were.

It was very strange.

I had a few more days before I could enter the portal and return home. Curiosity dictated I find out as much as I could about the woman I'd been mistaken for; the Lady Margaret-Jane. Assuming that the more prevalent clues to who she truly was would be in her suite, I headed up the stairs.

I'd almost reached the door to her rooms when I came face to face with Isabelle as she stepped out of the shadows. I couldn't believe my eyes! A slight squeal escaped my lips as I hugged her tightly. Never had I been so happy to see anyone!

She placed her hand over my mouth and made a "shush" sound as she pulled me into the shadows.

"Quiet!" she said. Her tone was soft, but urgent. "They must not know I am here."

"Oh," I replied, clearly confused.

"Where are your rooms?" she asked firmly.

I pointed to the door.

It was only after we'd padded our way as fast as we could across the short distance left to my rooms and were securely behind closed doors that she spoke freely.

"What a foolish thing you did," she scolded.

I looked at my feet in shame.

"No more foolish than you coming to get me," I replied softly.

"Duncan is in a rage," she continued as she paced the floor. "I had all I could do to subdue him when he discovered what you'd done."

"I don't want to hear about Duncan," I said with an impatient scowl.

"What?" Isabelle asked with surprise.

"I know about Lady Margaret-Jane Chapman," I spat as I pointed to her portrait on the wall. "Isn't it a convenience that I look exactly like her? It must take some of the sting off losing her like he did."

"You have no clue what you are saying," she said softly.

"Don't I?" I hissed as I reverted back to my native Manhattan tongue. "Why didn't he tell me about her? Why? Was it because if I knew that I was a suitable substitute... a fill in... I'd leave him? Because I am, you know. As far as I'm concerned, Duncan and I are toast."

"You cannot mean that. Do not say such things," she said as she wrung her hands and continued to pace.

"To think I thought he loved me.... me... not her. I even risked my life to come back here and help him. The worst of it is, I missed my mark. I'm too late. He isn't even here," I said, a little louder than I should have.

Recognizing my emotions were running dangerously high, I started breathing deeply to help calm myself down. It wouldn't do to have the household staff rushing in to see what was the matter.

"He never asked you to do this. He never wanted you to do this. You cannot blame him for your folly," Isabelle said quietly.

48

I looked at her closely for the first time since we'd entered the room. She looked tired and old, much older than I last remembered her. It suddenly dawned on me that she'd risked her own life to come to me.

"How old would you be right now?" I asked hesitantly.

"Do not worry about me," she replied.

"Are you losing your magic?" I gasped.

"It is fading," she moaned.

"Oh no. Why did you come? You have to go back! Go back now!" I wailed.

"I cannot. My magic is not strong enough to take me back. You must do it for both of us," she said softly.

"What? I don't know how! I couldn't even send myself back to the right time. I've barely learned enough magic to claim to be magical. I'm a baby at it!" I blurted with despair.

I couldn't believe what she was saying.

"You are more than you think," she said breathlessly.

I rushed to her side.

"Are you alright?" I asked in a tone that bordered on panic.

"I must lie down," she panted. "I just need a little rest and then I will be fine. The transfer here was exhausting."

CHAPTER EIGHT

I remembered all too well how tiring the transfer through time was. I'd also needed time to adjust. I led her to my bed and helped her get comfortable. Elizabeth hadn't been notified of my return and she wouldn't be looking for me until it was time to dress for dinner. This gave Isabelle a few hours of rest before we had to worry about her presence in my room.

I moved around the room as quietly as I could so as not to disturb her. Even though I'd been the recipient of Isabelle's surprise visit, I was still anxious to learn as much as I could about Margaret. After fingering through her meager belongings, I sat in one of the armless baroque chairs placed against the wall opposite the room's entry. I took a moment to admire the remarkable comfort of the seating while stroking the thick floor to ceiling tapestry that hung on the wall. Its intricate wooded scene was breathtaking. I couldn't resist running my hand along the artful design. I became so obsessed with following the fine lines of the artwork that I stood to make it easier. As I did, the heel of my riding boot slipped from beneath me and I lost my balance. Rather than catching myself with my hand against the wall, I fell even further as I quickly discovered that the tapestry was covering a large opening in the wall.

I was about to look behind it when I heard Elizabeth in the adjoining sitting room of my suite. I couldn't believe how the time flew by. She was obviously coming to help me dress for dinner. I looked out at the position of the sun and was surprised to see that it wasn't in the right position to indicate the approaching dinner hour.

I looked worriedly at Isabelle as she lay peacefully on my bed. Panic was creeping in. How would I explain her presence to the household? I'd been so focused on studying Margaret's belongings that I hadn't taken the time to devise a story. My heart beat wildly as I listened to Elizabeth approaching my door. She wasn't alone. I assumed it was a servant with my bath. I went riding, after all. My mind raced at what to do. Memories of my lessons with Isabelle flooded forth. Thoughts and ideas of magic she hadn't even gone over were almost overwhelming.

Without even thinking I said in a firm, hushed voice, "In the light of day or the dark of night, hide this woman from their sight. If by chance her face they see, let it look exactly like me."

I watched the energies swirl around Isabelle's peaceful body as her dark features transformed into my light ones. Satisfied, I slid into the opening behind the tapestry just before Elizabeth entered the room.

I heard her gasp and shush the servant accompanying her when she saw my friend and mentor's sleeping form.

"I had no idea m' lady was returned," she whispered. "Be as silent as you can, Garth. 'Twill not do to disturb her rest."

I heard heavy footsteps cross the wide planked floor toward my bed. I held my breath and waited.

"She looks the angel," Garth whispered. "I have ne'r been this close before."

"You should not be so now. Be about your business and be gone," Elizabeth snapped.

I listened intently to the bustling of Garth and Elizabeth as they prepared my bath and laid out my clothes. I worried over the fact that their activity did nothing to disturb Isabelle. I wanted to check on her to make sure she was okay and prayed the servants would leave soon.

To my dismay, Garth left, but Elizabeth stayed behind.

I had no idea what to do. It was only a matter of time before Isabelle woke up. With Elizabeth in the room, I certainly couldn't just pop out from behind the tapestry. I had no idea what was behind me, but it seemed like a deep dark hollow or corridor. It was definitely creepy. I didn't like the feeling I got while hiding there and it had nothing to do with the fact that I'd cast a spell to disguise Isabelle and I wasn't sure how long it would hold. There was something about this hidden room or hallway that bothered me. It was more than the fact that it was dark and dank. Since the castle was primarily built of stone and there was no electricity, dark and dank was a common thing in rooms that didn't have a fire or proper window for light and ventilation.

I heard Elizabeth gently waking Isabelle and I went into action. No longer was I thinking about the fact that Isabelle looked like me. No longer was I worried about how I'd explain Isabelle's presence to Elizabeth. My only concern was the danger to Isabelle should she be woken from her slumber too soon. I leapt from behind the tapestry and grabbed Elizabeth from behind, placing my hand firmly on her mouth to muffle her startled screams.

I was about three inches shorter than Margaret's lady's maid. The heels of my boots gave me some added height, but the height difference still made it difficult to maintain leverage as she struggled to be free. I was grateful for the martial arts training Duncan insisted I take after the mugging. It helped me throw her off balance and sit on top of her until she calmed down enough for me to release her.

The shocked look on Elizabeth's face would have been classic, had I not known how superstitious people of that era could be. I'd grown fond of Margaret's personal maid in the short time I'd been there. had no desire to frighten her like I clearly was. My heart went out to her as I scrambled for an explanation for the situation. There seemed to be none except the truth.

So, I told it.

To my surprise, Elizabeth calmed down almost immediately. She confided that the Margaret-Jane she knew before going to the future and coming back with amnesia was able to perform such spells. To my surprise, the girl was totally comfortable with it. She was actually more comfortable with the spells than she was with the concept of my not being Lady Margaret. That, she told me, was impossible.

Apparently, not only did I have a face that was identical to Lady Margaret's face and a name that matched hers as well, but I had marks in the same places on my body. I had to agree with her that it was a bit odd. I had no explanation for it. None at all.

Isabelle slowly roused during my tussle with Elizabeth and managed to catch most of our conversation.

"I can explain it, if you wish," she said softly, "but first, can you undo the spell. It feels rather odd to be you," she smiled.

I eagerly retracted the words I'd spoken and smiled as my beautiful friend resurfaced. Elizabeth gasped in appreciation and then affection.

"Greetings, m' lady, it has been some time since you graced us with your presence," the excited gentle woman said as she curtsied deeply.

I looked on curiously, but said nothing. Through my experiences on this journey, I'd learned firsthand that observation often times provided more answers than questions.

"Ah, I see you have met my mother," Isabelle said sweetly. "Alas, although I appear to be Rosalie, I am not she. I am Isabelle, daughter of Rosalie Johanna Remoras who reigns over the Spanish world of magic as queen. She is powerful, beauteous, loving, fair, and most of all, a dear woman."

Elizabeth stood up and walked closer to the bed.

"The resemblance is so that I could not tell you are not she. Now that I look closer, there are some differences; although very slight," she said calmly.

"From my father," Isabelle chuckled. "He is a privateer. Did you know this?"

"I have heard it spoken, but knew not if 'twas to be believed," my attendant replied demurely.

"Believe every word," Isabelle said wistfully. "He is the one person my mother cannot control. It is probably why she loves him so."

"When did he die?" I asked.

"Oh, he is not dead yet," Isabelle replied, "Nor is my mother. In fact, I should not yet be born."

"Yes, I forgot, sorry," I muttered, suddenly feeling foolish.

"It is an easy thing to forget," Isabelle sighed.

"May I ask something m' lady?" Elizabeth directed her question to Isabelle.

"Of course," she replied.

"You appear unwell. What causes you to arrive here a sickly adult instead of the wee babe that you should be?" Elizabeth asked hesitantly.

I held my breath. I knew the answer, but I still dreaded hearing it come from my friend's lips.

"I have been in the future with Lady Margaret and Lord Duncan," Isabelle said to Elizabeth while locking eyes with me.

I received her telepathic message to keep quiet loud and clear. Of course she would claim me as Margaret. Until we knew what happened to her and had a clearer picture of our own future, it was probably best to keep certain things to ourselves. I was feeling a little overwhelmed with the information we'd already shared and was grateful not to have to divulge any more.

Elizabeth looked at me cautiously as she said, "You mentioned nothing about finding Lord Duncan."

"I remembered nothing," I replied and then addressed Isabelle. "I have been suffering amnesia since my return. Perhaps you will be able to shed light on the darkness I have been living in."

"I will do my very best," Isabelle replied as she lay back against the pillows Elizabeth had painstakingly puffed and fluffed. "For now, I must rest."

CHAPTER NINE

My water was cold by the time we realized we'd better get me dressed and down to dinner before someone came looking for me. I shivered through my bath like a trooper and dressed as quickly as possible. It was of the utmost importance to keep Isabelle's presence a secret. Elizabeth proved a valuable ally in this cause. Her admiration and reverence for Rosalie spilled onto Isabelle. There was nothing the lady's maid wouldn't do to guarantee my friend's safety. Although grateful, I couldn't help being a little jealous. I got the impression that if it came to a choice between saving Isabelle or me, I'd lose.

With Isabelle tucked safely away under the watchful eye of Elizabeth, I went about my daily routine as Lady Margaret while I furthered my discoveries of the type of person she was. I learned that she'd been born into a magical family. When I learned her parents were kin to the faeries, but had only the faintest of blood in them, I had to spend some time digesting that fact. I believed in magic and -thanks to my relationship with Duncan- I believed in vampires. I supposed the faerie story could hold some truth to it.

Dinner had almost come to a conclusion when I learned about the grimoire Lady Margaret's mother once possessed. It wasn't the same grimoire they'd stolen from Lady Vivian. It was far more complete and complex. Unfortunately, when she died, so did the information on its hiding place. That was why they'd stolen the one from Lady Vivian. Had they possession of Lady Margaret's inheritance, there would have been no need.

My mind went back to that afternoon and my time spent hiding behind the tapestry. Could it be that Lady Margaret's mother hid the grimoire there? No, that couldn't have been it. From what I'd learned, Margaret came to live with the Colliers after her parents were killed in a carriage accident. If she allowed them to steal Vivian's grimoire to send her to the future, then she must not have had her family grimoire in her possession. I decided to brave the hole in the wall behind the tapestry, even though I doubted I'd find anything of significance there.

I was forced to endure the company of Lady Andrea Somers and her daughter Juliet for an hour or so after dinner before I was able to beg off with a headache. Having amnesia and not acting normal was proving useful.

When I returned to my rooms, I found Isabelle was up and moving around. She appeared to be in good spirits even if she had aged a few more years in my absence.

"How long do you have?" I questioned without really wanting to know the answer.

"A week, maybe longer," she said with a shrug. "When do you have the portal set for?"

"Two days," I replied.

"Then we have two days to throw me into the mix," she said matter-of-factly.

"Oh, lord," I moaned.

"Be careful the phrases you use here my dear and always be on your toes with the language. These walls have ears," she whispered.

My back stiffened as I looked around. My eyes rested on the tapestry.

"There is a hollow or a hall or something behind that tapestry. I hid there for a while this afternoon when Elizabeth first entered," I informed her.

"Let us check it out then," she whispered as she moved toward the beautiful thick fabric and lifted it way from the wall.

After poking her head behind the tapestry, she slid behind it and motioned for me to follow. I wasn't able to go far before my claustrophobia kicked in and my breathing grew labored. Not only was it pitch black, but the stone walls were within reach on either side of me. I could touch the stone ceiling as well. I felt Isabelle grab my hand and urge me forward. I tripped a few times on the hem of my skirt, but, other than that, the journey down the confining primitive corridor was uneventful.

I marveled over Isabelle's ability to maneuver in the pitch blackness. She confided she'd been down many corridors of the like and they were all pretty much the same. It had something to do with the magical traditions of her people. Even the paths leading to the sacred space had to meet certain specifications.

Although her explanation seemed complicated, it also felt surprisingly familiar.

When I thought I couldn't stand blindly following Isabelle one second longer, -no matter how adept she was at maneuvering- we came to the opening of a cave. I stood in it and breathed in the cool night air. It was sweet and refreshing after the interminable trip through hell to get there.

I looked out upon a large quarry with a round clearing. In the center of the clearing was a stone alter. Two large statues of hawks were placed on the ground on both ends of the alter. Their proud, majestic stance projected a combination of regal and threatening.

As I followed Isabelle out of the cave, I felt a buzzing sensation when I stepped into the outer perimeter of the clearing. It was like a mild electrical current flowing through my body. I didn't like the feeling.

"What's that buzzing feeling going through me?" I asked.

"You have a buzzing feeling? I have none. I wonder why," Isabelle replied.

"What do you feel?" I asked.

"Nothing," she said quizzically. "Perhaps you should step outside the circle, just to be safe. There is probably a protection spell around it."

"Why would I react and not you?" I asked.

"There are many reasons," she said thoughtfully. "The one that comes to mind and concerns me most is a sensor placed around the circle to notify the keeper of the circle when you returned."

"Returned? This is my first time here," I insisted.

"True, but you are a dead ringer for her," Isabelle said cautiously, as she surveyed our surroundings.

Before we could travel down that road of conversation any further, at least a dozen hawks swooped down upon us. As we battled to protect ourselves from the onslaught of their fierce beaks, Isabelle fell to the ground. Blood oozed from her temple. I screamed and tried to get to her, but the entire flock turned its focus on me. Rather than take me down like they had Isabelle, they took me up; literally. Their thick sharp talons dug into my tender flesh as each bird gripped my body, my clothing, my hair, etc. and carried me off into the wild blue yonder.

They were surprisingly strong and managed to get my bulk above the tree tops where they could fly more easily with their burden. The scent of dirty feathers and bird feces assaulted my senses as I struggled to maintain my composure. I had no idea where they were taking me or why, but I did know that if they dropped me I had a crippling distance to fall that could prove fatal. I thought it best to just let them take me wherever and deal with escaping afterward.

We traveled for quite a distance over the tops of trees until we finally hit the rolling hills of the local farmland. I recognized a few cottages and began to get my bearings. If I was correct, we weren't far from the cave where I'd hidden my belongings.

I could feel the strength of the birds' heavy wings waning and our position in the sky lowered ever so slightly. I feared for my safety as we flew over an enormous lake at a frighteningly lesser speed than we'd been traveling. Clearly the hawks were tiring under their burden. Their ability to carry both me and themselves ended just as we reached a small cottage in a clearing at the edge of yet another wooded area. A scream purged from my throat as they released me and I fell about twenty feet onto a large haystack. Although the hay provided a cushion for my fall, it also hurt like hell when little pieces of it pierced my flesh. I was filled with a mixture of relief for being alive and anguish over being stuck like a pin cushion with tiny shards of hay.

I lay motionless for a while and gathered my wits about me while I forced myself to work through the pain as I picked slivers of hay from my arms, legs and buttocks. As I looked at the bruising that was already surfacing, I reminded myself that it could have been worse. At least I was alive.

Thoughts of death brought Isabelle immediately to mind. I needed to reach her; but how?

I scrambled off the hay stack and brushed my clothing free of debris while straightening it as best I could. I'd lost a slipper in the fall and searched around the haystack in hopes of finding it. I was just slipping it back onto my foot when the infamous Lady Vivian Everhoust rode toward me on her enormous white stallion like a ghost in the night.

I have no idea how I knew it was Vivian. I just knew.

Perhaps it was when she spat out, "So, Lady Margaret, are you a glutton for punishment or just simple minded?" Or when she threw her head back, laughed, and said, "I believe simple minded is the like" that it struck me.

Her stallion paced and pawed the ground while it struggled against the flimsy looking restraints in its mouth. She seemed unbothered when it reared several times while its powerful whinny pierced the night air. Although I found her horsemanship impressive, I shuddered at the eeriness of the situation.

"Vivian," I said flatly.

"Lady Vivian to you, peasant!" she screeched.

I almost peed myself when her eyes flashed a burnt

yellow before returning to their normal dark brown. What was she? I'd only seen the eyes of those two vampires during my attack, but I didn't think they were flashing light exactly like that. The vampires repetitively flashed more red. Vivian's eyes had only briefly turned a definite burnt yellow before returning to their normal dark brown. Her facial features were also not distorted. In fact, I had to admit she was quite the beauty. If I had to describe her, I'd say she was a mixture of Amanda Seyfried and Angelina Jolie. She displayed the body type and spoiled cuteness of being that Amanda Seyfried carried off so well in her role in the film Mama Mia, but the sexy facial features of the actress icon, Angelina Jolie. I could easily understand why she was the belle of the season.

Thinking back on the people I'd met since my arrival, I recalled very few people who weren't on the attractive side. That seemed a little out of place compared to walking down the streets of Manhattan. There were so many people from so many cultures intermixing with each other, not only in cultural practice, but genetically. Sometimes these mixes and mingling of traditions and genetics weren't the best idea and you had to remind yourself that you weren't at a circus side show. I saw no sign of that here. The culture and the genetics were, for the most part, untainted. The purity came through as true beauty.

It's amazing how my mind just went off into that direction while in the face of danger. Perhaps Vivian was right. Maybe I was just simple minded. I'm sure most people of normal mind wouldn't be contemplating all the pretty people they'd met while some yellow eyed bitch on an enormous white beast taunted them.

Before I knew what was happening, I was besieged on either side by Vivian's men. They grabbed my arms and forced them behind my back. If I thought I was in pain from my encounter with the haystack, it paled in comparison to having my arms twisted behind my back as if I was some cotton stuffed rag doll.

I was about to make a complaint when a nasty, musty smelling sac was shoved over my head. It had clearly been used to carry some type of feed. I kept my mouth pinned shut and took shallow breaths through my nose to avoid inhaling too much of the rancid sediment of grain that remained within the fabric's weaves. Like the pain of the straw pokes paled in comparison to the pain in my twisted arms, so did the claustrophobia of the cave wane in comparison to the confines of the suffocating sac.

For the first time since I'd arrived, I questioned whether I would live or die.

I was unceremoniously shoved into a cart.

I was grateful for the thickness of the tightly woven silk I wore as I'm sure I would have met with an onslaught of slivers from the roughhewn planked floor of the cart, had I not had its protection. Had I realized the hole behind the tapestry on my wall led outdoors, I would have donned my cloak. As it was, I was not only depending on the layers of clothing I wore for protection against the cart, but for whatever warmth they could provide as well. Where I would normally silently lament about the unmerciful number of articles of clothing a woman was expected to layer onto her person simply to leave her room, at that particular time, I was extremely grateful.

CHAPTER TEN

I don't know how long I was in that cart or to where we traveled because we either went over an enormous rut and I hit my head and passed out, or someone hit my head for me. Whatever the means, I was unconscious for a while. When I awoke the sac was off my head, my arms were free, and I was in a large cage at the edge of the woods with six other battle worn females. After a series of cautious questions, I learned that we were all convicted of witchcraft and were to be hanged at dawn.

I experienced a whirlwind of emotions.

I feared for my life.

I feared for Isabelle's life.

I longed to have Duncan come rescue me.

I missed Duncan.

I hated Duncan.

I regretted meeting Duncan.

I regretted falling in love with Duncan.

I still loved Duncan, even though he was a shit who hooked up with me because Margaret was no longer available.

I regretted trying to save him.

I wanted to go home.

I was hours into my enumeration of why I regretted meeting Duncan, how I felt about Duncan, and how I felt about my foolish act of going back in time to save him, when two cloaked figures approached the cage. Amazingly my co-prisoners were sleeping; although how they managed such a feat just hours before they were to dangle from a rope until dead, I'll never understand. I was the only one awake and alert enough to notice Elizabeth and Garth creep up to the cage and slice through the thick leather hinges that prevented me from reaching freedom.

I reached out to shake one of my co-prisoners, but Elizabeth stopped me before motioning me to follow. The night had been a harrowing experience, but somehow I managed to keep my wits about me and followed them silently. I looked back briefly at the sleeping figures huddled together in the cage and hoped they woke early enough to realize their freedom was only inches away. I regretted not being able to alert them, but the slightest sound could have brought Vivian's people running. I considered throwing a stone into the cage, but if I startled anyone and they yelped it could mean not only my death, but the death of my rescuers as well. It was better to just leave the door ajar and hope the women noticed before it was too late. I prayed they would.

We ran a good distance through the woods until we reached a small clearing where our horses were tethered. Still, no one spoke.

Garth surveyed our surroundings before helping me onto my mount. This time I was allowed to ride astride, which made it so much easier for me to keep up with them. They were both remarkably adept riders.

It took the better part of an hour to reach the Colliers' Estate. We dismounted when we saw the buildings in the distance and walked our mounts the remainder of the way. This not only allowed us to approach quietly, but it gave the horses an opportunity to cool down after their long ride.

"Not a word of this to anyone," Elizabeth said firmly to Garth as she took my hand and pulled me out of the stables. "Follow me, m' lady. I know a short cut."

I wasn't sure I was up to any more secret passages, but I also didn't want to have to explain my condition or the fact that I was out of the Mansion in the middle of the night, so I dubiously followed her. To my surprise and delight, the short cut was nothing more than a stairway used by the servants.

When we reached my rooms, I leaned against the door,

closed my eyes, and took a moment to allow myself to react to the ordeal I'd just endured. My legs trembled and my body hurt from head to toe. My hair was littered with feed dust and I wanted a long hot bath more than I could remember ever wanting one. Elizabeth seemed to understand and left me alone until I was mobile again.

"Where is Isabelle? Did you find her?" I asked.

"She helped us find you," Elizabeth replied.

"Where is she?" I asked again as I looked around the room.

"You must rest, m' lady. Garth will set up your bath for you and, once we have washed away the filth of that place, you must sleep," she said softly.

"What of Isabelle?" I demanded.

"Alas, m' lady," Elizabeth said hesitantly, "she did not survive."

"What? How can that be? Did you not just say 'twas she who led you to me?" I asked with despair.

I was really struggling to stay in character. I'd had it with everything eighteenth century, especially their mode of speech. Trying to remember proper English and omit the slang of modern day when under such stress was all too trying. I wanted to go home and, when I did, I could guarantee I'd never accept an acting part that required I speak in this manner.

I had one day left to find Isabelle and get the hell out of there and I planned on doing just that. She couldn't be dead. She just couldn't.

"She performed a casting spell to find you," Elizabeth said. "It took the last of her magic. As you know," she hesitated, "'twas her magic keeping her alive."

My stomach flipped uncontrollably and what little I had left from the cuisine I'd dined on the night before came purging out onto the wide wooden planked flooring. Elizabeth might just as well have said I killed my friend. If it weren't for me, she would be going about her merry way in twenty-first century Manhattan without a care in the world. Instead, because of my stupidity, she'd returned to a time and place that didn't support her magical spell for longevity of life and used what little magic she'd been able to salvage upon her arrival to locate me.

I summed up my situation.

My dear friend was dead.

I'd miscalculated my jump back in time and Duncan wasn't even here.

I discovered I was a dead ringer for Duncan's true love.

An evil witch wanted me dead and I might not be able to go back to the future, in which case I'd die anyway.

Could things get any worse?

****

There was no funeral for Isabelle because there was no body; therefore, there was no closure for me. All I had to hang onto of my dear friend was a jar full of ashes that Elizabeth had the presence of mind to collect.

I spent the day in my room, feigning a headache. I had no desire to walk amongst the guests of the household. I found them artificial and stuffy. I wondered if I was getting a small taste of what life at court was like.

I was lying on my bed staring at the ceiling when I heard Isabelle say, "You are wasting time. Get up and get moving."

I sat up and looked around the room.

I was alone.

Puzzled, I walked to the tapestry and pulled it away from the wall. I had no desire to venture down that dank and stifling doorway to doom again, but I thought perhaps Isabelle was hiding there. Had she faked her death?

"I didn't fake my death. I actually died," she said. "Look behind you."

I turned and looked behind me, but saw only my empty room, nothing more.

"Really look!" she shouted.

I strained my eyes to look for whatever it was I was supposed to be looking for, but could still see only the room I stood in.

"What am I supposed to be seeing?" I asked with frustration.

"Me," she replied flatly. "Don't try so hard."

"First you tell me to really look and then you say don't try so hard. Which is it?" I demanded. It was only then that I realized Isabelle and I were using the twenty-first century style of speaking. "Is it wise to use modern English? Did you not just reprimand me about this?"

"You are the only one who can hear me," she said with a bit of humor in her voice. "Now relax and look again."

It finally dawned on me that Isabelle was a ghost speaking to me. I hadn't spoken with a ghost in quite some time, but I still remembered how to focus to be able to see one. I allowed my eyes to relax and my vision to blur. Sure enough, there before me stood a full apparition of my dear friend Isabelle.

"Hello, my friend," I smiled.

"Hello," she smiled back.

"I miss you already," I whimpered. "I'm so sorry."

Isabelle scoffed and waved her hand.

"Oh stop," she said casually. "I led a long, long, long life that was full of adventure. I have no regrets; so don't you have any either. Your only concern now should be getting the hell out of here before that crazy Vivian realizes you've escaped the gallows and comes looking for you."

"I'd forgotten about her," I moaned.

"Well, she certainly hasn't forgotten about you. So, get a move on. You have only one more day before you need to hightail it out of here,' she scolded.

"I know," I snapped.

"You've got it rough, whether you stay here or go back,"

Isabelle whistled.

"What do you mean?" She had my curiosity.

"Duncan is in a rage right now," she practically whispered, as if he'd hear her or something. "He was frantic looking for you and then he realized I was gone too. I finally had to pop in and tell him what was going on."

"He knows you're dead?" I started to shake.

"Yep," she said flatly.

"He blames me for your death," I wailed.

"Don't feel bad," Isabelle chuckled. "He went into an even bigger rage when he asked me to bring him back here and I said 'no can do'. There's no sight on this earth that compares to that of a raging vampire."

I did my best to subdue the mixture of panic and anger that rose in me. It was understandable that Duncan would be upset with me for the stunt I pulled that resulted in Isabelle's death. Well, maybe upset is a little mild. Anyway, I get that and that's why I panicked. I was, after all, a fill in for Margaret. How angry with me was he? Would I be safe with him if we encountered each other or would he want to teach me a lesson that could cost me my life? For the first time since I'd met Duncan, I was afraid of him.

The fact that he went into a rage because Isabelle wouldn't bring him back angered me. Since Isabelle was already dead and his returning would do nothing to help her -especially since Duncan hadn't inherited the magic gene from his father- then the only reason I could see that he'd want to return for would be to keep Margaret from meeting up with me. Wouldn't we have stories to share?

Well, since Margaret was in the future with him the joke was on him. It looked like we both lost out.

"You couldn't or you wouldn't?" I asked.

None of this was Isabelle's fault and I knew she deserved a better tone of voice from me, but my anger with Duncan just wouldn't calm down enough for me to pull "nice" off.

"Magic works differently here," she sighed.

"Well, he needn't worry about getting back to his precious Lady Margaret anyway. I hear tell she's in the future looking for him," I said with a shrug. "Besides, why did he wait so long to ask to come back? He's known you for centuries. You could've sent him back anytime during all those years. I don't get it."

"First and foremost, Duncan did not wish his family to know what became of him. This is why he allowed them to think Vivian teleported him into the future," Isabelle said as she leaned closer and spoke in a deep husky voice. "Between you and me.... Our wicked witch hasn't the power to do such a feat."

I couldn't contain my gasp. Was teleporting really that complicated? What kind of danger had I put myself into? This was a classic example of putting a child behind the wheel of a car and handing them the keys without driving lessons. It's a crap shoot whether they'll make it down the street without killing someone or themselves. So far, I'd killed Isabelle. I was probably next.

"I thought...," I managed to get out before she continued.

"Secondly," she continued. "Even if he had wanted to return, it took him most of this time to accept and adjust to being vampire. It is not that easy for the pure of heart to turn into something they consider a monster."

"He's not a monster," I blurted without thinking.

"Of course he's not a monster," she said assuringly.

He's a very sad victim of darkness who still holds within him enough light to keep from succumbing to the evil they tried to plant within him."

"Did Vivian make him a vampire?" I asked hesitantly.

Isabelle threw her head back and laughed as she said, "On my dear, dear Jane. You give that horrible creature far more credit than she deserves. Why do you think she tried to pin witchcraft on you and have you hanged at the gallows? If she was truly an adept magical being, do you think she would have to rely on the primitive means of man to do her bidding?"

"The birds," I mumbled as I rubbed my arms.

"She is a witch," Isabelle explained. "She has witchy comrades to do her bidding, but she and her friends are no match for you, my friend. No match at all."

I stared at Isabelle as if she had five heads. Was she kidding me? Had death altered her perception of things? I'd only started studying magic a few years ago and I'd proven quite skillfully that I hadn't a clue what I was doing. I was about to correct my ghost friend about her assessment of the situation when Elizabeth entered the room. Just like that, Isabelle was gone and I knew she wouldn't return again until I was alone.

I heaved a sigh of remorse and disappointment before turning to Elizabeth.

"How do you feel this evening m' lady?" Elizabeth asked with a sympathetic tone.

She was proving to be a reliable ally for me. It was time for me to see just how much of an ally she was. I needed help getting back to the portal in time. I decided to tell all and hope she'd be open minded enough to help.

"But, this is your home, m' lady. I do not understand why you might wish to leave it. If Lord Duncan is truly a vampire 'twould not do to mix with him. Vampires can be unpredictable," she uttered softly.

She didn't get it. My heart sank and, for some crazy reason that I couldn't explain. Suddenly my defenses went up. Was she saying Duncan couldn't be trusted? The look on my face was worth more than a thousand words.

"I am sorry m' lady," she quivered, "please forgive me... I... I did not mean..."

Realizing I was probably frightening the poor superstitious gentle woman I sighed.

"'Tis me who is sorry," I assured her. "Perhaps I need to lay down a bit more. I shall have dinner in my room tonight. Please inform cook."

With Isabelle gone, Elizabeth was all I had left. It wouldn't do to alienate her with my rash temper. I couldn't blame her for not understanding. She lived in a world of magic, superstition, secrecy, and fanatic religious control. Science had yet to interfere with imaginations like it had in the twenty-first century and politics had yet to invade the backward control of the masses. Electrical use didn't mute the elements of nature required to easily tap into the inherent magic of the earth. She existed in a world that was opposite mine in so many ways. Much of what they considered normal and every day, we considered fantasy, fake, or fanatical. What we considered natural was so unnatural to them that it could only be from the devil himself.

I'd tried to convince Elizabeth that I hadn't lost my mind and I truly wasn't Lady Margaret, but to no avail. Apparently the concept of a doppelganger hadn't been introduced yet. She was convinced my lack of recall was caused by one of two things; either Vivian-the-Horrid had placed a spell on me to make me forget Lord Duncan or the teleporting had confused my mind. She leaned toward the latter, but wouldn't rule out the first.

It took some convincing to get her to agree to help me slip away to the portal of return the following day. I assumed she decided it was better to humor me for a while. Whatever the reason, I was grateful. In a matter of hours, I'd be back in my own apartment and in my own bed. I felt peace for the first time since I'd arrived.

The thought of having to face Duncan when I returned flitted through my mind, but I forced it back out again. I knew I was being silly fearing him. I may have been a substitute for Margaret, but we'd spent far too much time together for his true nature not to be displayed. I knew that, no matter how angry he was with me, he'd never intentionally hurt me. I'd give him that, at least. I'd managed to send myself back in time successfully. If I could do it once, I could do it again. If sending him back in time to be with his one true love is what it took to appease my irate vampire, then so be it. My future with him was over with anyway. What did it matter where he went or who he was with?

It shouldn't have mattered. I told myself that it didn't, but somewhere in the recesses of my emotional body, tears were being shed. Duncan Collier was my one true love and I doubted I'd ever feel that way about anyone again. My heart was crushed and so were my hopes for the future.

CHAPTER ELEVEN

I found it humorous and fitting that I spent my evening in my room dining on oxtail soup; although it was far tastier and more robust than anything the cook at the inn provided. We always got the broth that was left over after she'd ladled the thick chunks of meat and vegetables to the paying guest. The occasional chunk of meat and vegetable were far and few between. The bread the estate's bakery produced was light and crusty and the sweet butter couldn't be compared with. It struck me for the first time that I'd been eating organic the entire time I was there. Even my watered down oxtail soup and crusty stale bread at the inn had been free of preservatives. Between the clean food, fresh air, and enforced exercise, I had to admit I felt better. I wondered if the benefits of this lifestyle on my body would teleport with me into the future or if I'd return to the Jane I was prior to my little adventure.

I'd decided to look at the experience as an adventure and not the catastrophe it felt like. Perhaps my change in viewpoint would help smooth over what time I had left until I returned to my own era through the portal. I finished my dinner and walked over to the opened window. The night air felt cool and refreshing. It helped to sooth my overheated nerves. The sun set about an hour earlier and the estate was settling down for the night. I saw no harm in taking a short stroll through the gardens. I hadn't been out of my room since Elizabeth and Garth's heroic rescue of me from my near hanging.

I had my cloak in hand when I noticed the tapestry on the wall sway ever so slightly. That tapestry was so heavy, only one of two things would disturb it; a huge gust of wind or human hands. Since the night air was amazingly still, it had to be the other.

I stopped in my tracks and waited. The room was so quiet that my breathing rang out in my ears. I hoped I wasn't really breathing that heavy or whoever was on the other side of the tapestry would know I was terrified. It wasn't good to give your attacker clues of that nature.

I inched my way toward the edge of the heavy fabric. My heart pounded to the point I was sure it would lodge in my throat and suffocate me. My legs felt weak and unable to support my fabric laden body. Sweat covered my brow and saturated my armpits; which activated the cloves in the musky underarm powder Elizabeth encouraged me to wear. If I hadn't been so worked up about who was stalking in the secret passageway, I might have actually enjoyed the exotic scent.

I had my hand on the edge of the tapestry and was just about to peek behind it when Elizabeth entered the room. I dropped my hand quickly and moved away from the wall. I held my finger to my lips and nodded my head toward the tapestry that just happened to move noticeably at the same time.

Elizabeth scowled and stormed to the fabric covered hole in the wall. She yanked the material aside to display a very chagrinned Garth standing on the other side.

I gasped in horror, "What are you doing? How long have you been there?"

"M' lady, I..." he stammered.

"'Tis my fault, m' lady," Elizabeth interrupted him. "I asked him to guard the opening of the passageway against intruders who might be coming to fetch you back to the gallows."

I gasped at the thought.

"He was expected to remain at the opening," she explained while she shot him daggerous looks.

"They might come after me?" I asked timidly.

"'Vivian has ill humor for losing and you have given her losses right along," she said.

"I have only just met her. How could I be giving her losses, other than my escape from the gallows that is?" I asked.

As the words came out of my mouth, I realized that they still believed me to be Lady Margaret and apparently Lady Vivian and Lady Margaret were involved in an ongoing war.

"Refresh my memory," I urged, "Why are Lady Vivian and I at war?"

"M' lady recalls nothing?" Garth asked.

He looked shocked.

"M' lady suffers memory loss from a... a fall," Elizabeth volunteered.

Okay, so now I knew that not everyone in the household was privy to the time travel thing. I made a mental note to question Elizabeth as to who within the castle was privy to their underground world of magic.

"I do not recall hearing of it," Garth mused indignantly.

I am to be informed of such things."

An uncomfortable silence settled through the room. Garth obviously felt his position had been usurped. I'd only met him when he brought in my bath, and even then I was hiding behind the tapestry. I just assumed he was a servant used for grunt work. Apparently I was mistaken.

"I asked Elizabeth to tell none about it. 'Tis my fault," I volunteered.

Elizabeth shot me a look of gratitude and relief.

"His lordship charged me with looking out for m' lady's wellbeing," Garth puffed his chest out with self-importance.

"'Tis my duty to know about such as this."

"I apologize. I shall be sure to have you summoned to assist should I fall or feel peril again," I cooed.

Garth flashed me a grin that displayed wide gaps where teeth had once been before bowing low and disappearing into the darkness of the tunnel.

"I do wish that hole gone," I pouted.

"Oh no, m' lady. 'Tis a good space that you make great use of," she beckoned me to follow her behind the tapestry.

I hesitated. It hadn't been that long ago that I'd followed Isabelle behind that tapestry and look how that turned out.

I soon discovered Elizabeth knew what went on behind the tapestry as fully as she did what happened in front of it. She lit a candle and then another until we were adequately illuminated. I saw my surroundings were more than just a passageway to the outside. To my immediately left was a low door. Elizabeth opened it and walked through as if she expected me to follow without having to be asked. So I did.

I had to bend quite low to avoid hitting my head on the top of the door frame as I stepped cautiously into a small chamber. In an era where owning one or two books was a big deal, I was shocked to see a narrow bookcase filled with leather bound books of all shapes and sizes. There had to be at least twenty-five of them. I walked over and lightly caressed a row. They were well polished and free of dust; as if recently attended to.

"Who owns these books?" I asked in wonder.

"You are the owner, m' lady," she explained. "'Tis in this very chamber that you work the magic to keep Lady Vivian from overtaking the earl's estate and possessing Lord Duncan body and soul."

"Do you believe Lady Vivian has such power?" I asked.

"I do, m' lady, as do the others," Elizabeth nodded her head vigorously.

"Why?" I asked.

"She is part devil," she hissed.

"I realize she is an unpleasant sort, but I saw no serious magic used against me," I mused aloud. "Other than the unpleasant flight to my captivity, she showed me no signs of being a powerful evil sorceress." Then I said to myself more than to her, "Although her eyes did flash some light briefly."

Elizabeth took a deep breath and let it out slowly. I wasn't sure if this was because she was losing patience with my inability for recall or if she was simply preparing for a long speech. Maybe it was a little of both.

"You bound her powers before you teleported," she explained. "She recruited a less adept witch to help her until she finds a way to undo your spell. This witch is still a very strong witch, but her magic cannot compare to your own. The flashing eyes are proof of magic being channeled through her by another. 'Tis why Lady Vivian was depending on including you in the hanging. The end of your life signifies the end of the spell."

"Or it could just be taken off as it was put on," I blurted without thinking.

"You would do that?" she gasped.

"Rather than die? Of course I would... if I knew how," I mumbled.

"You do know how, m' lady," she said eagerly, "Even if you cannot recall the spell, I am sure 'tis in one of these books. You have always kept a ledger of your spells performed. Surely the one you did on Vivian is in it."

I felt excited for the first time in I couldn't remember when.

"Where is this ledger?" I asked as I looked around the alcove eagerly.

"'Tis hidden even from me," Elizabeth said. She sounded deflated when she asked, "Truly, you not recall?"

"Truly," I sighed.

Elizabeth was Margaret's personal maid. I just couldn't believe she wouldn't believe that I wasn't Lady Margaret. There had to be differences in us, even subtle ones, to prove we were two different people. Yet, no one, not even Elizabeth, could see them. I found this both amazing and frustrating.

"Well, 'twill matter not soon. Tomorrow I travel to the cave and await the opening of the portal and return to the future," I said with relief.

Elizabeth looked uncomfortable, but said nothing.

I think I would have preferred she spoke.

The reality of my situation hit me like a brick. There was a crazy woman who practiced magic that wanted to kill me. Since I'd botched the timing in returning, how could I be sure I hadn't botched the return trip as well? Was I able to leave here at all, and if I was, would I be returning to the right time and place?

I decided to forgo the walk. I had no desire to risk being captured by Lady Vivian's cronies and miss my one opportunity to return to the future. If I did, it wouldn't matter how I died; at the hands of the hangman or because the magic that kept me there ran out. The fact of the matter was that I would die.

CHAPTER TWELVE

I'd been awake for hours before Elizabeth entered my room with hot chocolate and warm sweet buns. I had to admit that there were some things about my time there that I'd miss. Their hot chocolate was chocolate mixed with water instead of milk. It had a bitter base and was sweetened with an oversized dollop of whipped sweet cream and their warm sweet buns would rival any bakery in Manhattan.

I felt good. This was the day I was going home. Bye-bye eighteenth century, hello twenty-first century. I felt excited, yet relaxed. Since I was never one to eat in bed, after a long cat-like stretch, I climbed out of bed and padded over to the small table Elizabeth set my breakfast tray on.

"Today is the day I return," I managed between alternating mouthfuls of sweet bun and hot chocolate.

"Yes, m' lady," she replied hesitantly.

I questioned Elizabeth about her hesitancy and, once again, she expressed her concern for my lack of recall and insistence that I could return to the future without the use of a spell. Although she had no desire to see me leave again, she had concerns about my going so far from the estate alone; especially with Vivian hot on my tail. She practically begged me to let her confer with the earl about my plans and see if he thought the spell could be worked again without my magical participation. Apparently a spell like the one that was cast to send Margaret forward into the future required an incredible amount of magic from the castor. This information didn't surprise me, since I'd had to save up magical energy and use what Isabelle, and I had banked as well, in order to cast my own spell.

I knew I didn't have the same magical skills and power

as Margaret, but I had enough to get me back in time. I was banking the spell was also strong enough to complete the cycle and return me home. I just needed to be there when the portal opened. This was vital.

I tried not to think about the fact that I'd missed my mark in the timeline for the eighteenth century and that I might have done the same for my return trip. I couldn't worry about that. I just needed to keep focused on the fact that my magic spell would cease to exist after the portal opened and closed and, if I didn't pass through that portal, I'd eventually end up like Isabelle. Since I was supposed to be alive when I cast the spell and not keeping myself alive like Isabelle had been doing, I wouldn't disintegrate as quickly as she did. The fact was, I had no idea how long it would take me to die, but I would die.

Unfortunately, Elizabeth confided my kidnapping episode to the earl. I couldn't take the chance that he'd be able to ensure my return back to the future if he tried to do the spell without Margaret's participation. Since he truly believed I was Lady Margaret returned without her mind -so to speak- I was afraid he'd refuse to allow me to make the journey to the cave.

By the position of the sun, I estimated I had about five hours left before the portal opened. I didn't want to take any chances. I asked Elizabeth to have cook pack me a light picnic lunch and to ask the groom to ready my mount. She insisted on going with me and I didn't refuse. I needed someone to return the horse for me, after all. Not to mention the fact that in the short time I'd been with her, I'd grown quite fond of Elizabeth and was a little saddened about leaving her behind. I welcomed spending as much time with her as I could until the portal opened.

We passed the time away during our long ride to the cave discussing Margaret. Elizabeth volunteered as much information as she could come up with in hopes I'd remember that I was Lady Margaret. I asked as many questions as I could think of in order to understand my doppelganger a little better.

I also had Duncan to think about. Now that I knew he'd been engaged to someone who was my doppelganger, or vice versa, I was more than curious about their life together before he turned vampire. I also had to consider the fact that Margaret was at that very moment in the future searching for Duncan. What would happen when she found him?

I'd managed to tame my initial reaction of rage and jealousy when I discovered Duncan's fiancé was the image of me. I had Isabelle to thank for that. Somehow she'd managed to infiltrate my dreams and communicate some sense into me. I still thought he was a shit for not telling me up front that I looked just like her, but I'd give him the opportunity to explain. After all, I did love him and love doesn't die with a lie. If it did, then it wasn't love to begin with.

I discovered that Margaret and I had more in common than our looks. We were both magical and both orphans. Her parents were killed in a carriage accident a few years earlier. Mine were killed in a car crash a few years back. Margaret was lucky enough to be tucked safely in bed when her parents met their demise. I wasn't so lucky. I was actually in the car with them when a big rig swerved and sent our car tumbling off the highway. I don't remember the particulars. In fact, I don't remember much of anything prior to the accident. It's almost as if my life began the day I woke up in the hospital with a Jane Doe tag on my wrist.

I'd been found wandering the side of the highway a few miles from the accident. I'd managed to escape without a scratch on me, but my head was pretty messed up. I couldn't even state my own name. Fortunately, they found enough evidence in the remains of the car crash to connect me with the older couple and when they checked on the couple they learned they'd had a daughter my age. So, through the powers of deduction, my identity was salvaged.

I spent a while in what they called a rehabilitation home. I called it an institution. Whatever it was, I wasn't allowed to leave until I'd passed their psychiatric evaluation and proved I was just fine. My roommate was an internet fanatic who was more than happy to help me find as much information as I could on the Wells family. Between public records, social networking, and ancestry.com I'd managed to piece together a good deal about my family. As far as my childhood memories went, I just made something up based around the events I'd managed to discover. It worked to the point I eventually began to believe they were true.

Because of the way I'd discovered my identity, I ignored the Margaret on my name and went with Jane, taking the Doe away and replacing it with my family name of Wells. It seemed more fitting.

Eight months after my accident, I was released into my own competent care. The first thing I did was to visit my parent's grave. Even if I couldn't remember them, I could feel the loss of them deep inside me. I spent the majority of the day talking to them, crying for them, and asking for their help from beyond.

Someone must have heard me and decided to oblige because just before I was about to leave and look for a hotel, Chuck approached me. He'd been visiting his grandfather's grave and noticed me earlier in the day. For reasons unknown to him, I plagued his mind until he returned to find me still at my parents' gravesites. He introduced himself to me in such a fun-filled, bubbly fashion that it was impossible not to like and trust him immediately. I followed him home, where he introduced me to his lover and roommate, Doug.

It was Doug who encouraged me to follow my dream of acting. In truth, I wasn't aware I had ambitions of acting until Doug pointed it out to me. He insisted I was a natural. Once I investigated, studied, and entered the theater, I couldn't have been happier.

It was through the theater that I met Linda. We were immediate friends. We seemed to have the same viewpoint on the world and a similar sense of humor. Her interest in the world of magic was infectious. It wasn't long before I was pouring over every book I could get my hands on and attending every gathering open to me. The option of joining a coven was offered to me on more than one occasion, but I declined. I had an aversion to the term witch and didn't consider myself one. I was an alchemist and magician, not a witch. I had no particular religious belief attached to the magic I performed. It simply fascinated me and came easy to me, so I did it.

Once I'd connected with Duncan, Linda slowly faded away. She felt uncomfortable in his company and made no bones about telling me. Of course, I understood the reason, but I wasn't free to share that with her. It put a small wedge between us. I wouldn't say it ended our friendship, but it definitely left a gap in my life. Duncan's introducing me to Isabelle filled that gap splendidly. She was the female friend I desired, the magic professor I needed, and in many ways the mother figure I lacked.

It was clear to me that Elizabeth had been Margaret's closest friend and confidant. She wasn't a magician, but she had a strong understanding of that world and supported those who walked in it; the earl being one.

I questioned her about the fact that Lady Margaret and the earl were magical, yet Duncan was not. A cloud of sadness swept over her as she explained how Lady Vivian had stripped Duncan of his magic without his knowledge just moments before he was attacked by a creature. Although they were certain the creature was made of darkness and sent by Lady Vivian to seek revenge against Lord Duncan for thwarting her, they had no idea what it was so they were powerless to combat the poison that raced through his body. They thought he died for a while. They'd even laid him out in state and prepared his body for burial. By the sheer grace of God, he revived on the third day. Laying one out for several days was a standard practice because of the fact that the person may be mistaken as dead when, in fact, he was in an unconscious state that shuts down his body to the point it is difficult to detect life. What puzzled them was the fact that Lord Duncan lost almost all of his blood from the horrific gash on his neck where the beast tore his meat from his bones, yet when he revived, not only had the wound healed miraculously, but so did Lord Duncan. He seemed as healthy, if not healthier, than he was prior to the attack. The only difference being that his magic was lost. No matter what he did, he couldn't get it back.

Lord Duncan confided in his father and Lady Margaret that Lady Vivian had threatened to teleport him to another time in order to keep him from his love. He warned that if he should disappear they shouldn't fret and look for him, but know that he was alive and well somewhere and would always hold them dear in his hearts. It wasn't long after that when Lord Duncan disappeared.

The earl was beyond himself with grief. He and the magical group I'd met at dinner my first night at the estate spent hours upon hours looking for a spell to get him back. They finally came upon the spell they used to send Lady Margaret into the future where their seer felt he was, hoping that once she was there she could cast a spell to return both herself and Lord Duncan.

So, Duncan told me the truth. His family didn't know he was vampire and didn't know he'd left on his own accord in order to keep this a secret. The only thing he'd left out was the fact that I looked like Margaret. The verdict was still out on how I truly felt about that. Now that I'd had time to process it, I knew it wasn't enough to break us up, but boy did he have some explaining to do.

We reached the cave with no mishap. The ride went far quicker with Elizabeth's good conversation mixed with a bit of laughter than it had at any other time. I was feeling pretty good and had almost forgotten about the fact that I'd be leaving my new friend behind within a few hours' time and would never see her again. It must have hit her as well because a thin layer of gloom fell over us as we dismounted in silence.

Elizabeth set out to find a secure place to tether the

horses while I spread out the blanket. The cave was located on the side of a rocky hill, but I managed to find a level spot with a soft grass covering to set our picnic up on. The cook wrapped the chicken especially tight before placing it in the pottery pail with fresh baked biscuits and roasted turnip. The aroma of the still warm food caused my mouth to salivate to the point I just had to have a nibble of chicken, no matter how rude it might be.

I was just swallowing a bite of succulent chicken when I heard Elizabeth returning. I quickly wiped my fingers in the folds of my skirt and turned to greet her.

"I have laid it all out. Cook did a spectac..." I began and then stopped short with surprise.

It wasn't Elizabeth's crystal green eyes that stared at me with enough venom to kill a full grown man. It was Lady Vivian's evil dark orbs. Elizabeth's terrified eyes could be seen above the thick hand of one of Vivian's goons that was planted over her mouth to silence any warning she might have been able to pull off.

"You again," I growled, not bothering to speak with an accent.

I was too enraged to think of anything but the fact that this bitch was once again on the attack.

This couldn't be happening. From the position of the sun, the portal would be opening very soon and I had to pass through it. I couldn't have evil Vivian spoiling my plans. My mind raced on what to do.

"You truly are a bother," Lady Vivian said with a pouty tone as she sat next to me on the blanket and helped herself to my picnic fare. She gnawed a sailor's bite of meat off the chicken leg before tossing it to one of her men, who stealthily caught it and immediately devoured what she'd left behind.

"By all means, help yourself," I said, not bothering to hide my distaste.

"Whoever you may be, you have spunk," she spat out while masticating the flesh in her mouth.

"Let's not forget manners," I added.

Lady Vivian, belle of the ball to all who were blind to her true self, dabbed daintily at her greasy grin with a linen napkin. The action was in such stark contrast to her eating display that I chuckled.

"Perhaps you would share the amusement?" she growled.

"Someone told me Lady Vivian Everhoust was the season's belle for the last two years. I just question the criteria," I giggled.

Big mistake.

With lightning speed Witch Vivian nodded her head and her goonies were upon me. It happened so quickly, I didn't have time to think; let alone act. Once again, I was caught in her trap and at her mercy.

I looked at the position of the sun. The portal would be opening any time now. I struggled against my captors, but to no avail. I was doomed. This just couldn't be happening.

They tied a rope around Elizabeth's waist and then continued on to mine. As if binding us together wasn't enough, they also bound our wrists in front of us, looping a lead between our wrists to pull us along.

We were made to follow their horses on foot. The length of my riding skirt kept tripping me up and more than once I landed face first in the dirt path. Elizabeth wasn't doing much better. I suppose we should have been grateful that we were in an outfit that was designed for activity and not in a typical day dress.

Although my riding boots were well made, they were intended for sitting atop a horse, not long walks down a hillside trail. I longed for my Reeboks.

The sun was in position. I could feel the vibration of the portal opening. It swept and swooshed the air past my face with abnormal force. I wondered if the others felt it. If so, did they understand what was happening?

"There be a storm comin' m' lady," the oaf leading me

said to his mistress.

"We shall have to pick up the pace," she replied.

With that, they spurred the horses into an even faster walk, mindless of whether Elizabeth and I were upright or not.

CHAPTER THIRTEEN

The sun was setting.

Elizabeth and I sat huddled together in one of the oh-so-familiar cages they placed their witch trial victims in to await hanging. It was dark when Vivian captured me the first time and tossed me into the confines of death. I'd had little opportunity to really inspect the cell's composition and structure.

This one appeared pretty much like the other. The bars were made of iron and spaced eight to ten inches apart. It was fortunate that none of the captive's height exceeded six feet or they wouldn't have been able to stand upright. The cage was slightly more crowded than my previous prison, making it difficult to tolerate the stench of dirt and sweat that was inevitable on such poor mistreated creatures as we.

The one difference I noted in the construction of the iron cell block was a major one and probably sealed our fate. Elizabeth managed to rescue me by slicing through the leather hinges on the door. The hinges on this door were made of the same iron as the bar. We were locked in tight with no way out even if someone did know where to find us. Since we'd left the castle on the pretense of taking a picnic on the edge of the estate grounds, I seriously doubted anyone would look for us here. By the time they realized we were gone, it would be too late.

I mentioned my fears to Elizabeth and, with tear filled eyes that clearly relayed her fear, she nodded her agreement.

It will never cease to be amazed at how I somehow lacked the common sense to be afraid. I wasn't afraid when I was attacked by the vampires. I wasn't afraid when I learned Duncan was a vampire. I wasn't afraid the first time Vivian captured me and I still couldn't muster the appropriate fear that the very real probability of being hanged at first light should produce.

What was wrong with me?

Although the moaning and tears of my cellmates never totally ceased, things calmed down to a tolerable degree as the day turned to night when my companions in misery eventually drifted into an exhausted sleep. I was once again able to hear myself think. I leaned back against the bars and laid Elizabeth's head in my lap. She'd mercifully fallen asleep about an hour earlier. My heart ached for her. It was bad enough to actually be a person of magic and be hanged for it, but to be innocent was frustratingly horrible. I looked around the cell at the dirty, forlorn faces and tried to pick out the true witches amongst the victims.

I found only one.

She looked back at me through the eerie star lit darkness with knowing eyes, but said nothing. Not wanting to disturb Elizabeth, I willed the woman to come to me.

She did.

"Cannot you do something to be free of this?" I whispered. "Surely there is a way..."

"Anna. My name is Anna," she whispered, "There is a way, but it takes more power than I possess."

"I am Jane," I said with a chagrinned smile over my lack of manners before asking hesitantly, "What if we worked it together?"

I hadn't tried to use magic since I'd arrived and I wasn't sure I'd be able to, but it was worth a try.

Anna looked at me long and hard before saying, "Only you and I shall be freed."

My heart flew up into my throat. What was she saying? Was she expecting me to abandon Elizabeth to the fate that awaited her? That couldn't be. I must have misunderstood.

"No, we shall do the spell for all of us," I said nervously.

I was finally afraid.

"It will only work for witches. Your friend is not a witch," she replied bluntly.

"I shall not leave her. 'Tis because of me she is here. I shant abandon her," I half wailed, half whispered.

"I have not the power to help her. I am sorry," she said with sincerity. "I am limited with my knowledge."

Since I still considered myself an apprentice, I would have been a hypocrite to complain to the witch about her lack of skills. I closed my eyes and took a deep breath. My heart broke in two at the thought of abandoning poor Elizabeth to such a fate. Maybe I should just go to the gallows with her. After all, I was going to die soon anyway. Why not forget about escaping with this witch and just get it over with?

As I mulled over my options, Isabelle's ghost appeared before me.

"Take heart, my friend," Isabelle said. "Help is on the way. Get out of this situation and come back for your maid."

"What help?" I said aloud.

Anna looked at me quizzically. It was clear she was unable to see or hear Isabelle and had no idea what I was talking about. I covered my mouth, feeling foolish for my outburst and looked around to see if anyone had awoken. They hadn't.

"I see spirits," I explained in a hushed voice. "My friend is here. She tells me help is coming."

"What help?" Anna asked.

I smiled, since that's exactly the reaction I had.

"I do not know. She disappeared before I could find out more," I whispered.

"Pray call her back. Find out... I beg you," she pleaded.

I closed my eyes and willed Isabelle back to me. It took a considerable amount of effort before I was successful. I attributed that to the fact that I'd missed the portal and was on my way out. Once again, I questioned why I was even bothering with escaping. My fate was already sealed.

Isabelle's ghostly figure was bright against the dimly lit night. I heard a gasp from Anna, who was finally able to see her. I wondered if this was the first time my new found conspirator had ever seen a ghost, but decided now wasn't the time to ask. We had more important things to worry about. Even if my fate was sealed, I could at least do what I could to help these innocents escape a wrongful death.

We questioned my ghost friend about who the help might be that was coming, but she just kept smiling and telling us to wait and see. She did, however, give us a spell to perform that would loosen the hinges enough to pop the posts from the barrels manually and free ourselves.

We did the spell and watched in wonder as the posts elevated in the barrels enough for us to pry them out the rest of the way. We looked for a tool to use for the task, but there was nothing within reach. Anna said a few words and a rock rolled close enough for me to grab and pull through the bars. Its round shape wasn't ideal for the task, but it was better than nothing.

Anna ripped a piece of her petticoat to place between the rock and the hinge so the sound of rock on metal would be muffled and we set to work. It was an exhausting task. We had to stop on numerous occasions when we thought we heard someone approaching or voices in the distance. Finally, after what seemed like an eternity -but was probably more like a matter of minutes- we each took hold of the door and walked it away from the cage. Then, as quietly as we could, we roused our co-captives and urged them to run into the woods as quietly as they could.

We didn't wait to see what happened. Once I'd roused Elizabeth and beckoned her to follow me, we left everyone else to their own devices. I could only hope one of them didn't do something stupid to bring attention to the escape.

We ran as fast as we could into the woods surrounding the clearing. Fortunately, Anna was from the area and knew the woods well. She led us to a small shack where we stopped to rest. We knew we still weren't far enough away from the hanging circle to let our guard down, but our bodies needed a little time to rejuvenate before we continued on.

It was eighteen hours since Elizabeth and I ate anything and our stomachs made it known as they echoed through the night silence. Anna looked mildly embarrassed by what I considered a natural bodily function as she walked to the edge of the shack's one small window to peer out.

I didn't feel right. My body was tingling from head to toe and I felt dizzy. I wondered if it was from hunger or if I was just going to die right there in that little shack. I looked around the sparsely furnished room. I could barely make out Elizabeth as she sat on the floor and leaned against the wide planked wall. She looked so forlorn. The fear of being caged to await a hanging sapped the spark of life I'd admired so much right out of my new found friend. I wondered if it was a wise thing for me to inform her of my situation. She couldn't help with it anyway. No one could. I'd missed the portal opening and now it was only a matter of time before I ceased to exist. I wondered if -after tampering with time like I had- I'd still be born in the future.

"Quickly," Anna urged softly as she motioned for Elizabeth and I to join her. "Stay down low. They are outside."

I grabbed Elizabeth's hand and squeezed it reassuringly as I pulled her close to me behind Anna.

"I shall cloak us with the spell of invisibility. Let us pray they do not linger. I dare not say how long 'twill hold," Anna said before she immediately spoke in rapid succession, "We shant be seen, we shant be felt, we shant be heard, we shant be smelt by any that seek. So mote it be."

It was an amazing feeling that blanketed us. A sense of peace filled me from head to toe and, from the way Elizabeth's face relaxed, I guessed the same happened to her. I had to hand it to Anna. She may not have known too many spells, but the ones she did know, she knew well.

The haze that covered us made visibility of our surrounding near impossible, but I could still hear well enough. The shuffle of feet was close. I was sure that if I reached out

I'd be able to grab whoever was walking around the shack. I wasn't sure, but I got the feeling it was only one person and it was male. Maybe the others were outside searching the area.

Suddenly, a few more sets of feet walked across the roughhewn planks. The rest of the search party, I assumed.

"Ho there!" someone shouted as yet another person arrived.

I heard a brief, chaotic scuffle and then a horrific gurgling sound before an eerie silence fell over the room. The hairs on the back of my neck came alive. Elizabeth's nails dug into my flesh, but I dared not move. I had no idea who the newcomer was, but I got the feeling that he was the last man standing.

The surviving footsteps were much lighter and far more deliberate as he walked around the interior of the shack. I heard him leave and made ready to move, but Anna grabbed my arm to stop me while placing her finger to her lips and shaking her head. After straining my ears to hear over the erratic pounding of my heart, I realized that the newcomer was just outside the door. One move from any of us would have easily alerted him of our presence.

I willed my muscles to relax and did my best to steady my breathing and slow my heartbeat before I passed out from the whole ordeal. Okay, now I was scared. Even if I was destined to die, I didn't want it to be in the manner of the man who'd just been killed. I didn't need to see him to know it was a gruesome death.

The haze around us started to fade. Anna looked at me with horror. The spell was wearing off. Apparently, her weak point wasn't knowing the spells, but knowing how to cast them in a manner where they'd stick.

As I peered through the haze, I wondered if the figure standing in the doorway would be able to see me as well. I shuddered at the thought. The sun was high enough for its rays to frame his large silhouette as it filled the doorway. He was very tall, but not particularly wide. His stance had an air of grace about it. There was something familiar about the way he clasped his hands behind his back while in deep contemplation. When he turned so that I could view his profile, my heart stuck in my throat. I felt Elizabeth tighten her muscles beside me. Whether it was out of sheer shock or mistrust of what we saw, neither of us spoke.

I rubbed my eyes as if to clear them of the vision and allow reality to return to the room.

It didn't.

No matter how hard I rubbed my eyes or squeezed them open and shut, the vision of Duncan Colliers remained. How could that be? Was my vampire boyfriend really standing in the doorway of this shabby excuse for a building? I looked at the remains of the bodies he'd killed. It was a little more gruesome a kill than I would have expected from Duncan, but then the only time I'd ever witnessed him killing was the night that gang of punks mugged me and he saved me from the rogue vampires. He'd torn them up pretty bad, but I assumed it was because he was angry with them for attacking me. Perhaps this was his normal way of killing.

It was Elizabeth who was the first to come to her senses and greet him with a polite curtsey. He nodded his greeting and appreciation for her assurances that he'd been sorely missed, but his eyes focused on me.

I remained frozen.

For reasons I couldn't explain, I was unable to move, to think, to breathe! How had Duncan managed to step back in time? Was Isabelle alive in the future? Had she helped him? Why had he returned? I was under the impression he didn't want his family to ever know he'd become vampire. Was he really that worried about the possibility of me encountering Margaret? Margaret was in the future, wasn't she? Nothing was making sense.

It wasn't until his long legs strode across the wooden planked floor and he held my chin while kissing me gently that I came back to life. I remembered those lips. His scent. His feel. This was not my imagination playing tricks on me. Duncan, my Duncan was there with me and he was very, very real. All of the stress and anxiety of the chain of events leading to this moment flooded my body and I collapsed into his strong, secure arms. All of the fear and emotions I'd thought were dead in me came pouring forth. My body trembled while I cried like a baby.

He swooped me effortlessly into his arms as I buried my soaking wet face into his neck. The last thing I heard before the world went dark was Duncan asking Anne to lead us to safety.

CHAPTER FOURTEEN

I awoke to the savory aroma of venison roasting over an open fire pit. An elderly woman stood diligently rotating the spit with a slow steady arm. My stomach roared in response to the savory aroma that filled the night air.

I sat up with a start when I realized it was night. I'd slept the day away and had no clue where I was. I also didn't see Duncan or Elizabeth. Panic threatened to overtake me until I finally laid eyes on Anna walking toward me with a smile and a mug of frothy grog.

Relieved that I was free and more than likely in her coven's camp, I accepted the grog gratefully. It was sweet with a bit of bitterness and a mild bite as it slid down my throat. I reminded myself to pace my drinking since my stomach walls were suctioned to each other from the hours of enforced fasting. The grog could easily get the better of me.

A warm soothing sensation filled my being by the time I'd drank half the mug. I smiled thankfully at Anna and questioned her as to our whereabouts. I was right. We were in her coven. When I asked about Duncan, she explained that he went to visit his father and would return as soon as he could. He'd taken Elizabeth with him, as he felt she needed to be removed from the dangers that lurked ahead. She was a loyal lady's maid, but loyalty was expected to go only so far. What Elizabeth experienced for my sake was way beyond what anyone would have expected of her. I agreed.

It wasn't long before Anna and I were dining on delicious roast venison with a side of boiled potatoes and carrots. I can't remember when anything tasted so good. The open air accentuated the freshness of the food. I was so delighted to be eating my fill of the delectable fare that I almost forgot where I was and what I'd been through. It all came rushing back to me when Anna introduced me to the temporary high-priestess of the coven.

Although she was clearly skeptical of me, Helen seemed an amiable enough sort. We chatted about where I'd come from, the fact that I'd missed going through the portal, and of course, Vivian the wicked.

Helen confided that I truly looked remarkably like Margaret and she would have believed I'd returned with amnesia had she not known Margaret so well. She claimed that even with amnesia, certain habits would remain the same. I agreed.

Helen saw no sign of those habits.

Since I still felt it might prove useful to know as much as I could about Margaret -plus, my curiosity about the woman Duncan truly loved ran high- I asked her what some of those little lacking habits were. Helen was reluctant to mention them at first, but then thought better of it and explained that Margaret tended to fidget from foot to foot due to an old foot injury she'd suffered while learning to work with horses as a young girl. Her left foot was mildly deformed and pained her quite often. She also had a tendency to either touch or grab at her neckline as if she found it too confining. After having worn her clothes for a longer period of time than I'd planned on or cared to, I could completely relate to that one. The biggest give away was that I was left handed. I held my mug of grog and pulled my meat from the bone with my left hand. Margaret did everything with her right hand. I was surprised Elizabeth hadn't picked up on these things. Helen's gifts of observation were admirable.

Finally, someone believed I wasn't Margaret. I didn't know where to go from there with this turn of events. It didn't take long before Helen took control of the situation and the decision was made for me.

Apparently what I'd learned about Margaret being sent to the future to retrieve Duncan was true. What they omitted to tell me was that Margaret was a powerful witch in her own right and was the High Priestess of the coven. Helen was only standing in during her absence. The coven felt the absence of their true leader and Helen believed it was important to get her back as soon as possible; especially since Vivian managed to infiltrate their little family and placed a wedge within their core. Helen feared mutiny at any moment.

I'd never considered myself a witch and the concept of a coven seemed corny to me in my old life. Somehow, in this life it all seemed very normal and very necessary. I sympathized with Helen's situation.

She was certain that she was the only one, other than Duncan, who knew my true identity and she wanted to play off this factor. The coven was falling apart. They wanted their true leader back. Margaret was their true leader. I was Margaret's doppelganger. This could work.

I nervously expressed my concerns about my weakening condition and odd sensations since I missed the portal. Adding to that concern was the fact that I would probably fall short in the magic department. I wasn't sure how I felt about pulling the wool over a bunch of witches. The consequences could be intense. One angry witch after me was enough.

She was undisturbed my concerns. She'd studied time travel in great depth while preparing Lady Margaret for her journey and felt certain that my fate was not to be the same as Isabelle's because I was technically naturally alive in the twenty-first century. Isabelle had been kept alive by magic. Her natural time to live had long ago expired and without the magic, even though she'd come back to her own era, she'd come back a little earlier than she'd been born. When she lost her magic, she had nothing, not magic or natural life cycle to pull life from.

Helen was certain my weakening condition could be remedied with a little balancing of my energy fields. Although I'd never been a part of a coven, she felt I'd learn the ins and outs quick enough. When I reiterated my lack of magical power she simply laughed, shook her head, and muttered something about modesty.

It was clear to me that my vote in the matter was moot. Since I was stuck in the past with the only semblance of hope in surviving being in the witch who wanted me to pretend to be the coven's high priestess, I saw no way out of the ruse. Hopefully, I could pull it off long enough for a solution to my dilemma to be discovered.

It was late and I was tired. I followed Helen to a little cottage on the edge of the clearing. I was guided to a small alcove in the back where a bed awaited me. For the first time since the nightmare began I felt safe and secure. I practically fell onto the bed and remember very little after that.

It seemed as if I'd no sooner closed my eyes than the morning sun was peeking over the treetops. Little by little my recollection of where I was and why I was there returned to me. I lay still with my eyes closed while I listened to the hushed activity around me. It was clear that my companions were as hesitant about waking me as I was about letting them know I was awake.

"I heard she has no recall of us. 'Twas removed by the transference," whispered a youthful sounding woman.

"Lady Helen shall care for her. She is almost as good as the lady herself. She shall make all right as rain. Just wait and see," said an older woman.

"What if she cannot?" the younger woman asked.

"Say nothing of such things or even think it! Whatever need be done to correct Lady Margaret, Lady Helen shall do. 'Tis as simple as that," the old woman insisted.

Lady Helen? She hadn't told me she was of noble birth. With the way people seem to be so stuck on titles, I found that odd. I definitely planned on asking her about it.

I could see figures moving about through my slatted eyes, but I couldn't make out if any of them were Helen. I doubted the women would have talked so freely she was amongst them. I got the impression the little abode I slumbered so peacefully in belonged to the high priestess. The trundle bed beneath mine was still pulled out, which led me to believe I hadn't been totally alone during the night. Is that where Helen slept? I'm sure she'd been occupying this space while acting as high priestess. My return... or Lady Margaret's return.... was probably unexpected. Since it didn't look to me like the encampment possessed much in the line of guest rooms, I assumed she'd used the trundle for the night.

"Ah, m' lady, good morning to you. 'Tis good to see you looking so fine. So, you slept well enough, then?" the old woman said with exuberance as Helen came through the door.

Her smiling face and booming enthusiasm was infectious as she stirred the ingredients of one of the kettles placed over the fire the great fireplace sported. Having had free access to the kitchens at the inn, I was fairly familiar with what was probably in those kettles. One had the morning gruel, the other an ongoing stew, and the third contained water for teas and other uses that may arise. I looked at the hems of the women's skirts to make sure they were soaked with water to avoid a fire. I was pleased to see they were. The inn's cook told me that was a private trick of hers, but I knew better and this proved it.

I decided to alert the group that I was awake. With a long, cat-like stretch and a yawn to match, I eased myself to the side of the bed. Before I was able to plant my feet on the floor, two maids were placing slippers on my feet and assisting me into a very ornate house robe. I felt like a queen. I suppose, since they were under the impression that I was their high priestess, in essence I was their queen; for a few days anyway.

I made my way outside to the common table and sat in the seat at its head. There was something surreal, yet invigorating, about the way their encampment was set up. Many of the members of the coven were of nobility, so they came and went in secret. The rest lived on premises full time. Their camp was their home and sanctuary. It was filled with love and friendship. Had I realized that such was a part of the coven experience, I'd have joined one long ago. Leave it to the movies to distort and exaggerate yet another image of something that is not what they considered normal.

CHAPTER FIFTEEN

After a tasty and hearty breakfast, I joined Lady Helen in the forest for some private instructions on how to be Lady Margaret, as well as to give her an idea of my magical powers and wisdom. She was more than a little surprised to discover how limited my knowledge was in comparison to my potential. I did my best to explain what life in the twenty-first century was like and how the magical arts became an underground fad over the centuries; only to start resurfacing as acceptable a few years ago. Even with the resurfacing, the acceptance was still not wide spread, but at least no one was hanged or jailed for practicing it.

My tutor was overcome with emotions as she embraced the concept of being able to perform magic and worship in the open without being hanged and not exercising that right. It was something she just couldn't fathom. The thought of people taking for granted the gifts of the gods and goddesses was almost as distressing as being hanged for it as a crime.

I found working with Helen fascinating and exciting. Isabelle's approach was far softer; with herbs and the basics of magic as her foundation. Helen's method of training was straight to the point with little, if any, reservation for my safety or wellbeing. It was as if she simply knew I'd be alright so the thought of protecting me never crossed her mind. Interestingly, it didn't cross mine either. It wasn't until the end of the day, after I'd manifested an innumerable number of fireballs, blown up a few boulders, influenced a few animals into doing my bidding, cast an invisibility spell on my cloak that was so powerful Helen was hard pressed to find me, and levitated three feet off the ground, before it even hit me what I'd accomplished.

My day was so full of wonders and magic that I'd completely forgotten about Duncan until I saw his tall silhouette in the moonlight as he emerged from the path in the forest. Curiosity immediately consumed me. He'd been with his father. Had he confessed to being a vampire?

I approached him cautiously. Lady Helen was so eager to school me on the magical arts and my role in the coven that she neglected to tell me how I should behave when I was in Lord Duncan's company. Did we embrace? Hold hands? Kiss on the cheek? Kiss on the lips? I wanted to run into his arms and kiss him until neither of us could breathe and then find a soft bed somewhere to finish our reunion. Of course, I knew better. I rummaged through my memories of couples I'd seen since I'd arrived and realized I'd met very few of noble class. The working class people were so tired at the end of the day it's a wonder they managed to say "hello", let alone do anything else.

This was awkward.

To my relief Duncan took control. He walked up to me with all the grace and dignity one might expect from a future earl and stopped just inches before me. My knees felt weak and my heart threatened to leave my body on its own accord. I inhaled his familiar scent deep into my lungs. Having been forced to use the cosmetics of the day, I now recognized the faint scent of clove mixed with lavender on him. It seemed an odd combination, but somehow, on him, it worked.

"Good evening, Lady Margaret," he said as he took my hand and bent over to lightly brush his lips against my fingertips. "You look far lovelier than I recall. Time has been kind to you."

"As it has to you," I said stiffly.

Duncan raised an eyebrow while his sea foam blue eyes twinkled merrily. He was obviously enjoying my discomfort.

"It seems centuries since we have walked together," he almost chuckled. "Might I convince you to join me in a light stroll around the camp's perimeter." He looked directly at Helen as he said, "We shall stay within the ring of protection, of course."

Helen nodded her approval and bowed sweetly. It seemed the handsome Lord Duncan could be refused nothing by the enchanted ladies he left in his wake. I didn't know whether to smile or scowl.

Without waiting for my reply, he tucked my hand in the crook of his arm and started walking toward the edge of the encampment. I had to pick up my feet and lengthen my stride to keep up with him, lest I end up being dragged along like a beast from a hunt. Images of Elizabeth and me bound together while being dragged mercilessly behind horses that were practically at a trot flashed through my mind and I shuddered.

"Are you cold?" Duncan said with concern. "I had not considered the chill in the air tonight. Shall we fetch your wrap before we continue?"

"No, I'm okay," I replied and then sucked in air as I realized my mistake in speaking to him in twentieth-century Manhattan accent.

Duncan scowled briefly, but said nothing. We walked the rest of the way to the parameter in silence. I used the time to admire how well he fit the style of the era. The sleek lines of his lean, muscular body were outlined and accentuated by the cut of his waist coat and long overcoat. His finely shaped calves were well displayed by his breeches. He even looked good in his wig. It was almost too intimidating for someone like me, who never really felt at home in my own skin. I think that's why I enjoyed acting as much as I did. I could be someone other than who I was.

"We can talk freely here," Duncan said softly as we reached the edge of the clearing.

"I'm afraid of the woods," I muttered before I realized what I'd said. Since Duncan looked at me with clear confusion written all over his face, I elaborated, "Every time I go near them I get grabbed by that maniac Vivian and placed in a cage to await the hangman."

"That can get old," he said matter-of-factly.

I may have spoken without thinking, but I would have expected just a little more empathy from him than that!

"You're angry with me," I pouted.

"'Twas a fairly foolish thing you did that cost a very dear friend her life and nearly cost your own as well," he said in a harsh whisper.

"Yes," I said meekly.

What else could I say? He was absolutely correct with his statement.

Duncan looked at me long and hard before expelling the air from his lungs and pulling me close.

"Do you have any idea how frightened I have been? I thought I lost you," he whispered in my ear as he nuzzled his face in my hair. "It is difficult enough to think of our eventual separation as I continue my miserable existence forever. You are the first person I have allowed myself to love. My hopes were that Isabelle would show you how to stretch your life as she stretched hers. Now those hopes are crushed."

"I only wanted to give you what you desire most. I wanted to give you back your mortality," I whispered back.

"Whatever made you think I desired mortality over you?" he managed to say, just before his lips consumed mine.

His kiss was like no other. I could feel the anguish and stress I'd caused, but I could also feel his love. It was real. All of it was real.

My mind whirled.

I'd worked myself up about the fact that I was a dead ringer for Lady Margaret-Jane. I truly believed Duncan hooked up with me because I somehow made him feel closer to her. His kiss threw doubts on this belief. Had he really worried about losing me? Was I enough on my own, or did he just not want to lose his precious Margaret-Jane again? I just didn't know. Where I once was certain, I now was unsure.

I must have tensed when he was kissing me because

he pulled his face back from mine far enough to search my eyes with his own. He looked long, hard and deep, but said nothing.

"What is it?" I asked.

"I was going to ask the same thing. Something troubles you. Tell me," he said softly as he adjusted his embrace to give me a little more space, but not completely releasing me. When I looked away, he persisted, "Jane, I know you too well to accept that nothing is bothering you. Please tell me."

After a moment of excruciating silent debating on my part, I decided to just confess my fears and come what may.

"I saw the portrait of Lady Margaret-Jane Chapman." I could feel him stiffen and it somehow spurred me to continue with more confidence and determination, "I could be her twin. Everyone thinks I'm her. I'm just curious why, during all of our long conversations about your past, you neglected to mention that I'm the spitting image of your long lost love."

"She is not my long lost love," he muttered at a pitch that was barely audible.

"What?" I reacted with a whispered screech and immediately checked myself.

The topic of our conversation was bad enough, but we were also speaking in modern English. The one thing that I quickly learned was that even without the benefits of modern technology, there were ears everywhere. We may be under the assumption that we were alone, but could we be absolutely certain someone hadn't followed us and was hiding in the woods within earshot? It wouldn't do to be overheard.

"We were very good friends and... well... until I discovered what true love really felt like, I will admit that I thought she was my love, but she was not."

"Oh," I hesitated as I recalled the affection that I often glimpsed between Duncan and Isabelle. "Isabelle," I whispered.

"What about Isabelle?" he asked.

"She was your true love?" I said reluctantly.

My own love for my lost friend was so powerful that I couldn't even be angry or resentful about Duncan's love for her.

He chuckled and stroked my hair.

"I loved Isabelle in a way one can hardly describe. She was my lover at one time, true, but that quickly faded as we both learned our attraction for each other was more that of a brother and sister than of a man and a woman... or in my case, a vampire and a witch." He sighed heavily, "She was my best friend for centuries. Yes, I loved her, but I was not in love with her." He took my face in his hands and looked me squarely in the face, "You, Jane. It is you who I love with all my heart. You are the one who coaxed the remnants of humanity from the depths of my hardened soul and brought it back to life. For centuries I lived a hollow being. Then, one night I walked into a dreary little sub-level pub and stumbled upon the sunshine of my life. True, your remarkable resemblance to Margaret-Jane was what drew my attention to you. The fact that your name was Jane was also a fascination, but over time I got to know you; the heart of you that cannot be duplicated by any-one or anything. That is what I fell in love with Jane. The true you."

Our next kiss was all consuming. Never had I ever expected to hear such a heartfelt confession of love from Duncan. I knew he cared for me, but I was always under the assumption that I was just another relationship to pass eternity with. It was me, I thought, who kept us strong and together. That was why I wanted so badly to give him the gift of mortality. I hoped that by doing so it would break the barrier that he'd built between himself and mortals to protect himself from the inevitable loss that awaited him. Now, I realized that I'd broken through that barrier without having to do anything but be myself. There were no words for the emotions that swirled through me at that moment. I felt love for Duncan; happiness at being his true love; pleasure in the depth of our kiss and his embrace; peace at knowing that for the first time in my life I felt like I truly belonged to someone; regret over my foolish-ness in attempting to retrieve his humanity without assistance from more learned magicians; and remorse over endangering and costing the life of my friend.

By the time he released me I was so affected by the moment that my legs failed me. I stumbled backwards and would have fallen had Helen not been behind me to prevent it.

"Please excuse me," she said sheepishly, "I come to fetch Lady Margaret for circle."

CHAPTER SIXTEEN

The star filled night reminded me of a quilt my friend Linda kept over her bed. Its deep navy background created the perfect palate for the brilliant white and gold stars that were too many to count. Linda's quilt didn't twinkle with life like the night sky did, but that was the only difference. Whoever crafted that quilt did a fine job of capturing the essence of a starry night.

As we approached the circle, the apprehension I'd been nursing about the ruse Helen and I were playing rose within me. This was not any ordinary group of people. This was a group of people who had magical abilities. Grant it some had stronger abilities than others, but they all had them to some level. I had no desire to anger any of them and find out who knew what.

Lady Helen seemed oblivious to the risks we were taking as she walked boldly into the center of the circle. Or perhaps she just didn't care. She held her hands up in the air and silence swept over the attendees as quickly as if she's flicked off a switch. I was in genuine awe of the influence she had on the coven and the apparent regard they held for her. I wondered if Margaret was held in as high esteem. It didn't take long for me to find out.

I listened intently as Helen announced the return of Lady Margaret and explained the tragedy of her memory loss that occurred as a result of her time-space travel. The group seemed to buy her story hook, line and sinker. I saw no doubt in anyone's face. What Lady Helen said was to be taken as absolute and that was that.

All eyes were on me as they waited expectantly for Lady Margaret to make her grand entrance into the center of their circle. I was so engrossed in the fascination of how one person could have such unquestionable obedience and respect from such a large group that it took me a few moments to realize that I was supposed to be Lady Margaret. Somehow Duncan's arrival shifted my thinking and I no longer felt the need to be someone I wasn't. Unfortunately, Lady Helen still felt there was a need and, since I owed her a great deal, I needed to continue pretending. If this wasn't a great exercise in the art of method acting I don't know what was. It was a shame it couldn't be used on my resume.

I took a deep breath and pulled on my best smile as I glided across the firm ground to stand next to their true leader. I found it interesting that I'd stood in the face of the threat of death on numerous occasions and never broke a sweat, but standing in front of this group of magical people scared me to death.

Go figure.

I addressed the group with as much confidence as I could while apologizing for my lack of memory. I went around the circle and had each attendee introduce themselves to me as well as tell me a bit about who they were and why they were part of the coven. Although some found it an odd request, the majority not only obliged willingly, but actually enjoyed themselves. They teased and poked at the appropriate times without ever showing disrespect to one another. I found them to be a wonderful and tight knit fellowship. On more than one occasion during the process of introductions I caught myself wishing I could take them back to the future with me. What I wouldn't give to have such loving and kind people as my circle of friends. Of course Daryl, Doug, and Linda were certainly kind and loving people, but they were so few in number that it couldn't compare with being a part of a family such as this. Plus, they weren't magicians. There was a lot to be said for surrounding yourself with people just like you. I would miss it if I was able to return to the future; especially now that Isabelle was gone.

The thought of Isabelle saddened me. I looked for Duncan for reassurance as I did my best to regain the mood I'd so enjoyed just a few minute earlier. He was nowhere in sight. I allowed my mind to wonder at his whereabouts briefly before I returned my focus to the matter at hand. I was sure Duncan hadn't gone far and would return when the circle meeting ended.

I was correct.

We finished our meeting and the group dispersed quickly and quietly. I looked around the clearing in awe. There was very little sign that we'd even been there not five minutes earlier. Even the fire we'd used had been extinguished and disguised. I was certain you would have had to either been an attendee or a skilled tracker-hunter in order to recognize the signs that a fire ever existed. To add to their security factor, the coven performed a powerful cloaking spell over the area.

I felt Duncan before I saw him standing before me. He looked a little disarray, but I wasn't in the mood to find out why so I said nothing. All I wanted at that moment was to make love to my vampire. It may have been only a day or so for him in his reality of the future since he'd seen me, but it had been weeks for me and I missed him dearly. My emotions were especially erratic and in need of quenching after the turmoil I'd endured over my insecurity about his love. I needed more than his words to assure me that we were secure.

He seemed to know what I wanted without my saying it. Without a moment's hesitation, he swooped me into his arms and leapt into the air. I hadn't been carried like this since the night he'd rescued me from the vampire attack. Then it had been the buildings of Manhattan we scaled and flew over. This time it was an English forest of maple, oak, birch, pine, and elm trees of all shapes and sizes, followed by rolling meadows and neatly trimmed gardens. Instead of street lights illuminating our way, nature provided us with a sky blanketed with brilliant stars and a glowing full moon. It was like a scene from a fairy tale.

We landed silently on the balcony of my room at his family castle and he set me down gently. Neither of us spoke as he waited for me to regain my equilibrium and then guide me into my rooms. I looked briefly at the tapestry on the wall, wondering if eyes and ears might be behind it. He followed my stare and smiled knowingly before lifting his hand and gesturing some sort of symbol in the air. The tapestry disappeared, leaving only solid wall in its wake.

I gasped in surprise, but said nothing. In truth, he gave me no time to question him about his new found magic. His lips consumed mine and his arms wrapped me in them possessively as soon as his hand completed the spell.

I bathed in the passion of the moment as he guided me to the bed, never releasing me, never stopping that long, libidinous kiss. My head spun and my heart beat wildly. My ears roared with the thunder of my blood as it bounded through my veins. I shuddered with delight as his hands slid the length of my legs beneath my skirt. He released my lips so he could follow those strong, aristocratic hands with soft tender kisses. I knew where this was leading and my body contracted with anticipation and desire. Passion mounted within me with every tortuous move.

His hands reached my most private part only seconds before his lips took over. He was soft, gentle, teasing, arousing…. he was mine.

I lost count of how many times his expert ministrations brought me to my peak of ecstasy before he finally relented and allowed my exhausted body a brief reprieve. As he lay next to me, I clumsily did my best to relieve him of his clothing. This was my first experience with the workings of sixteenth century male attire. It was far more complicated than the modern day tee shirt and jeans.

Unable to wait any longer, Duncan freed himself of the confines of his breeches, pulled me beneath him and entered me swiftly. I found his actions surprisingly sensual. There was something arousing and naughty about coupling passionately while in the confines of modest attire. It was as if we'd managed to pull one over on our stuffy social critics.

I wrapped my legs around him and steadied myself to enjoy the driving passion that only a vampire possessed. I'd often wondered if I'd even be content making love with a mortal again after having the erotic experience of coupling with a vampire. Vampires were naturally sexual. They not only had a stamina to perform that was borderline exhausting for a mortal, but they emitted the most powerful pheromone that added to the experience. A mortal man simply couldn't compete, no matter how badly he wanted to or how virile he considered himself.

I was on the verge of explosion with another type of explosion occurred.

It took a moment for both Duncan and me to realize that someone entered the room and was now bellowing her indignation at the top of her lungs. He continued his thrusts, until it finally registered that we were no longer alone. He stopped, but remained inside me as he looked around the room for the intruder. I felt his body stiffen as he slowly pulled himself free of my embrace and quickly secured himself back into his breeches.

I lay paralyzed in stunned disbelief while Duncan covered me with my skirts and I stared at the angriest version of me I'd ever seen. Duncan's father and Elizabeth stood in silent shock behind her.

Reality that we'd been caught in the act of sex struck me like a brick. If this was in the twenty-first century, I'd have been a little embarrassed, but would have probably laughed it off in the end. Unfortunately, this was not the twenty-first century. This was the eighteenth century and things like this just weren't supposed to happen before nuptials were performed. We'd performed a major fopah.

Of course that wasn't what occupied my mind or my attention. The enraged look on the face of Lady Margaret-Jane as her glower shifted from me to Duncan and then back again is what grabbed it. She seemed less surprised to see me than she was to see what we'd been doing.

"Father...Lady Margaret," Duncan stuttered.

Surprised to discover my vampire lover was actually nervous, I glanced at him with my peripheral vision while never taking my eyes off Margaret.

The Earl of Winterspring's face was almost purple as he moved toward Duncan's side of the bed. He stopped at the edge and pushed his face dangerously close to my lover's face while strongly suggesting, through clenched teeth, that he meet him downstairs immediately. The look of disgust he sent my way was heartbreaking. I'd grown to like and admire this man. The thought of him disliking me saddened me deeply.

Duncan's father stomped out of the room; slamming the door soundly behind him for emphasis. Duncan stood at the side of the bed and looked at me apologetically before silently bowing to Margaret and strolling non-too securely out of the room.

I found it remarkable that these people had the power to bring my vampire lover to his emotional knees like that. It was clear that the beliefs of his upbringing were strongly instilled within the depths of his being. I couldn't help wonder what this meant for us.

"Remove this trollop from my bed and away from my sight," Margaret barked at Elizabeth. Without warning she flew to the bed and slid her hand beneath my skirts to fondle the sticky proof that Duncan had truly been with me. I gasped, but was too shocked to do anything about it. She pulled her hand free and stared at her fingers in disgust. "Make certain the bedclothes are immediately disposed of!"

Silence permeated the room as Lady Margaret-Jane left the room as majestically and as quickly as possible. I remained on the bed, still stunned into silence, while I processed what just happened. Elizabeth was the first to come to her senses and begin moving around the room.

"'Tis most irregular m 'lady," she said nervously.

"My name is Jane," I replied softly.

"Pardon? Yes... yes, Jane," Elizabeth wrung her hands. "'Tis most irregular. 'Tis wrong to address you as Jane, m' lady. I do not know who you are, but you are clearly someone Lord Duncan cares for and you... well... you are the image of Lady Margaret. I do not feel right calling you by your given name."

"Well, I'm not a lady," I boldly stated in my own American English, "and I'm not from this time. I'm from the future and in the future we aren't called m' lady, or Lady, or whatever," I flipped at her as I hopped out of bed.

My shock was replaced by anger and indignation.

"Oh?" Elizabeth gasped and backed up.

"In the future, Duncan and I are lovers. We live together openly as a couple. What you saw when you unceremoniously barged in on us was a reunion between a couple and I resent being called a trollop because of it!" I declared. I knew it wasn't right to take my anger out on Elizabeth, but she was the only one in the room to listen to me and I needed to vent. "We don't use the word trollop anymore either!" I puffed. "It's slut!"

I stepped behind the privacy screen and tended to the task of cleaning myself up as I continued to spurt and sputter about my eagerness to be free of the eighteenth century and return to my own time with Duncan in tow. The problem was that I didn't know how to go about it.

Elizabeth wisely worked silently at the task of stripping the bed free of its bedding and calling for the maids to remove the offending material before her true lady returned. When I stepped out from behind the screen, she'd finished her task and was standing at the foot of the bed looking at me.

Neither of us said a word for what seemed like eternity. I never did feel comfortable in total silence.

It was Elizabeth to spoke first.

"I truly thought you were Lady Margaret. You told me different, but m' lady, you are the image of her. I could not believe...," she began.

"I know," I sighed as I gestured her to be silent. "I doubt I'd believe it either."

She giggled as she said, "You speak in an odd fashion. 'Tis how they speak in the future?" When I nodded she added with sincerity, "You did well with the language of today."

"Why, thank you," I replied as I curtsied.

We looked at each other briefly and the giggling began. I don't know if it was nerves or humor that struck Elizabeth to the point of such silliness, but whatever it was, it was infectious and it wasn't long before our giggle fest turned into a full blown laughing fit.

Soon the mood between us switched from an uncomfortable lady's maid and a lady to that of two women who simply liked each other and enjoyed each other's company.

We spent the majority of the following hour getting to know each other more intimately. Elizabeth explained that her true given name was Mary and her surname Elizabeth, but it was the practice to refer to the staff by their surname. Using her given name would have been far too intimate a relationship. I found this bit of information fascinating.

Elizabeth was full of questions about the future. She was both impressed and shocked by the social promiscuous and freedom men and women enjoyed. She found that fact that Duncan and I lived openly in the future as man and wife, while not man and wife, astonishing.

Our conversation eventually came around to time travel and Isabelle. I reluctantly confided my actions to her. In doing so, I also confided Duncan's true state of being. A skillful listener, Elizabeth remained quiet until she was certain I'd finished.

"'Tis not uncommon to perform actions that may not be considered the wisest for love of a vampire. We do what we feel is right at the time and pray we are correct," she said solemnly.

I rubbed my ears. Had I heard correctly? I'd just informed Elizabeth that Duncan was vampire and rather than be shocked or repelled she came out with, 'We perform actions for love of a vampire.' What was she saying?

I questioned her about already knowing that Duncan was vampire and she shook her head. I thought carefully about her words. She'd used the expression "we" instead of "you". This meant that if she didn't know Duncan was a vampire, she knew of a vampire. When I made this statement she nodded slowly while watching me warily.

CHAPTER SEVENTEEN

My conversation with Elizabeth proved enlightening and fascinating. She admitted to me that she loved a vampire named Patrick. She was actually discussing becoming a vampire as well, but agreed to wait a few more years so that she and Patrick would be more compatible in age when it happened. It seemed Patrick was much older than she when he was turned and felt self-conscious about the age difference their bodies displayed. That, in itself, I found fascinating. Unfortunately, she told me, just like there are good and bad people, there are good and bad vampires. This was something I knew first hand. It seemed Patrick was on the side of right when he came up against wrong and he didn't survive. Since no one was aware of their relationship or the fact that Patrick was a vampire, Elizabeth was forced to mourn in silence. Our conversation was her first opportunity to speak her pain.

I held her close while she wept for her lost love and thought of Duncan. What would happen to him now that he'd returned? It was clear magic was much more prevalent in this day and age and vampires seemed the same. Would he have to defend himself against the wickedness that abounded here? How many good vampires were there? Was it an even match? Did one outnumber the other?

I sat at the window of Lady Margaret's room and looked out onto the dew covered garden below while I pondered this fact. The sun was peeking over the horizon to display a blanket of moist rolling green as far as the eye could see. It was a stark contrast to looking out of my studio apartment in the east side of Manhattan at the dirty brick buildings that surrounded it.

Elizabeth left to see to the needs of her mistress. After

some deliberation, it was decided to move Lady Margaret-Jane to a less offensive part of the castle since the rooms she once occupied now repulsed her. It was all fine with me since I'd grown accustomed to the rooms. I glanced at the newly made bed and sighed. I would have much preferred they'd left the remnants of Duncan and my lovemaking alone. I had no idea what was about to happen. For all I knew, my memories of him could be all I had left.

My attention flew from the picturesque scene out the open window to the man and woman walking below me. I wondered if Duncan and Margaret were aware that I was just a few floors above them and within hearing range. As their conversation progressed, I doubted it.

I felt almost criminal as I listened to Margaret reprimand Duncan for his deplorable behavior in her bedchamber. It both amused and saddened me that Duncan didn't bother to defend himself. Instead, he listened intently to her ranting until she finally ran out of insults and complaints. Then, and only then, did he come to my defense.

My heart swelled with pride and love as I listened to my vampire explain to his onetime fiancé that he'd finally found the love of his life in me and he had no intention of giving me up, no matter what the earl, or tradition, or society felt he should do. He admitted that what attracted him to me in the first place was the fact that I looked so much like Margaret, but when all was said and done, I was nothing like Margaret.

I thought at first Margaret would take offense and begin yet another tirade. Instead, she looked thoughtfully for a few moments and then nodded her head. She admitted that, although she loved him dearly, it was truly more like the love one would have for a brother than what one might have for a husband. She'd settled on the marriage for the sake of the earl since he was her acting guardian, but secretly desired to marry for love. She longed for a love like the one Duncan and I shared.

I was relieved on two accounts. My eavesdropping provided me with a clear picture of where I stood and where Margaret stood with Duncan. He loved her as a sister, she loved him as a brother, and we loved as lovers should. All was well. I was even more delighted when I heard him approach the true coven leader about helping us get back to the twenty-first century. Although she hadn't quite made it that far when she'd traveled through time, she felt she knew what she'd done incorrectly and would make the adjustments. The worst case scenario, she explained, would be for her to have to perform a life elongating spell, such as the one Isabelle used to stay alive. The only drawback with that was that it would have to somehow be adjusted to accommodate my traveling back in time. Although Duncan appeared to be following her conversation, it sure sounded complicated to me.

I was so engrossed with my eavesdropping that I never heard the brute enter my room through the tapestry opening and was completely taken by surprise when he slipped a dirty sac over my head. My first instinct was to scream, but before I could utter a sound I felt a blow to my head and everything went black.

When I awoke, I was once again in a cage with other forlorn captives and was harboring a splitting headache. I cradled my temples while my thoughts immediately went to Vivian. Would that woman never give it a rest? I couldn't believe it was happening to me once again. I looked around the cage at the others. There was something different about them. They held a fear of dying, but it wasn't of hanging. I closed my eyes to better concentrate, but couldn't grasp what it was I was picking up. It didn't take long for me to find out.

With the regality of an anointed queen, Lady Vivian Everhoust positioned herself a few feet away from the cage.

"So, you arouse. Arthur can be heavy handed at times. I questioned if he was so with you. 'Twill not do for you to leave us without my having the pleasure of seeing you go," she practically cackled.

"Oh, will you just stop?" I roared. "I'm not even Margaret,

you damn fool. I'm Jane." Vivian stopped short and stared. I seized the opportunity to continue, "I'm her doppelganger or something. I came from the future without knowing anything about her or you or your stupid feud. That's between the two of you. I know nothing about it. What I do know is that, if you kill me, you still won't have your stupid powers back!"

Vivian strolled around the perimeter of the cage while never taking her eyes off me. I could see the wheels in her head turning. She was definitely weighing my words carefully. I decided to press further.

"Let me ask you this," I said boldly. I waited only briefly for her nod before I continued, "It's a fact that Lady Margaret is the head witch of a coven, right? Doesn't that make her most powerful? She took your powers from you?"

"That was only because she took me by surprise," she scoffed.

My chest heaved as I struggled to keep the adrenaline in my body at a healthy level. I grew impatient.

"Whatever the way she did it, she did it," I said. "If Lady Margaret was powerful enough to strip you of your power, what makes you think she's not powerful enough to blast her way out of here and just kill all of you? There's no one as powerful as she is here, right? You are the only one who's a match for her and she one upped you and took away your powers. Now, does it make sense that I'm not her?"

"I cannot follow the words you say," Vivian muttered while she clearly struggled with what she did understand. "What manner of speaking is this?"

"This manner of speaking is my manner of speaking. It's the speech of the future. I-am-not-Lady-Margaret! I-am-Jane-Wells!" I said as slowly and plainly as I could.

"Lady Margaret is where?" she asked hesitantly.

"The last I saw her, she was walking in the gardens on the arm of Lord Duncan," I spat.

It suddenly meant more to me to get under Vivian's skin than gaining my freedom. I'd had just about enough of her kidnapping and caging antics. She still had me at her mercy, but I somehow didn't care. I'd worry about that later. Right then, all I wanted to do was torture her in some way that might equal the torture she'd been piling on me. Telling her that Margaret and Duncan were strolling through his castle gardens arm in arm seemed like it just might have done the trick.

I sat back smugly as I reveled in the emotions I felt pouring from her.

She stared at me as if not seeing me. It took a while for me to realize that she actually wasn't seeing me. She was scrying for Margaret and Duncan. From her reaction, I assumed she'd found them. It made sense that she could still scry; since it wasn't a witch's gift, but a psychic gift. Although not all witches were psychic, many were. Like me, Vivian had psychic gifts. I wondered if Margaret had them as well.

"No, Lady Margaret does not have the sight," Vivian said with smugness that equaled my own. "It appears that you just might. I question why I did not notice." She walked around the cage, bent down and picked up a small rock, and tossed it into the cage. "Toss it back to me," she ordered.

Confused, I did as she asked.

"There! You are left handed. That swine Margaret it right handed," Vivian almost gloated.

"So, you believe me?" I asked impatiently.

"That I do, Jane Wells, that I do," she replied.

I walked to the door of the cage and stood expectantly waiting for her to open it and release me. She walked to the other side of the door and pushed her face close to the bars.

"Do you think that because you are not Lady Margaret that I shall set you free?" she cackled. "That shant happen. I have spies everywhere and my spies tell me that Lord Duncan was discovered in your bed. I heard tell he was discovered with a Lady Margaret by Lady Margaret, but I could make no sense of it until now. It seems I have to rid myself of two pesky witches. Lord Duncan will have me or he shall have no one at all."

"Isn't it bad enough that you turned him into what he is?" I bellowed.

"What he is?" she pondered. "What might that be?"

I hesitated. Could it be possible that Vivian had no idea Duncan was a vampire? Hadn't Duncan told me that it was she who had him turned? I was confused and unsure what I should say. If the wicked witch didn't have a clue that Duncan was a vampire, was it wise to let her know? I'd spoken only to Elizabeth about it. I had no idea who else, if anyone, knew about it.

I decided to lie.

"He's a broken man, of course," I said quickly. "You broke him when you cast whatever spell you cast on him."

She threw her head back and laughed as she said, "I threatened him with darkness to frighten him, but I did nothing more. He has wandered about under a false illusion. Oh, this is good. This is very good. I managed to thwart his marriage with a mere idle threat. I would have thought more of Lord Duncan. Perhaps I should reassess my feelings for him."

What was she saying? She took his magic and sent vampires after him. He told me so himself. How could it be that she stood there now denying the magic part and seeming ignorant of the vampire part? Something wasn't right. I needed to get out of that cage and go to him. If Vivian wasn't his nemesis, then who was? Better yet, was that person still around and did he or she know Duncan had returned?

"Please release me," I said with urgency. "I believe Lord Duncan to be in trouble and I must warn him."

She laughed a full belly laugh.

"If Lord Duncan is in true danger," she hissed, "'tis I who shall warn him. You shall remain where you are until I decide what best to do with you."

With that she was gone.

CHAPTER EIGHTEEN

They moved me to a cage all my own. Although still completely exposed to the elements, I was at least spared the aroma and company of the other captives. One of the things I truly had difficulty adjusting to was the poor hygiene habits of the underprivileged, of which I found myself amongst more often than I cared to admit.

Minutes turned into hours as I waited impatiently for Lady Vivian to come riding up on her white stallion and release me from my prison. I spent my time looking into the future as best I could. It was my first attempt since I'd traveled back in time. Prior to my meeting Lady Helen, I wouldn't have been able to do it, but she'd done something to balance me out and enhance my skills. I was actually more powerful than I thought I could ever be; certainly more powerful than I'd been in the future.

Vivian returned angrier than ever. She'd tried to see Duncan, but was sent away without being received. It was the ultimate insult.

"I have never been humiliated thus! The hoddypeak at the door denied me entry. He refused my card. I had no way to inform Lord Duncan I was visiting. Such behavior is unheard of. I cannot believe it!" she ranted.

I could understand why Duncan wouldn't want to see Vivian, but that type of behavior seemed very odd for him. Something was wrong. I simply had to get out of that cage.

"'Tis not the Duncan I know. Something is amiss. If you will let me out I shall investigate the situation. I shall convince him to see you," I said as convincingly as possible in her own style of speech.

At this point, my desire to annoy her was replaced

by the hope of allying her. Speaking in my native mannerism would hardly ally her.

She looked at me for a moment before saying, "So now you speak as should be?"

It seemed a little risky to explain that I was trying to speak so she could understand me and possibly like me. As testy as she was, she would have probably taken offence. So, I shrugged my shoulders and remained silent.

After a mini stare down between us, she shook her head and walked away.

I leaned against the bars of my confine and slid to the floor. It was clear there was no dealing rationally with Lady Vivian. I was tired, hungry, and pissed off. Something had to change. I spotted a stone similar to the one she'd had me toss earlier on the ground just outside of the cage. It was a painful stretch, but I managed to grab hold of it and pull it to me. Holding it tightly with on hand, I pounded it as hard as I could against a bar. The sound of rock hitting metal rang through my head. I waited. Nothing. I did it again. Still nothing. Holding the rock as firmly as I could, I walked along the interior perimeter of the cage. The rock to slam against each bar as I did. After a few minutes of this annoying act, a big, burly, and incredibly hairy fellow emerged from what seemed like thin air.

"Stop that racket!" he bellowed in a surreal kind of voice that sounded like it originated from somewhere outside his body and then was funneled through his vocal cords.

"I am hungry and thirsty," I said defiantly.

He looked at me quizzically for a moment -as if to decipher just what hungry and thirsty meant- nodded his head, and disappeared back into the nothingness he came from. I was just starting to wallow in self-pity when, with remarkable speed, he returned with a basket. Its contents were hidden by a fabric covering.

After barking for me to step to the back of the cage, he waited for me to oblige and then opened the door just far enough to slip the basket inside. I considered charging him and forcing my way out, but the fact of the matter was that his size equaled at least two of me and I felt weak from hunger and dehydration. I was certain that all charging him would have accomplished was the removal of the much needed food basket and greater punishment. Since I was trying to shorten my prison sentence, not lengthen it, I stood still at the back of the cage until he'd secured the door once more.

When it was clear I could approach the basket, I did so with caution. It was brought to me by a goon type of fellow who seemed to struggle with the concept of hunger and thirst. That made me question what might be in the basket under that covering. I kicked it lightly with my toe to see if I might disturb any live creatures lying in wait. Nothing. That was a good sign. I picked up the basket and sniffed. It had a fresh baked bread aroma. Another good sign. Setting the basket back down, I quickly removed the covering with one swift jerk while jumping back in case something jumped out at me.

I waited.

Nothing.

I finally braved a look into the basket and was delighted with what I saw. My mouth salivated at the sight of a half of a round loaf of freshly baked bread, a small square of cheese, an apple, and a wide mouthed jug of Meade. After seeing the Meade, I was grateful I hadn't kicked the basket any harder than I had or I'd have been out one jug of delicious brew. As dehydrated as I was, that would have been a tragedy.

Knowing what I know about the necessity of water for the body, I looked for a jug of that as well, but found nothing. I shrugged and let it be.

The food before me was as well received as that of a five-star restaurant and just as good to my poor hungry palate. I was hard pressed to eat like a human and not some starving dog. Once satiated, I curled up in the corner of the cage and fell asleep.

It was night when I was awakened by Isabelle coaxing me to arouse and make haste. I rubbed my eyes to help the process of my body's return from sleep while I sat up. Isabelle's body glowed in a way that surprised me. I'd seen many ghosts in my day. Some were transparent, some were as dense as a human, some were black, some were white, but never had I seen one that glowed.

"You're glowing," I said about the obvious.

She looked down at herself and held up her hands and twisted them to and fro.

"Will you look at that?" she said with amusement. Then with more seriousness she continued, "You must wake up and get moving. I have learned they intend to sacrifice you to the goon leader, Larkin, tomorrow night. It is far too difficult to escape in the daylight. I have waited to get past these goons all day!"

"They can see you?" I asked incredulously.

"Not only can they see me, they can touch me and harm me as well!" she said in a hushed tone. "The glow you see around me is from an attempt I made to protect myself with an invisibility spell."

"There's no magic there?" I said with disappointment.

"There is plenty of magic here. Unfortunately, it works very differently than on this side of the veil. It is far more complex, yet much easier once it is mastered. I am still learning." She heaved a sigh, "It is a horrific handicap at a time like this."

I stood up and reached out to touch her. She felt like thick cotton candy. My hand penetrated her only a smidgeon before it felt like I was wrapped up in the weaves of soft, sticky cotton.

"The stickiness is the ectoplasm used to help us materialize," she explained. "How does it feel?"

"A little gooey," I replied.

A cough sounded in the distance and brought both of us back to reality.

"We need to hurry," Isabelle whispered. "Take heed to be more careful. These goons have ears sharp enough to hear a pin fall on a pile of hay."

"Where are we hurrying to?" I asked a little sarcastically as I spread my arms around the cage.

"You are going to say a spell to get you out of here," she said briskly. Before I could reply, she raised her hand to stop me and continued, "I know you have been diligently working with Lady Helen. I also know she performed magic to balance your body flow and keep you alive while you are here. Because your body thinks it belongs to this timeline your powers have come into their own. You are stronger than you think. Your only handicap is your lack of knowledge of spells. I will tell you what to say. You will repeat what I say and do exactly as I say. Then you will run like the wind behind me as I lead you to safety. There will be no time to converse once we begin. It is important you comprehend what to do beforehand. Are you clear?"

I wanted to ask her to slow down and let me think about things. I'd just been woken up from one of the best sleeps I'd had in ages by a glowing dead friend who informed me my powers were great, but my knowledge was small. The repeating of her words verbatim and running like the wind I could understand and easily do since I'd been her student for so long; but not the powers. Instead, I nodded that I understood and took a deep breath.

Isabelle chanted, "Ballaí de chuid cruach le haghaidh dom agus a leagtar dom saor in aisce! Ballaí de chuid cruach le haghaidh dom agus a leagtar dom saor in aisce! Ballaí de chuid cruach le haghaidh dom agus a leagtar dom saor in aisce!" while she raised her arms wide to the heavens. When she'd finished she looked at me and nodded.

I held my breath and hoped I'd remember the words correctly.

Without a moment's hesitation I said in a soft but firm voice, while holding my arms exactly as Isabelle had done, "Ballaí de chuid cruach le haghaidh dom agus a leagtar dom saor in aisce! Ballaí de chuid cruach le haghaidh dom agus a leagtar dom saor in aisce! Ballaí de chuid cruach le haghaidh dom agus a leagtar dom saor in aisce!"

I learned later that all I was saying was the simple command in an old language that the ancient steel could understand. The command was "Walls of steel, part for me and set me free."

Can you believe it?

I'd only just repeated the last of it when the bars of the cage bowed to create an opening large enough for me to squeeze through. Isabelle waited for me on the other side. As soon as I was free, she tore off into the woods at a pace I was hard pressed to keep. Somehow I managed to keep going until she mercifully stopped to allow me a rest before I had a heart attack.

When my heart finally left my ears and receded back into my chest, I detected the faint sound of dogs braying in the distance. Isabelle informed me that it was not dogs, but goons hot on our tail and we needed to pick up the pace. I couldn't believe she expected me to be able to run any faster than I had been, but I nodded and waived my hand for her to lead the way. Off we went.

The goons were almost upon us by the time we passed through the protective shield of the coven's encampment. As it appeared before us, the braying faded away.

I was exhausted! When Lady Helen rushed to my side, I was too out of breath to speak. I merely waived my hand in the air while more and more members of the coven surrounded me. I looked for Isabelle, but could see no signs of her. I was disappointed that I hadn't been able to thank her properly for her help or spend more time conversing with her about the other side of the veil. I'd never really spent time speaking to the ghosts I'd seen over the years and I had a bunch of questions about what it was like. I'd hoped to have those questions answered by Isabelle.

When I was finally able to convey my tale of woe to Helen and her group, most of them were aware that I was not the true Lady Margaret and were supportive, if not sympathetic, to my plight. Those who seemed hostile listened long enough to get the gist of what I was saying and then skulked away mumbling that I deserved what I got for being such a lying 'so and so'. - Of course 'so and so' isn't the true term they used but there's no need for that kind of vulgarity in this story. -

Helen pulled me aside as soon as she was able to confide in me some of her recent discoveries. Although she was furious with Lady Vivian for what she kept putting me through, her main concern was with the fact that she'd learned someone within the coven was responsible for Duncan losing his powers and suffering the attack that made him vampire.

I sucked in air when I learned she was aware of Duncan's state of being. Did anyone else know this? She assured me she'd shared this information with no one else, but intended to go to Lady Margaret with it at the first possible opportunity.

Lady Helen seemed far more open minded about things than the Lady Margaret I'd met in my bedchambers and eavesdropped on in the wee hours of dawn. From the way she'd been interacting with Duncan, I doubted she was aware he was vampire and I wasn't altogether sure it was wise to tell her. I expressed my concerns to Helen. After much debate, she agreed to withhold the information from her leader for a bit longer.

I spent the remainder of the evening telling all to Helen. I needed a comrade to help me through this mess and she was the most likely to agree. From what I'd heard and learned while interacting with the coven, she was also probably the most qualified. Many even whispered that Lady Helen deserved the position of high priestess over Lady Margaret. They felt her skills and wisdom exceeded that of their leader's. Unfortunately, her position in society fell short. It seemed that, even in the world of magic, there was a class distinction to uphold. Lady Margaret's family lineage was enough to earn her the position. Her association with the Earl and Lord Duncan sealed the deal. Lady Helen was of a lesser noble birth and just couldn't compete in that arena.

Although she never spoke of it, I sometimes wondered how Helen felt about the way positions within the coven were determined. It seemed a bit unfair to me.

CHAPTER NINETEEN

Duncan arrived at the encampment with the dawn. He was furious with Vivian; as well he should be. When I managed to calm him down enough to be cohesive, I filled him in on the conversation I'd had with Helen. He listened intently without one interruption. When I'd finished, he paced the floor of the little cottage with his hands behind his back and his head held low in thought.

"I have often thought back on the night I was attacked and wondered about it. Nothing added up. Vivian was angry with me, true, but it made no sense for her to damn me to a soulless eternal life. I witnessed her work her wiles on men who felt it wise to seek female companionship elsewhere. She was amazing at it and always accomplished what she set out to do. My rejection of her was given only once. For her to give up so easily just did not seem something she would do. I expected more from her," he said.

"Helen and I believe there is another witch who is working with the vampires. She's the one who bound your powers and told them where to find you. We're sure of it," I said with agitation.

The more I thought about it, the angrier I became.

"I cannot think who would wish to do such a horrendous thing. I had no enemies that I can recall. This was not done lightly. Someone wanted me out of the way. I cannot think who that might be," he said, clearly puzzled.

"Helen said the same thing," I replied.

Silence permeated the little cottage while we each pondered over this new twist of information. We'd been focusing on Vivian for so long -especially Duncan- that it took some time to digest the fact that his twist of fate may not have been a result of her doing the evil deed. After all, she'd also lost her powers. Maybe it wasn't Margaret who'd removed her powers like we all thought. Maybe the same witch who stole Duncan's powers and set the vampires on him stole Vivian's as well.

It suddenly occurred to me that Duncan regained some of his lost powers. When I questioned him on this he, informed me that his father cast a spell to unbind him. As simple as that! I asked if all of the powers had returned. They hadn't, but that was to be expected after centuries of binding. It would take some time before they were completely renewed.

I questioned Duncan on whether someone other than Margaret would be able to restore Vivian's powers. He thought it was worth a try.

We headed back to the estate in search of his father. It was time for me to face him after our last encounter. I didn't look forward to it. Duncan assured me that he'd caught his father up to date on everything, including the fact that he was a vampire and that we lived openly together in the future and society was just fine with it. He even went so far as to add that he'd informed him that the only reason we weren't married was because he was vampire and I was mortal.

I wondered if that was true.

Lady Margaret was nowhere to be found when we asked about her upon arriving at the castle. I was grateful, as I still felt hesitant about divulging all to her. I couldn't explain why, but I assumed it was because I carried an inherent insecure and jealous streak down my back where she was concerned.

We waited in the study while the earl was informed of our desire to speak with him. My body was covered in nervous perspiration by the time he entered. It was my concern over my sweaty condition that made me remember that I'd been held captive for two days in a nasty cage with other sweaty people and I never took the time to clean up before barging into his study with Duncan. I was horrified. If Duncan was bothered by this fact, he gave no signs of it.

The Earl of Winterspring eyed me curiously while he walked silently to the brandy decanter. He helped himself to a few shots before turning and motioning for us to be seated. Duncan took my hand and led me to the settee, but he remained standing. I could see the all too familiar twitching of his jaw muscles and understood he was far too agitated to sit.

I said very little while the earl and his son discussed the concept of returning Vivian's powers to her. When the conversation eventually led to my capture, I finally joined in.

"In truth, I believe her quite harmless. She may possess magic, but at her core I do not think she is evil enough to follow through with her threats," I interjected.

"She was planning on sacrificing you," the earl bellowed.

"She may have planned such, but I cannot believe she would do it," I replied.

"I disagree," said Duncan. "I believe she would have left you to the mercy of the goons and turned her back on the thought."

I thought for a moment. Leaving me to the goons to do with as they will and turning her back so her conscience stayed clear did sound a bit like something the Vivian I'd met might do. My habit of seeing the good in people may be something that Duncan found endearing, but it also could get me killed. I nodded and stayed silent for the remainder of the conversation.

After long deliberation, it was decided that they would meet with Lady Vivian to discuss a truce. Should she agree, the earl would order the return of her magical powers. I was surprised to discover that it was the earl, and not Margaret who'd removed them to begin with. Apparently when Duncan's powers were stripped, the earl went into a rage and, believing Lady Vivian to be the culprit, cast a spell to bind hers as well. Vivian assumed it was Margaret who'd done the deed and the earl never said differently.

I mentioned her angst at being turned away when she

came to call and both men looked at each other quizzically. Neither of them was even aware she'd been there. This left me with the opinion that Lady Margaret was behind the socialite's humiliation.

The earl promised to speak with his ward at his earliest convenience and remind her of the code of etiquette that holds firm under all circumstances and we parted company. After the earl expressed his deepest sympathies for my ordeal and looked me up and down from head to toe, Duncan led me to my room and ordered a bath be prepared. Although his father hadn't brought up the last time he'd seen me, I brought the topic up to Duncan. He simply kissed me long and hard and assured me that all was straightened out and I was not to fret over it any longer.

I smiled as I noticed that, even in private, Duncan was slowly returning to the eighteenth century pattern of speech. Although he'd never lost it completely, it grew far more distinctive as time progressed.

My bath arrived and Lord Duncan excused himself with all the pomp and circumstance expected of a man of his station. As he bent over to kiss the back of my hand, I caught a faint twinkle of amusement in his eye as he winked and left the room.

As I soaked in my bath, I suddenly noticed an enormous armoire in front of the tapestry on the wall. It looked incredibly heavy. I had no doubt it would take several men to move it in order to pass behind it. Thus the threat of the element of surprise had been eliminated. I don't know who was to be credited for this stroke of genius, but, whoever it was, I thanked them. I can't even express how tired I was of having a smelly rag bag shoved over my head to suffocate me while I was carried away and deposited in an equally stinky cage.

Grant it, the first abduction was performed by birds with no sac over my head, but their stench was none the better.

Dinner was brought to my room without my asking and I was all too happy for it. I was tired and in no mood to socialize; especially with Lady Margaret. Although I'd listened in to her conversation with Duncan and was aware of her true feelings for him, my last encounter with her was humiliating and I just wasn't in the mood to deal with how a future encounter might be at that moment. Although I believed every word Duncan said, for all I knew Lady Margaret could have been feeding Lord Duncan with a bunch of lip service simply to get on his good side. I wanted to be at my best for our next meeting.

CHAPTER TWENTY

I was grateful for the refreshing night's sleep when I entered the breakfast room and came face to face with my doppelganger. I suppose, technically, I was her doppelganger since she was born first. I wasn't really sure how that worked. It really didn't matter at the moment. What did matter was that we were completely alone and the air was so thick you could cut it with a knife.

"You have returned, I see," she spat as she walked to the buffet to help herself to a hearty breakfast of scrambled eggs, boiled ham, roasted venison, and a thick and juicy raspberry pastry.

My eyes went from her plate to her waist and then back again, as I pondered over how an appetite such as that managed to maintain a figure like the one she sported. Her diet resembled the Atkins Diet or possibly the South Beach Diet. I vowed to check both of them out when I got back to the future. In the meantime, I helped myself to a cup of tea, a small amount of eggs and a thin slice of ham before settling at one of the numerous round tables that graced the garden style dining room.

"I knew you were full of shit," I said as I stuffed a forkful of eggs in my mouth.

"Pardon me?" she almost bellowed.

"I said. I knew you were full of shit," I repeated. "If you don't understand, I'll clarify in your language as best I can. You are a liar and a deceitful pile of cow dung and I see right through the show you seem to feel Lord Duncan is too blind to pick up on." I popped a piece of ham in my mouth before asking, "Is that clear enough for you?"

"Well, I never," she spat as she slammed her plate on

the table and marched from the room.

I chuckled as a footman, who'd been standing against the wall, immediate began the task of cleaning up the food that had plummeted to the floor when Margaret's plate slammed so unceremoniously on the table. Although his head was lowered, I was sure I detected a hint of a grin.

"'Tis not the wisest to anger a high priestess," said a familiar female voice.

Although her words were sincere, the glint of humor in her eyes told me that she too enjoyed my little interaction with the precious Lady Margaret.

"I did not see you there," I said to Elizabeth as I eyed the footman.

I wasn't sure who knew I was from the future and who simply considered me an imposter who looked remarkably like Lady Margaret.

"I was just entering when you exchanged words. I slipped back out before she saw me," she said. "I wish to speak with you if I could." I nodded and continued stuffing my mouth with ham. "In private," she whispered.

There was something about that sentence that sent a chill down my spine. It wasn't the words or even the way she said it. It was more like a premonition of sorts. I nodded hesitantly before wiping my mouth with the embroidered linen napkin that matched the embroidered linen tablecloth on the table I'd chosen to sit at and following her out of the room.

I trailed behind Lady Margaret's gentle lady's maid through a part of the castle that I was unfamiliar with. It was shut off from use most of the time and opened only when there was an event being held and extra rooms for guests were needed. I couldn't imagine why she'd be taking me to such a secluded part of the castle or what was so vital to speak about that it required such seclusion.

We ended up in a small suite that she explained once belonged to the original part of the house. When the castle was enlarged, the current lord moved their living quarters to the new wing, leaving these beautifully detailed rooms void of life.

I gave a wry smile when she informed me that Lady Margaret suggested I be moved to this suite, but Lord Duncan wouldn't hear of it. Thank you Duncan! As beautiful as these rooms were, they felt incredibly cold and lonely. I couldn't imagine having to house myself in such a remote part of the castle, cut off from the rest of the living.

One day the lords of the fine estate would come to realize that sweet, gentle, prim and proper Lady Margaret wasn't all she let on to be. I just hoped it was soon.

Elizabeth begged me to sit. I selected an absolutely gorgeous crewel embroidered winged back chair that I was certain had seen only a handful of bottoms on its overstuffed seat cushion before being abandoned. As I let my hands move gently over the intricately stitched floral design, a young housemaid that I'd never seen before wheeled in a tea cart that was laden with tea and the same raspberry pastries that Margaret had heaped upon her plate.

Since I hadn't satiated my hunger before being asked to leave the table, and the pastries looked out of this world delicious, I accepted the plated one offered to me along with a cup of tea.

Elizabeth seemed nervous, so I dove into my fare with a little more gusto than I might had I not been trying to ease the tension in the room. When the raspberry juice spilled down my chin and I caught it with my fingertips, the mood immediate lightened and I joined Elizabeth in light laughter over my crudeness.

"This part of the house is lovely," I said as I boisterously licked my fingers. "It must have been a difficult decision to abandon it for the new wing. Of course the new wing is gorgeous as well." I heaved a sigh of admiration as I said wistfully, "In my time, people only dream of living like this."

"The castles are gone?" she gasped.

"No, most still stand, but times are different. Only a

handful can actually afford to live in them. Many are forced to give tours to the public for payment in order to help them make ends meet," I explained.

"They charge a fee to tour their homes? I cannot believe such a thing. 'Tis demeaning!" she exclaimed.

I'd managed to get Elizabeth talking comfortably with me. We continued to discuss the differences in lifestyles between the eighteenth century and the twenty-first century for a few more minutes before I brought the topic around to why I was asked to speak with her in such private quarters.

"I have someone who wishes a meeting, but cannot be seen," she explained.

I was immediately on the alert. Although I thought Elizabeth was my friend, she was also Margaret's lady's maid. Had Margaret set me up for yet another abduction? Adrenaline built up inside me until my ears roared with anxious anticipation. Sweat beaded on my forehead and I gripped the arms of my chair in preparation for flight.

"Oh, dear m' lady. Pray fear not. He is not here to hurt you. Truly, he is not," she said gently as she knelt before me and grabbed my sweaty hands. "He wishes only to warn of the danger awaiting Lord Duncan and you."

"Why has he not presented himself to Lord Duncan?" I asked, doing my best to maintain their pattern of speaking.

There was no telling what or how many ears were listening in on this conversation. That was a condition of the times I'd learned quickly.

"'Tis complicated and he shall tell you better than me. If you wish it, I shall remain in the room the entire time. He shant mind. He has no secrets from me. He is my brother," she said softly.

I detected sadness in her voice, but before I could ask her about it a tall, light haired man who looked very much like he could be Elizabeth's brother entered the room. They both had the same straight nose, high ruddy cheekbones, well defined chins and doe-like brown eyes. I noticed right away that his were more thickly lined with lashes than hers. I remembered Linda complaining about the unfairness of men having thicker lashes than women and smiled. I hadn't thought of my friends from the future for some time. It felt nice to reminisce.

"M' lady, may I introduce my brother, Rufus Elizabeth the Third, if you please," she said as she stood and backed away.

"I thank you, Mary," he said as he smiled at her affectionately.

I could detect an array of energies radiating from the handsome man before me. It was clear that he adored his sister and had a strong loyalty for her. He gave me the impression that he also had a strong sense of honor. There was something else I was feeling that was familiar, but I couldn't quite place. I decided to wait and see if it would surface on its own.

"M' lady," he said as he bowed and kissed my fingertips.

It was then that I remembered that the Elizabeth family was also of noble birth, although not as high in station as the Collier family. I found myself wondering if he and Duncan were friends. They looked to be about the same age.

"Pray, m 'lord, be seated," I said gently as I retrieved my hand from his.

My entire body relaxed as I watched him lower his handsome, lean frame into the seat opposite mine. Although I still couldn't put my finger on what it was that I was feeling about him, I sensed I was safe in his company.

"How may I help you, Lord Rufus?" I asked.

"I wish to speak about a delicate matter, yet one of great importance for your safety and that of Lord Duncan," he began.

My body shifted to attention as I prepared to listen to what Lord Rufus had to say. When he'd entered the room, he was the epitome of aristocratic confidence. Now, as he sat opposite me, I could see that confidence ebbing away to be replaced by an insecurity that seemed abnormal. Whatever it was they felt I needed to know, neither of them was eager to tell it.

"Mary informed me you came from the future," he began.

It took me a minute to remember that Mary was actually Elizabeth. When I finally did, I smiled at her and nodded. He shifted closer to the edge of his seat.

"She spoke of witches and vampires who remain hidden from the future world," he continued.

"'Tis true for the most part. Witches are quite open about their beliefs and practices. In the future, science has circumvented magic and placed it in a category of myth. Vampires, werewolves, and the like are not considered real. Their stories are told for amusement only," I explained.

"How incredible!" he gasped. "Yet, 'tis my understanding you lived with a vampire in the future?"

I looked at Elizabeth hesitantly. Had she told him that Duncan was that vampire? I wasn't sure.

"'Tis correct," I said guardedly.

"Yet, you remain mortal?" he asked.

"I remain mortal," I replied.

"Incredible," he whispered.

I was beginning to get impatience and feel uncomfortable with the way the conversation was turning into a cross examination of me and my choices rather that providing me with information on the danger they claimed I was in.

"Please forgive me, Lord Rufus, but I fail to see how my living conditions in the future has any relevance on whatever danger awaits me here," I said politely, but firmly.

"Yes, yes," he said with mild embarrassment, "it may appear that way, but it does play a role in what I am about to say. Will you humor me for a bit longer?"

"Certainly," I replied and then added, "forgive me."

"There is nothing to forgive, m' lady," he said firmly. "I shall get to the point of why we speak." He stood up and walked to the unlit fireplace. Leaning his shoulder against the mantle he proceeded to say, "I am a vampire."

When I gasped, he moved toward me and then stopped, as if concerned I'd bolt from the room or something. Instead, I leaned forward to inspect him more closely. Since we'd only just met, I had no idea how he should look. His features were quite distinct, true, but they were certainly not ghoulish like those of the vampires I'd encountered in the future. The only vampire who looked like a normal person that I'd ever met was Duncan and his complexion was a lot paler than Lord Rufus.

"You look far too ruddy and healthy to be a vampire," I said as my curiosity got the better of me.

Obviously expecting a far different response from me, he tossed his head back and gave a full belly laugh. Elizabeth followed suit. I realized that it was not a laugh of amusement as much as it was a laugh of relief. It seemed they were both very concerned about divulging this enormous secret to someone they weren't altogether certain they could trust. I didn't take offense, since I'd been entertaining the same concerns myself.

"I have to ask how you manage to maintain a complexion of such health," I persisted. Since everyone in the room knew I was from the future -and I sensed, more than saw, that we truly were alone- I saw no reason to continue the language ruse. In truth, I was getting annoyed with having to remember to speak prim, proper, and stiff. I finally bit the bullet and brought it up. "Since you know I'm from the future, would you mind terribly if I ceased with the antiquated speech pattern? I'm finding it more and more difficult to stick to it as the drama unfolds."

Rufus tossed his head back in laughter and smiled while saying, "You certainly can. I don't mind dropping it myself. Modern English is so much easier for me, even if I was born in this century."

I gasped, "You're kidding me! How old are you?"

He raised an eyebrow for a moment at my frankness

and then chuckled, "I became a vampire two- hundred and thirty years ago."

I quickly did the math in my head and realized that he was from my time frame. I couldn't believe I was in a castle with two two-hundred plus year old vampires roaming about not knowing the other was nearby. What were the odds? Even more so, both vampires were unbelievably hot!

We spent the next few hours discussing his life and times as a vampire. Like Duncan, he'd been attacked at night and, like Duncan, he abandoned his family rather than tell them the truth. It was only upon his return through time that Mary discovered him and learned the truth. He admitted he found it surprisingly refreshing to learn what an open and accepting mind Mary possessed. He attributed it to her servitude to witches. Had she been working in a normal household, he would have considered her unapproachable. As it was, she'd proven to be a valuable ally and assistant for him.

I asked him why he'd return, but somehow the conversation swayed to lighter subjects such as members of the Collier household. Elizabeth amused us with anecdotes about Margaret and Lilith. She was even able to share stories about Duncan, since, in her time, he'd only been gone a year.

I watched as Elizabeth removed her cap and slippers and sat unabashed at her brother's feet, using his knees to support her head. When he rested his large palm on her firelight curls I marveled over the freedom I hadn't seen since I'd come to this place. It was uplifting.

I couldn't resist asking them about their home and childhood. Since I didn't remember mine, it was always interesting to hear others tell their tale and see if perhaps something that happened to them might create a spark of memory for me.

They were raised not far from Winterspring on at Habersham Heights, owned by the viscount Mortimer Elizabeth and his wife Lady Martha Elizabeth. Rufus was a few years older than Mary and the second son. The first son died not long ago, leaving Rufus to inherit the title and lands when the time came. This was the primary reason Rufus returned. Unlike Duncan, he was prepared to figure out a way to live as a vampire and still mingle amongst the mortals. The most difficult thing to achieve was the fact that he didn't age as he should. He covered that by having a witch cast a spell for people to see him as he should be instead of as he truly was when it was needed.

I'd learned spells of that nature from Isabelle, but I'd never thought about using it for Duncan. I made a mental note to remember to mention it to him and see if it was something he desired.

My biggest question was about how he'd managed to maintain such a ruddy complexion. Compared to Rufus, Duncan looked sallow and sick. Duncan's diet consisted of vegetables, fruit, and animal blood. The only thing he couldn't tolerate that a mortal could was meat. He could easily pass for a vegetarian. When I questioned Rufus on his diet, he laughed and said, "One should not believe all one hears about vampires and how they survive," and that was that.

I won't deny being disappointed by his response, but since it was our first introduction, I thought it rude to persist. I was sure our paths would cross soon enough and I'd broach the topic again.

CHAPTER TWENTY-ONE

Duncan and his father had business with the tenants on the estate to tend to and weren't expected home for a few days. He'd met me for mid-morning tea to explain how trouble was brewing between tenants on the far end of the estate and the estate manager requested their assistance. The explanation of what type of trouble wasn't volunteered, and I never bothered to ask. My mind was still whirling from my meeting with the very handsome Lord Rufus and I was finding matters of the estate difficult to focus on. Plus, did it really matter in the scope of things what happened to the estate? After all, Duncan and I would be finding a way back to the future soon and all that went on in the eighteenth century would be insignificant. All I remembered was that the estate consisted of two thousand acres and they had to go to the very far end of it. At best it was a one-day ride, but usually two.

Although I longed to take dinner in my room, Lord Collier requested I dine with his guests as their representative in their absence. He was regretfully leaving a small party of associates who he'd invited to spend the week, but there was no way around it. Since they were fully aware of both Lady Margaret's return and my existence, he expected us both to entertain in his and Lord Duncan's absence.

She sat at the head of the table in the earl's place while I mixed myself into the middle of the group. I had no desire to stand out in the crowd. Of course, Lady Lilith was in attendance and so was her glower, only this time it was aimed in the right direction. It seemed there was more than the rival for Duncan between the two. Had that been the case, and having heard the rumor of Duncan and my love tryst -and with the absence of her guardian- she surely would have been throwing eating utensils at me like darts. We were just being seated at our respective places when Lady Lilith shocked the dinner party by asking the dowdy looking Lord Dunbar to switch seats with me so that I would be seated directly next to her. A hush came over the room as he obliged.

I wasn't sure if it was the wisest idea, but I went along with her request and took the seat next to her. Since I wasn't all that hungry, I guessed it didn't matter if my dinner was ruined by her sour, biting conversation. To my surprise, it was anything but. Other than the cutting looks she sent to the opposite end of the enormously long table, she was the epitome of politeness.

She questioned me on how I was enjoying my stay at Winterspring. She shared some enjoyable anecdotes about her childhood growing up with Duncan. We touched a bit on my relationship with him, but I was quick to change the subject to something more neutral considering the company we were in.

I would occasionally glance in Lady Margaret's direction to find her openly glowering at me. Her distaste for my presence at the table was fully displayed. Most of the dinner party ignored the undercurrent and enjoyed the good food and conversation, but there were a few who felt it necessary to join the royal high priestess in her glowering fest. I suppose I couldn't blame her for her behavior. Not only had I taken Duncan from her, but it appeared I was making a friend of Lady Lilith.

Double whammy!

Relieved when the meal ended, I made my excuses and left Lady Margaret to preside over the party of friends while I went back to my rooms. I didn't even need to feign a headache. I felt like someone was playing racket ball with my brain. This was one of the few times I truly missed modern day medicine. Their headache powders just took the edge off. They still required you lie down for several hours the stress could leave your body.

Elizabeth helped me out of my gown with the ease and efficiency of an adept lady's maid. I'd just crawled beneath the security of the thick cotton bed cover when the chamber maid asked for entry into my rooms. She needed to collect the piss-pot early. She'd been informed that the washerwoman's normal schedule for pickup of the estate's inhabitant's urine was thrown off due to her daughter's delivery of a healthy baby boy. The washerwoman's husband would be collecting the urine for her while on his route for dung collection and would take it all to the tannery on his own. I have to say, I found the whole process disgusting and had to shudder the thought of it from my mind whenever I encountered an article of wearing apparel or item fashioned from leather. I guess it's what one is accustomed to, because I thought nothing of it whenever I saw a dog owner walking the streets of Manhattan with the dog's recent dump wadded in a little plastic bag.

Elizabeth waited in silence for the maid to leave before approaching the side of my bed.

"I want to thank you for assisting me. I hope you are not being reprimanded by Lady Margaret for it," I said sleepily.

"She is unaware of my doings of late," she explained, "There are matters with the coven occupying her thoughts. As long as I attend her needs when she requires me, she pays me scant mind."

I'd been so focused on the drama of traveling back through time, pretending I was Lady Margaret, continual kidnapping, Isabelle's death, and Duncan's arrival that I'd never really paid Elizabeth all that much attention. True, I spoke with her whenever she was around, escaped kidnappings with her, and so forth, but I'd never truly looked at the woman like I was doing through the mirror as she combed out my golden locks to make me ready for sleep. I loved the tradition of brushing the hair long and hard with a soft bristled brush before bedtime. It felt so good that, at times, I had to prevent myself from drooling.

The closer I looked at her, the more other worldly she

appeared. That's the only way to explain it. It wasn't anything in particular that stood out with distinction. It was more the energy around her and the tiniest of hints of something different. If I hadn't been sitting there with my body's abilities completely relaxed and open, I probably would never have noticed.

"What is it about you that is different?" I asked with my acquired eighteenth century lilt.

Elizabeth smiled and said, "You can speak normally, m' lady. There are no ears tonight."

I smiled gratefully and repeated in modern English, "You're radiating energy that I don't remember being there."

Her eyes grew wide and she gasped, "You have the sight?"

I chuckled and nodded.

She confessed it never occurred to her that I might have the sight since, once again, she'd assumed I was exactly like Lady Margaret; who was a powerful magician, but didn't have the sight. She relied on the coven's seer for her information. Not so with me. I don't know if you'd call me a true seer, but I had certain psychic abilities that I used on occasion or that popped up when I was relaxed; like I was at that moment.

Realizing the topic was being shifted away from her and placed on me, I swung it back around and asked her once again what it was that I was sensing. Her hands shook as she continued to brush my hair. Whatever it was that I'd picked up on, it was definitely something she wished I hadn't.

The shuffle of footsteps on my balcony caught both our attention. I leapt to my feet, knocking Elizabeth off balance as I focused on who or what might be on the balcony.

"You said there were no ears," I whispered.

"Truly, there were not," she pleaded.

"I bid you come hither!" I commanded with a boldness I didn't feel.

I held my breath as the footsteps made their way toward the entrance to my rooms. My only thoughts were that I knew I couldn't undergo another kidnapping by that crazy witch Vivian. I grabbed the fireplace poker. The other times I'd been taken by surprise. I wouldn't be this easy to capture this time.

The brilliant moonlight cast a shadow of a male figure long before his tall, lean body filled the archway of the balcony. I gasped as he stepped casually into the room as if I'd bid him entry from an actual door instead of the balcony of a second story suite.

As the light cast from the candles fitted securely in the sconces on the wall illuminated his figure in what could only be called a romantic light, I was hard pressed to subdue a gasp of awe and keep my chin from dropping to the floor and my tongue from hanging even farther as I stared like a groupie who'd finally come into the company of her idol. There before me stood Lord Rufus Elizabeth in attire that looked more suited for the turn of the twentieth century than for the late eighteenth century. The lines of his short waist, black flocked dinner jacket fit perfectly. Its tails cascaded just right over a lean lower frame. The pewter silk vest matched his pewter top hat perfectly. The expertly tied cravat brought attention to the white collar that covered his muscular neck. The walking stick he nonchalantly leaned on finished the ensemble off perfectly.

"Lord Rufus," I said stupidly.

"At your service," he said smugly while bowing low.

"Whatever are you wearing?" Elizabeth asked warily.

"'Tis the dress of eighteen-ninety-six England my dear sister," he replied.

"Eighteen-ninety-six. I do not understand," she whimpered.

"You time traveled?" I asked incredulously.

"That I did," he smiled.

"Wow," I said as I plopped myself down on the stool I'd only recently stood up from. "Have you been back to the twenty-first century?" I asked after I'd regained my composure.

Rufus looked down at the floor and sighed, "Alas, the formula eludes us. Be assured we are working on it and expect to discover it soon. The cusp of the twentiety century is as far forward as we have been able to get."

"We?" I asked.

"I do not work alone," he replied, "'Tis a group of us diligently working on cracking the code."

"A group of ... vampires?" Elizabeth asked hesitantly.

How odd it was that I'd forgotten Elizabeth was still with us. Lord Rufus' presence filled the room to the extent it was difficult to see or know anyone or anything else. I put myself in check and forced my mind to break free from whatever spell it was under. After all, I already had a handsome vampire as a boyfriend. The problem was that, although I felt connected to Duncan, I didn't feel that powerful draw to him that Lord Rufus created. I'd done nothing other than look and admire, but for some reason I felt like a guilty cheater.

I suddenly remembered I was standing in my chemise and rushed to don the embroidered cotton robe Elizabeth laid out for me earlier. As I glanced sheepishly in his direction, I was sure I saw a hint of amusement in his eye before he addressed his sister more seriously.

"Do you think my only associates to be vampires?" he asked defensively.

"No," she said quickly.

It was nothing that stuck out. Once again it was more my psychic abilities coming to play, but I could sense a dark side of Rufus that I hadn't noticed before when he spoke so defensively and an extreme vulnerability in Elizabeth. This, once again, led me back to the question of what it was about her that I was picking up. Rufus was easy. He was vampire and vampires had a dark side, but Elizabeth... well, that remained a puzzle.

CHAPTER TWENTY-TWO

After some lighter conversation about why her brother felt the need to visit Lady Jane at such an hour and why he chose the balcony to enter rather than the door, Elizabeth reluctantly made her excuses. It was time for her to tend to the needs of Lady Margaret and she dared not be late. She cast me a worried look and made her leave.

I pondered briefly over why Elizabeth would be concerned about leaving me alone with her brother. After all, hadn't she been the one to introduce us and assure me that he wouldn't harm me? The look she shot me was clearly a look of worry or concern. Things just weren't making sense.

An uncomfortable silence spread through the chamber while I debated if I should ask the dangerously alluring Lord Rufus to leave or invite him to stay and converse with me a bit longer. There were still many questions that I had for him about the time traveling he was doing. If Duncan and I were to get back to the future, we needed information on how to do it and possibly some help. I also had questions about his vampirism. It seemed somehow different than Duncan's. I'd eliminated many of the myths of vampires -such as they can't go out in daylight and they can't eat much of the same food as humans do- from my experience with Duncan. He wandered freely day or night, although he admitted to a resurgence of strength that occurred from the energy of the moon and he deplored meat of any kind.

Duncan was a loner. He associated with very few vampires. Rufus, on the other hand, was clearly a social butterfly. I had no doubt he'd mixed and mingled with many. If one wanted to learn more about them, he would be the logical vampire to query.

I watched the sleek vampire as he leaned his shoulder against the stone wall of my chamber and fiddled with his fingernails as if he hadn't a care in the world. It was as if he knew I was wrestling with a decision and was patiently awaiting it. His relaxed and confident pose also led me to believe he expected me to invite him to stay.

He was right.

He was reluctant to converse about his associates in time travel so I shifted the topic to his vampirism. Perhaps, once we got to know each other better, he'd feel more comfortable sharing information he considered private. In truth, I was more interested in the actual time traveling than I was in who he was working with anyway.

He motioned for me to sit in one of the wing back chairs near the fireplace and then seated himself in the chair opposite me. The seating wasn't placed very far apart. I felt staggeringly near his long legs as he stretched them out before him in a manner that only a man without a care in the world would do. His smile was much softer and gentler than I'd have expected from a vampire; other than Duncan, of course. This just raised my curiosity all the higher. I was driven to discover as much as I could about this breed of human, for no matter how often Duncan declared he was no more than a monster, I only saw a man with a hollow chest that needed to be filled with light. To me, he was less a monster than those spike haired punks who attacked me the night I learned he was a vampire.

We spent the next few hours laughing and joking and sharing information. He wanted to know as much as he could about my life in the future with Duncan. I wanted to learn as much as I could about vampires. He never asked the name of my vampire lover and I never volunteered. I certainly didn't volunteer that he'd returned through the portal I was supposed to use when I was held captive by wicked Lady Vivian. He seemed more intrigued about the fact that Duncan and I lived together without him ever biting me, not even a nibble.

He questioned me about the health and stamina of my

vampire. I admitted that, although his state of health seemed strong, my lover's appearance was far less robust than his own. This pleased him. He leaned closer. I could smell and almost taste the exotic spices on his breath. I could make out a few of them. Had I spent more time in the kitchen I might have recognized them all, but as it was I identified only clove and cinnamon.

The longer I spent in his company, the more I was affected by the pheromones he emitted. This was a new experience for me. It was like I was under his spell. The problem was that I knew I was under his spell and I didn't want to do a darn thing about it.

I questioned him about his daily habits as a vampire. From my time spent with Duncan, I'd observed that he slept very little, enjoyed long walks at dawn, responded to cold and heat only when they were at the extreme, drank alcohol, ate grains and vegetables, and drank only enough of the blood of animals to satiate himself, but not enough to kill the creature, was respectful of his footprint on the planet, and was the most passionate lover I'd ever encountered. I wondered if this was true of all good vampires.

Rufus confirmed that his daily habits were quite similar to those of my vampire lover, with the exception that he drank the blood of humans, not animals. When I gasped, he smiled and assured me that he had no intention of forcing himself upon me and he too only took enough to satiate his hunger. He attributed his robust appearance vs. my lover's pale one to their difference in feeding habits. He was of the opinion that his body originated and remained of human composition, not animal, and it required human blood to maintain it. Duncan, on the other hand, was a vegetarian in his mortal years so getting him to consume even a drop of animal blood had been a tortuous ordeal that took years for him to overcome. Asking him to feed on humans was near impossible.

We touched on my psychic abilities. He seemed fascinated with them, as well as the fact that he hadn't been able to pick up on them. He explained that most psychics were easy to spot, yet somehow this ability in me eluded him.

"I have to wonder what else I might discover about you," he said in a breathy whisper as he leaned forward and lightly brushed his lips to mine.

Our contact was for the briefest moment, yet it lingered on my lips; a tantalizing tingle that tasted of exotic spices from the other side of the world. A shiver of delight crept slowly up my spine. I savored every agonizing second of it until it burst into an orgasmic explosion throughout my body.

I stayed perfectly motionless while I tried to decipher what just happened. It was an experience I'd only read about in romance novels and, in truth, considered it a part of the whole fantasy read. Never in my wildest dreams would I have thought these erotic romance scenes were based on actual events. Wow! Wow! Wow!

Rufus stood and took my hands in his. He felt warmer than I'd expected him to feel, another difference to note between him and Duncan. As he pulled me to my feet, my mind screamed for me to remember Duncan and demand Rufus leave, but my body had other ideas and my body was in command at the moment.

I felt his strong arms encircle me as his lips closed in on mine. His kiss was heady and all consuming. Every inch of my body stood at attention. My head spun out of control and I soon lost my equilibrium as yet another scene from a romance novel was acted out by me.

I was vaguely aware of my breasts pressing against him for relief and my hips grinding into his in anticipation. I thought about how wanton I might appear to this man of the ages, but it was a fleeting thought at best. I allowed my hungry body to be swept into his arms as we shimmered to the bed. Shimmer is really the only description for the speed in which we traveled from one location of the chamber to the next.

The mattress beneath me gave me a small semblance of grounding as he tore my chemise from my body in the heat of passion. It was such a hot and sexy move I could barely contain myself. I wasn't quite as efficient or successful in removing his attire, but, with his helping hand, it didn't take long for our hot naked bodies to be stretched out side by side on the freshly laundered bed linens.

His long, well-manicured fingers traced my body. He left nothing unexplored. When he finished and was satisfied he'd prepared me for the next step in my journey to bliss, he shifted from tracing my body with his fingers to tracing it with his tongue. Starting at my toes, he worked his way up, slowly, languidly, until he reached my private area. My body pulsed and contracted with anticipation, but I did my best to maintain control. I wanted to savor every second of this experience and feared any response, other than my uncontrollable moaning and mild writing, would shift his actions. He pleasured me just long enough to torture me, but not long enough to allow me release and then continued up my torso with that expert tongue of his. Years of love making had taught this vampire well. I could say, without a shadow of a doubt, that he rivaled Duncan with technique.

Duncan. In the recesses of my mind I felt guilt and shame over my unfaithfulness to him. It wasn't like me to act this way, but I just couldn't help myself. As Rufus's soft lips consumed my nipple, my carnal instincts took control and all thoughts of Duncan flew out of my head.

I could stand no more and demanded, rather firmly, for release. He emitted a low, satisfied chuckle from somewhere deep in this throat before entering me with a power that matched my need. Almost instantaneously I reached heights of erotic perfection that forced all thoughts and reasoning from my mind. I could think of nothing. I was so consumed in the ecstasy of the moment that I couldn't even think who I was having sex with. I couldn't call it making love. Duncan and I made sweet, gentle love. This was pure, erotic, animal coupling.

It took a moment for me to realize that Rufus was no

longer suckling my breast. He was drinking from it instead. He'd managed to sink his fangs around my areola and was feasting on my blood. The pain of the piercing of my tender flesh mixed with the erotic sensation of my nipples still being worked and I went out of control. Instead of pushing him away and salvaging my life giving blood for myself, I pushed his head against my breast even harder. At that point and time he could have drained me dry of blood and I wouldn't have minded as long as the ecstasy remained.

When he finally pulled his mouth free of my breast and focused on completing his own orgasm, I was out of control. If I hadn't known better, I would have thought I'd been slipped some type of aphrodisiac. My body met his powerful thrusts with equal passion.

When he fell beside my exhausted body, it dawned on me that we hadn't used protection. Panic immediately replaced passion. One of the myths of vampire lore was that they couldn't procreate. This was far from the truth. In fact, they were probably more fertile than any other creature on the planet. Duncan always took precautions not to impregnate me because he feared for what might happen to me during the birthing process. Most mortals didn't survive. The only way to walk away from giving birth to a vampire baby was to become a vampire yourself during or immediately after the birthing. Since Duncan longed to be free of vampirism, the last thing he wanted to do was to turn me into a vampire or create a vampire child. It was his dream to find a way to become mortal again and have a normal family existence with me.

What had I done?

I rolled away from Rufus, mindless of his attempts to pull me back.

"What is troubling you, my love?" he asked.

"Don't call me that," I panicked. Whatever effect his pheromones had on me were long gone. "I can't believe I just did such a thing to Duncan. How could I do such a thing?" I wailed.

"Duncan?" he repeated quizzically.

"Never mind!" I screeched.

Rufus lay back with his arm over his eyes and remained silent while I paced the room.

"You impregnated me, didn't you?" I spat.

"Yes," he whispered.

I stopped, frozen in mid-step as his confession sunk in.

"Why would you do that to me? Don't you think I know what happens next? Did it ever occur to you to ask me if I wanted to become a vampire before you sealed my fate?" I asked through gasps of air.

"I thought it was what you wanted," he said, somewhat abashed.

"Are you kidding me? What the hell gave you a damned fool idea like that?" I demanded.

It didn't matter to me that I was confronting a vampire who could crush the life out of me at any moment. All I could think about was how I'd been taken for a ride down a road of no return. Not only was I going to become a vampire and give birth to a vampire child, but I would have to explain the whole scenario to Duncan. Could things get any worse?

"You were so into it. Since you lived with a vampire as man and wife for quite some time, I assumed you understood," he explained.

"You assumed correctly. I do understand. I understand that you slipped something in those drinks you plied me with to create an aphrodisiac effect on me like nothing I've ever experienced before and you took advantage of the moment and planted your vampire seed in my mortal womb!" I roared. "Don't you think if I wanted to be vampire I would have been one by now?" I bellowed, "My lover is a vampire after all. I've had plenty of opportunity."

"'Twas no aphrodisiac, my love. What you experienced was the art of love making... real love making," he cooed. "Can I help it if I drive you wild?"

"Oof!" I spat and stomped behind the screen to clean myself up as best I could.

I tended to the stickiness between my legs before focusing on my swollen nipple. Tiny droplets of blood still oozed from the piercings of his fangs and I was incredibly sore, but I had no doubt it would be a clean heal. I knew that if I asked him to heal it for me it could be done instantaneously. I just didn't know if I wanted to give him the satisfaction of my having to present my nipple for healing. His selfish, thoughtless actions caused his appeal to dwindle and I now flinched at the mere thought of being ogled by his lusty orbs.

It was a difficult thing to do, but I saw no way around it. Duncan would be returning prior to the wound healing if I didn't get help from my vampire fling. It took every ounce of will I possessed to walk out from behind the screen and ask him to tend to the wound he'd created.

With a knowing smile, he smugly bit his wrist and gently massaged his blood over the piercings of my nipple. Of course his touch was far gentler and slower than need be, as if he was once again trying to arouse me, but I jumped back before it took effect.

Once was enough!

CHAPTER TWENTY-THREE

"You need to leave," I huffed as I nervously paced the room.

My mind darted in all directions. I didn't want to die and become a vampire. I didn't want to give birth to a vampire baby. More importantly, I didn't want to have to tell Duncan that I'd been unfaithful with another vampire and I was carrying that vampire's child.

"I can't lose him," I murmured.

"I am right here, my love. You shant lose me. There is nothing to fear. I will remain by your side the entire time," Rufus cooed as he hopped out of bed and moved next to me.

My psyche kicked in and I heard loud and clear that I needed to avoid looking into his eyes. Perhaps the myth of them glamoring their victims wasn't a myth after all? I wished I'd gotten that message about an hour earlier. I growled at my own lack of capabilities. He put his fingers beneath my chin and I pulled away. Making a point to look down, my eyes settled on his naked manhood reacting to my nearness. It was only then that I realized I hadn't a stitch on. I raced for my robe and slipped into it as quickly as I could.

"It's a little late for modesty, don't you think?" he chuckled.

"Oh, just go away," I huffed.

"You can't mean that, my lovely" he said softly as he crossed the room to stand near me once more.

"I mean it. Oh yes, I mean it!" I hissed.

"I apologize for misreading your signals. Had I realized your former vampire lover was inadequate to the extent that my love making would release your wild side for the first time, I would have done things differently," he said in a tone that reeked of amusement.

"He's not inadequate. He's also not former!" I cried out.

"No, my love. There is a code ... a law if you will... amongst vampires. Impregnating a mortal is as good as marrying them. He may have been your lover, but he is no more. You belong to me, my beauty," he replied in a firm, yet sultry tone.

"What? What are you... What?" I stammered. My mind was reeling. "No! You can't... no... I... we love each other."

"Truly? Is that so?" he chuckled, "Your behavior in bed leads me to think otherwise."

I held my fingers to my temples and pressed as I mumbled, "This can't be happening."

"You can't make me believe you aren't attracted to me, so don't try," he said. "In time you will forget your lover and love me as I love you."

"What? You don't love me... how can you... what do you mean you love me?" I huffed.

This was all too much.

"I fell in love with you the minute I set eyes on you," he explained. "When you reach my age, you can tell the difference between love and infatuation. You are who I want to spend eternity with." He looked at me smugly. "So I will."

"Do you always get what you want?" I asked.

"Why not," he said matter-of-flatly as he shrugged his shoulders.

"No matter who gets hurt?" I said more than asked.

"I shall do my utmost to never hurt you, my love. I shall cherish you and the children you bear me always," he said with earnest.

"Children?" I choked out.

I couldn't contain my shock.

"Of course. You have a young and healthy body. Once you are made vampire, your body will be even stronger. You'll be able to bear many children," he responded.

"This is a nightmare," I moaned. "You really need to leave."

"Oh, my dear, this is no dream. This is very, very real," he assured me.

It was clear Rufus was getting annoyed with my refusal to accept what was happening. I knew it was dangerous for me to anger a vampire, but I just didn't care. What was the worst he could do to me? Kill me? Well, that was going to happen sooner or later; so what the heck.

I continued with my tirade as I spat, "You are the sneakiest, most conniving beast I have ever encountered. What would possibly make you think that you can waltz in here, impregnate me without my permission, tell me you love me, and expect me to run to you with open arms?"

His eyes twinkled with amusement as he said in a tone that sounded like he was talking to a child, "You are a spitfire."

His response sent me into a blind, frustrated rage. I must have gone temporarily insane. That had to be the only explanation for my rushing at him with claws extended, ready to do whatever ever damage I may. It wasn't only foolish, but stupid of me to think he couldn't thwart my efforts with minimal exertion. All my little tantrum did was land me right back into his naked grasp.

That was not a good place to be.

Typical man that this vampire was, my display of rage had an arousing effect on him and he was ready for action once again.

As if to prove his point of possession, he tossed me onto the bed -as if I was nothing more than a stuffed toy he'd tired of playing with- and ripped the tie from my robe. I struggled to cover my body with the fabric as it fell opened with one hand while fending his advances off with the other.

Looking back, it was foolish of me to even try to fight a vampire who was twice my size and four times my strength, but I did the best I could to the bitter end before he gained entry to my womanhood. Without the aphrodisiac affects to push my body to heights unknown and with all desire for him terminated, the experience was nothing short of tortuous. To add to the agony of the situation, he was driving into me with a pounding force that clearly showed how angry I'd made him.

As if to solidify our bond, once again he planted his seed within my womb.

I made no move to get up and clean myself. What was the sense in trying to wash away the inevitable? Deep down in my core I knew I'd conceived. I now belonged to this beast that lay atop me grunting the remainder of his sperm into me.

I'd lost Duncan -my one true love- forever and I had no one to blame but myself. I lay stiff as a board while I waited for him to release me.

As if knowing my thoughts, he growled in his native eighteenth century voice, "You shall love no other. I shant have it."

His fiery lips burned as they forced mine to respond. His frustration mounted. He was a vampire who was accustomed to getting his own way. As handsome as he was, I had no doubt he'd also gotten his own way as a mortal, at least with the ladies.

My mind flew to our initial meeting and the hesitation I had when we'd met. Why hadn't I paid attention to my own intuition? I'd been so trusting of Elizabeth when she told he her brother wouldn't harm me. Had they planned this together?

"Why do you want me? There are plenty of beautiful women. I mirror Lady Margaret. Why not take her?" I practically wailed.

I couldn't believe the words were coming out of my mouth. Even so, I felt no loyalty toward that evil woman or shame in offering her up to him. As far as I was concerned, it was her comeuppance.

"You might resemble her in looks, but that is where it ends. She has a heart as black as coal. 'Twould be a life of hell with that one," he mumbled as he nuzzled my neck. "No, my lovely Jane, 'tis you I have waited all these centuries for. You are the sunshine of my dreary life,"

I gasped in horror. Those were the exact words Duncan said to me. Had he somehow found out? I had to know.

"Those are the exact words my lover said to me when we met. Is that a coined phrase for vampires?" I asked bitterly.

"He said this?" Rufus sounded agitated at the thought. I nodded.

A dark cloud of jealousy consumed his face and a faraway look came into his eyes. I dared say no more. For the first time, I was afraid.

"Tell me the name of this vampire that said this to you," he commanded.

"What does it matter? He's in the future and I'm stuck here," I said quickly.

Something warned me that it wouldn't be the wisest thing to divulge Duncan's name or whereabouts to Rufus.

"It matters. Tell me his name!" he growled.

Without a moment's hesitation I blurted out, "Sebastian McDougal."

I have no clue why I came up with the name. There was no reason for my madness, except to protect Duncan from this vampire who was crazy with jealousy.

"He made it to the future?" he asked incredulously.

Oh no. Leave it to me to select a name out of thin air that actually belonged to a vampire; and one Rufus knew no less. I was batting a thousand in this game of hell.

"Do you know him?" I asked hesitantly.

"Only by reputation," he replied.

I took a chance and said confidently, "He's a force to be reckoned with."

"Aye, that he is," he mumbled absent mindedly.

"I wonder his reaction when he hears you raped me," I said boldly.

That was definitely the wrong thing to say. Without a moment's hesitation he growled that my body belonged to him in all ways and there was no such thing as raping what belonged to him. Whether he was trying to drive his message home or was simply fed up and frustrated and knew no other recourse, I don't know. All I do know was that when he sunk his fangs into my neck it burned like nothing I'd ever experienced before. I think a hot iron might have felt better. What a stark contrast from the erotic experience I'd had while in the throes of passion.

Tears flooded my cheeks. I whimpered and begged for him to stop. The sound of him sucking my blood from my body thundered through my ears. I could feel my life force leaving. I was sure he was going to kill me right then and there. When he finally did stop, I had barely enough where-with-all left in me to breath, let alone do anything else.

I lay weak, limp, and lifeless. I was fully aware of all that was happening, but powerless to make a move or participate in conversation. I could hear him mumbling his apologies about losing control and felt him rubbing my body as if trying to rub life back into me. He bit his wrist and held it firmly against my mouth. I had no choice but to ingest his blood. As the metallic taste of the rich fluid oozed past my lips, I slowly began to breathe life back into myself. Minutes later, I was opening my eyes and looking around.

Relief consumed his face and real tears slid down his cheeks. I was so intrigued by the concept of a vampire crying I did nothing to resist him when he cradled me against his chest and rocked me back and forth. All the while he cooed in my ear about his undying love and the bond we'd created between us that night. He assured me that he'd tend to Sebastian, if need be, and begged me not to give it another thought.

When I finally felt myself again, I decided to use a different tactic. I needed to be alone so I could think about all that just occurred. It took a while for me to convince Lord Rufus to leave. He finally agreed, but not until he'd arrogantly informed me that he'd be back. Now that I carried his child, I was considered his mate and he had a right to come and go as he pleased.

My tortured mind was working overtime, as were my tear ducts when Elizabeth slipped into the darkness of my room and lay down next to me on the bed. No words passed between us, but I knew she was aware of what happened and she was offering me the only thing she had to give; her sympathy and support. It was then that I remembered her look of warning as she'd left to attend to Margaret. She'd feared something like this would happen.

"By my troth, I knew not when I introduced you. I trusted his word. He disappoints us both," she whispered.

"He more than disappointed me, my friend. He's written my death sentence," I sighed.

A loud gasp in the dark clued me in on the fact that Elizabeth had no idea of the consequences of my encounter with her brother. I explained in great detail all I knew about what happened to a mortal female who was impregnated with a vampire's seed. She admitted to me that she'd believed vampires weren't able to procreate and one needed to be drained of blood in order to be made vampire. Since her brother was a vampire, this surprised me. I expressed my surprise to her and she explained that he'd only just returned into their lives and she was still getting used to the idea of him being a vampire. She'd taken no measures to truly understand vampirism -after her vampire love was killed- out of superstition and fear.

"Did you inform him of your lover's identity?" she asked cautiously.

"No," I whispered.

"Good," she said before pulling me close and stroking my hair.

Although her actions bordered on intimate, I inherently knew Elizabeth was displaying a sisterly love and desire to protect me. I cuddled into the crook of her shoulder and nuzzled my face into her neck. Her long locks fell over her shoulders and tickled my nose.

"He deliberately impregnated me and he says that it's vampire law that I'm his wife now that I'm pregnant with his child. What will I tell Duncan?" I murmured into her neck.

"Perhaps we can reverse the pregnancy," she replied.

"Abortion?" I asked.

"'Tis only a seed seeking claim on your womb, m' lady. An herbal potion and a bit of magic should do the trick. We shall seek the council of Lady Helen in the morning," she soothed.

"'Tis a most splendid idea," I murmured as I drifted into

blissful sleep.

CHAPTER TWENTY-FOUR

Dawn was barely upon us when Elizabeth summoned Garth to my chambers and, after swearing him to secrecy, had him assist us in moving the wardrobe far enough away from the tapestry to allow us to slip behind it. We decided it was best to travel with Garth along. Now we not only had to worry about Vivian and her crazy abductions, but we needed a watchful eye for Lord Rufus as well.

Although neither of us was eager to bring Garth into our confidence, we were forced to divulge a bit of information to him concerning Lord Rufus' obsession with me in order to get him to cooperate. Even though he now realized I wasn't Lady Margaret, I'd won him over during the time he thought I was and his loyalty to me was astounding. Although I'd paid it little attention, I was now extremely grateful for it.

Elizabeth informed Garth of our early morning rendezvous and had asked him to make certain we had horses waiting for us at the opening of the tunnel. To my relief, he'd selected well behaved steeds that required a good seat, but minimal coaxing. I hadn't ridden since Elizabeth and I were captured during out picnic near the cave that afternoon. Remembering the coaxing and begging I had to do with the horse I first rode when I searched for my belongings in the cave, I prayed I would end up with a cooperative beast on this very important mission. My prayers were answered.

My mare was gray, sleek, and fit me like a glove. She moved beneath me as if she sensed the urgency of our reaching the sanctuary of the coven in record time. Garth was good enough to forgo the side saddle, so I was allowed to straddle her back and hang on with my thighs. I regretted the tenderness of my groin from my encounter with Rufus, but it couldn't be helped. I gritted my teeth and urged my mount to keep pace with the others. Now wasn't the time to be a wimp.

Lady Helen greeted us with all the warmth and love one might expect from a great leader. I felt saddened to think she had to step back and allow Lady Margaret her rightful place as high priestess of the coven. I was certain Margaret didn't deserve the title, just as I was convinced Helen did. Sometimes life was just screwed up.

Helen took us to a remote section of the encampment. Even though the majority of the few permanent residents were yet to rise, she didn't want to take any chances of being overheard. Once we reached the selected location, she cast a privacy spell around us for good measure. It was so impressive that I made a mental note to learn how to do it when all this was over.

I was grateful we'd left Garth to tend the horses so he wouldn't be privy to my tale as I reluctantly confessed to both Lady Helen and my friend and pseudo sister about how I'd fallen under the spell of Lord Rufus and conceived his child. I didn't have to tell Helen about Duncan because she already knew, as did Elizabeth. I left nothing out of my story, feeling it important for Helen to know and understand absolutely everything that was said and everything that occurred.

Elizabeth was practically overtaken with grief at the discovery of a side of her brother she had no idea existed. She apologized repeatedly for placing me at risk by introducing me to him. When I asked her why she did it, she grew silent in thought before stating he'd asked to meet me. Helen looked concerned at that comment, but said nothing.

My shame and humiliation at my confession of wantonness was far more overwhelming than I'd imagined it would be. It appeared the prudence of the eighteenth century had infiltrated into my twenty-first century thought process. Helen eased my discomfort by explaining that vampires not only had the ability to glamour their victims into doing their bidding, but she suspected my wanton behavior was a result of some form of aphrodisiac being slipped into my drink. The only puzzling factor was that I hadn't taken a drink in my chambers. If I'd been slipped anything in my drink, it would have had to have been given to me in my mead at dinner.

Since most aphrodisiacs required time to get into the system, Helen wasn't thrown by that concept. What concerned her was the fact that someone was obviously in cohorts with Rufus. If it wasn't his sister, who could it be? This bit of realization brought to light the fact that there was someone within the mansion walls who was Jane's true enemy and whoever it was consorted with vampires. Extra precautions would need to be taken until they discovered the mystery person's identity.

The ultimate task at hand was to dislodge the seed that was planted not twenty-four hours earlier. Lady Helen praised Elizabeth for her quickness of thought and said she was fairly confident we'd be able to correct the situation because of that quickness. I realized when Elizabeth puffed with pride that the poor girl probably never received a complement, or, if she did, they were far and few between. I made a mental note to be freer with them where she was concerned. It must be difficult to be born of privileged blood, but still have to be in a position of service to someone of higher rank.

Lady Helen queried Elizabeth long and hard about her knowledge of Garth. Elizabeth assured us that he was of the highest caliper of men and could be trusted explicitly. Once he swore loyalty, he could be loyal to a fault. Although it pained me to do so, I felt I needed to remind her that she'd assured me Rufus wouldn't hurt me as well. With a look of hurt that cut my heart in two, she once again apologized and confessed she had no idea why she said such a thing to me as she hardly knew her brother. She had been sent away as a young girl to work as a woman's gentlewoman and had very little exposure to him. Helen presumed she too had been unwittingly glamored. It made sense.

Garth was summoned to our meeting and was filled in on everything. His reaction to the news of Lord Rufus being a vampire was mild in comparison to his reaction of what had been done to me. His loyalty to the lords and ladies of Winter Spring went back generations. His father and his father before him all served as protectors to the master of the estate and his loved ones. Lord Duncan was the son of the Earl of Winter Spring and next in line to inherit the title. He made it clear to Garth that Lady Jane was his love choice and was to be protected at all times. The fact that Lord Rufus managed to access her chambers without his knowledge put him into a state of outrage. He vowed it wouldn't happen again.

Satisfied that we had at least one male protector within the estate to monitor the other residents' actions where I was concerned, Helen focused on deciding on the selection of potion to dislodge Rufus' seed. We also needed to find a place to hide me while the abortion process took place. This would be tricky because it would take a week to complete. I suggested I just go back to the estate and continue with my daily routine, but she was concerned that Lord Rufus might visit my bed during the process and plant more seed. The potion was only so strong. We couldn't take that chance.

Disappearing while Duncan was absent from the estate was no big deal. Elizabeth need only announce I was a bed with a condition and no one would even think to check on me, but when Duncan returned it would be a different matter altogether. We needed a story to explain my absence to him. That was a challenge because Duncan knew full well that I was not from that era and I had no one to visit. He was also quite intuitive and could smell a lie from a distance. Convincing him of our story would be difficult.

Elizabeth suggested telling him the truth, as did Garth and Lady Helen. I went into a panic over losing him because of my infidelity and was assured by all three that he wasn't the kind of man to abandon his love because she'd been tricked into behaving badly. I assured them repeatedly that it was abnormal behavior for me and I appreciated their support, but I just wasn't convinced telling Duncan was the wisest thing.

Unfortunately, majority ruled and, since I was at their mercy and in need of their aid, I had no choice but to agree to comply with the plan.

When it was settled that I'd be the one to present the situation to Duncan when he returned, we went over the various places I could be hidden where Lord Rufus wouldn't know to look. We decided on the little shack that Duncan had found Elizabeth, Anna, and me hiding from Vivian's goons in. Since Elizabeth was required to wait on Lady Margaret, Anna was summoned to watch over me.

The look of surprised delight when Anna saw me standing next to Lady Helen was heartwarming. She breathlessly exhausted words as she went on and on about wondering where I was and how I was, etc. When she finally ran out of breath to allow someone to get a word in edgewise, she was given the basics of the story and asked to be my caretaker during the aborting process. I was grateful to Helen for her omission of the circumstances that led up to my conceiving the child of a vampire. She left that up to Anna's imagination and judgment.

What was being asked of her was a dangerous task and she well knew it. She'd be participating in the abortion of a vampire seed. Should the vampire discover this, it would most definitely mean her death. It didn't surprise me that it took minutes of quiet deliberation before Anna nodded her head in agreement to the assignment.

Unbridled tears of joy and gratitude gushed forth as I hugged her close and whispered my thanks. This was the second time she'd participated in my escape of impending death. I owed her big time.

They whisked me off to the shed without a moment's hesitation. Anna cast her spell of invisibility around the entire shack while Elizabeth received orders from Lady Helen on what to do when Lord Duncan returned that evening. Garth was cloaked in a spell of protection to help enhance his ability to stand guard over me.

It was no more than an hour or two after I'd settled into the little shack made cozy by the efforts of my protectors that I was given the most disgusting tasting, thick, black sludge to force down my esophagus.   It was with great effort that I managed to get it down. While I was struggling to keep it down, I overheard Helen giving instructions to Anna that I was to take this sludge every three hours for the first twenty-four hours and then twice a day for the remainder of the week. Oh happy day.

As the contractions in my abdomen seized my body and my stomach threatened to escape through my throat, I lay doubled over wondering if I had what it took to survive the next week.

CHAPTER TWENTY-FIVE

I don't remember much of the next twenty-four hours. I slipped in and out of consciousness; which was probably for the best because when I was awake I was writhing in pain from the contractions of my uterus as it tried to free itself from Rufus' embedded sperm. Anna explained to me that vampire sperm was far more difficult to abort than mortal sperm, but it could be done and not to fear. She also assured me repeatedly that I was stronger than I thought and I'd get through the ordeal and live to enjoy life again. There were moments when her reassurances were the only thing that got me through and gave me the strength to endure.

We spent the few moments I was pain free and lucid enough to converse discussing the books in the alcove of my bed chamber and whether or not they contained a spell to help me return to the future. I questioned how long the work Helen did to shield me from Isabelle's fate would last, but she had no idea. It was a spell far more advanced than anything the temporary high priestess was known to cast. It must have been the look of horror that came over my face upon hearing this that prompted Anna to continue with the assurance that Lady Helen was the best around when it came to spell casting. Many believed her abilities exceeded that of their high priestess, though none would say it openly for fear of the consequences. Apparently disrespecting the coven's high priestess brought about unspeakable punishment.

Anna suggested we ask Elizabeth to bring us the book Lady Margaret recorded her spells into. She admitted she was surprised to discover the high priestess was so careless as to leave her library unattended in such a way. When I explained the difficulty one would have in finding the location and that the only reason I was aware of it was because Elizabeth was under the impression I was Lady Margaret and was showing it to me in hopes of jogging my memory, she relaxed and nodded in understanding.

Although I trusted Anna to care for me, for the first time I questioned if she trusted me in return. After all, I wasn't who I'd been convinced by Lady Helen to claim to be, so right off the bat I'd lied to her. It was understandable if she had doubts floating around in her mind.

Elizabeth managed to slip away from the castle once a day. When asked to bring the spell book, she hesitated, but agreed to see if she could slip it out unnoticed. Lady Margaret was preoccupied these days with a secret matter that she refused to share with Elizabeth, therefore it might be possible. Elizabeth confided that there had been a changing in the personality of Lady Margaret since her return from the future. Although she'd never been the gentlest of humans she was even less so now. Anna confirmed this. I'd noticed no changes in myself, nor had Duncan mentioned them, so I could give them no reason for it except that perhaps it worked differently when you went to the future and returned to the past verses going to the past and returning to the future.

An unbelievable pain shot through my gut without warning and I fell to the floor. Anna and Elizabeth gasped worriedly as they helped me stand. I followed their stare to the floor and couldn't believe the pool of blood I stood in. It was gushing out of me like someone stuck me with a blade. I'm not sure if my body trembled from the loss of blood or the shock of seeing it pouring out of me.

Anna ran to the door and shouted for Garth. He appeared within seconds. His face went ashen when he saw the scene within the small shack. Anna only had to ask him once to fetch Lady Helen and he was mounted on his gelding and kicking up dust as he galloped off.

The encampment wasn't far off. The girls made me comfortable on the small cot I'd been occupying and I watched while they cleaned up the pool of deep red blood. Elizabeth was the first to rush outside to vomit, but Anna wasn't far behind. When my eyes were finally able to focus I understood why. There, in the middle of the pool of thick red goo was an overly large blob that looked to be taking shape!

I could hear Garth returning with Lady Helen, but I couldn't bring myself to open my eyes. I was sick from head to toe. The only thing that was keeping my stomach from lurching out of my mouth was my tonsils.

I felt her hand on my forehead and rolled onto my back.

"M' lady," she whispered. "Lady Jane, 'tis Helen."

"I know," I said flatly.

"You have aborted, dear Jane. 'Tis done," she said gently.

"Why was it so big?" I asked.

It had been about a week since I'd been with Rufus. I couldn't believe even a vampire could grow that fast.

Her sigh was heavy, followed by a long pause, before she spoke, "The babe was in your womb longer than one week. Did you not realize?"

I sat up in panic.

"I killed Duncan's baby?" I asked.

She closed her eyes tight and nodded.

"How could that be?" I blurted as if Helen knew all.

"You showed not, true. Some women have no knowledge of these things going on within their womb until they begin to show. This must be with you," she said as she brushed a tear from the corner of her eye.

"What will I do?" I wailed as I tried to get up.

"You shall lay still and let me tend to you, that is what you shall do," she commanded as she pushed me firmly back onto the cot.

When the girls returned to complete the task of cleaning up the horrific murder scene, Helen whispered something in Anna's ear. She looked at me briefly, nodded, and left the shack. Within minutes she'd returned with a small box. Shuddering with timidity, she placed the blob that was the beginning of Duncan's unborn child in the box and wrapped it in cloth before leaving the shack again.

With the tragedy out of sight, Elizabeth was able to focus more clearly on cleaning the mess from the floor. It took the better part of an hour and Garth's assistance, but she eventually got it all cleaned up.

I had no idea where Anna went with my unborn child. Truthfully, I don't think I wanted to know. All I wanted to do was to bury my head in the ground and wish away the recent chain of events. Instead, I allowed the world around me to go black and I slipped off into blissful nothingness.

I awoke to hear muffled voices of a man and woman in deep conversation. My head was still unclear, but I was certain I recognized both of them. One was Helen and the other was.... Duncan! Duncan was here in the hut! He was standing not five feet away from the very spot where I murdered his child. I groaned at the misery of it all and turned my back to the room.

My movement and groan caught their attention. They stopped their discussion and came to my bedside.

Lady Helen was the first to reach me. Without a moment's hesitation she began checking my vitals. How long had I been sleeping? I felt incredibly groggy. I remembered being given a drink just before I dropped off into blissful nothingness. With the condition of my head being as it was, I assumed it was drugged. No matter. I was just as happy to escape the reality that I just couldn't face. I moaned for more drink, but got water instead of drug. I choked and spit with disgusted surprise.

The water had a cleansing effect on my head and I was soon alert and coherent. Satisfied, Lady Helen stepped aside to allow Duncan access to me. He knelt down beside my cot and took my hands in his. With his forehead against mine he whispered of the distress he'd been in since he returned to find me gone and no one able to tell him of my whereabouts.

He moaned of his fear of losing me. He uttered his undying love for me. He declared me as his forever.

Under normal circumstances I would have been dancing on the ceiling at such confessions from the vampire I loved. Unfortunately, this wasn't a normal circumstance. I was the worst of the worst of people for what I'd done to him and I didn't deserve his love and devotion. Instead of smiling and telling him I loved him back, I, once again, rolled on my side and nudged my face against the roughhewn wall. It stunk of earth, smoke, and animals, but I didn't care. I deserved to breathe in the stench and suffer. In fact, I deserved a whole lot more.

I took everyone by surprise when I demanded to be left alone. I could feel their eyes on me as they did my bidding and left the shack. Their worried murmuring beat at my head as if they were standing right above me, so I covered my ears with my hands and wished them away. I was a horrible person. I didn't deserve love and I certainly didn't deserve anyone worrying over me.

I wondered if Duncan would have announced his undying love to me if he'd realized what I'd done. We'd decided I'd be the one to tell him and, since I hadn't, then his declarations were meaningless. He'd take them back as soon as he heard my confession anyway. There was no sense in dragging out the inevitable.

Blissful dark emptiness beckoned me once again. I went there willingly.

CHAPTER TWENTY-SIX

The rich savory aromas of chicken stew wafting under my nose was all it took to roust me out of my slumber. It was at least a day since I'd eaten and my stomach walls were beating and growling for attention. They were so loud I couldn't blame Anna for the giggle that escaped her as she leaned forward to slip a spoonful of the delicious broth between my parched lips.

"What day is it?" I asked after swallowing the hot broth and savoring its delectable flavor.

"'Tis the end of your second week, Lady Jane," she replied. "Ye have been sleeping for most of the days, with little coherence in between."

"Ach," I moaned as I pulled my body into a sitting position.

I was weak. Although they'd given me sponge baths daily, I longed to immerse my entire body into a soothing lavender bath. I felt like tiny creatures took residence in my head and were chopping wood or something on a consistent basis. It was a barely noticeable sensation, but it was there.

I assured Anna that I was well enough to feed myself and she warily handed the bowl to me. Admittedly, I was a bit shaky, but after a few more spoonfuls my movements grew progressively steadier. By the time I'd cleaned the bowl, I was feeling very close to my normal self.

Anna watched me with a smile of appreciation.

"'Tis splendid to see you up and alert, m' lady, you had me worried for a while," she whispered.

I stretched my body in a catlike manner and muttered, "I long for a bath."

"'Tis a simple enough request. I shall check with Lady

Helen to make sure you are fit for bathing. Should she agree, I shall have one set up right away," she assured me as she hurried from the shack.

Since Anna was only gone a minute or two, I deduced Lady Helen was just outside the door. I was right. Her beaming face was quick to follow Anna through the door upon her return.

"Ah, Lady Jane, you look much better," Helen exclaimed, "How do you feel?"

Her hand radiated a soothing coolness against my forehead.

"Methinks I shall live," I replied quietly.

With a light hearted chuckle, she reached to the small table next to my cot and handed me a trencher of stew. I sat up immediately and took it gratefully. I was ravenous!

"You have a splendid appetite. 'Tis a sign of quick healing," she boasted.

"I can't thank you enough," I replied, too tired to bother with shifting my language.

"'Twould not due to lose thine habit of speaking our way," she whispered. "I fear we are not as secure as I hoped for. It appears Lord Rufus works with a very powerful witch. Your use of improper speaking could tip off the winds."

"Pray tell, whither is this witch?" I asked, taking heed to her suggestion.

"We know not the location or identity of the witch," she replied. "What we do know is the power is profound. 'Tis equal to that of our high priestess."

"Does it match your own?" I asked.

She looked away as if embarrassed and shrugged her shoulders in a non-committal way.

"The power of the spell we detect is strong enough to be of a coven leader," she explained, "a high priest or priestess for certain."

"Can you match it?" I persisted.

I cannot say," she sighed. "'Twould depend if the magic is worked by one or many. I suspect 'tis more than one."

"They desire what?" I asked, already knowing the answer.

"To find you, of course," she said flatly. "Lord Rufus sends a small army in search of you. He becomes desperate."

"Is Lord Duncan aware of this search?" I ask hesitantly.

"I think not," she sighed. "Perhaps he should."

"Why do you think such a thing? 'Tis madness," I hissed.

"'Tis sensible," she hissed back. "Let vampire protect against vampire. I have not the magic on my own."

"What about the coven?" I demanded.

"None with the skills required," she said sadly.

"Truly, I say Lord Duncan is not to task for such a battle. He has not the constitution to equal Lord Rufus. He dines on vegetables and occasionally the blood of animals. Lord Rufus feasts on humans." I touched my neck, "Of this I know first-hand. 'Tis what makes him so robust."

"You underestimate Lord Duncan," she said softly.

"Perhaps... but 'tis better to be safe. I could not bear losing him in such a way," I replied.

I was determined to keep Duncan and Rufus apart. I knew inherently that Duncan wasn't up to fighting Rufus. It was more than their difference in diet. There was something about Rufus that seemed different. It was like a force flowed through him that wasn't present in most vampires. I wondered if this force had something to do with the witch he was working with. I discussed this at length with Lady Helen, who was heavy hearted when she agreed it probably did.

Garth arrived with a beaten and banged copper tub in tow. Following close behind him were several maids with buckets of water. I watched as my bath was prepared with the utmost care and attention. It didn't matter that the little tub looked like they'd salvaged it from a junkyard and only half my body would fit into it. It didn't matter that the sides were full of bumps and lumps. At that moment and time, it was the most luxurious, wonderful vessel of lavender essence on the planet.

It took a moment for me to find my footing. Having always had an independent streak running through me, I politely waved away Lady Helen's offer of assistance and forced my legs to do my bidding. It was bad enough that I needed their assistance for protection from Lord Rufus and Lady Vivian and whoever the mysterious witch was... oh yes, and the anonymous person in the mansion who was helping them... the very least I could do was to walk on my own. I needed that small semblance of control over my life.

I allowed the maid, Gwendoline, to help me undress and lower me into the copper tub. My knees were practically tucked under my chin. but I didn't care. The soothing lavender scented liquid swirled around my aching body like tiny massaging fingers. The girl pulled my braided locks free and poured warm water over my matted hair. As she worked in the lathering oils created by Anna's expert hands, I just knew I was in heaven.

I was so content with the experience that I never notice the mood of the little shack change from warm and cozy to cold and frosty. It took a few minutes of immobility on Gwendoline's part for me to open my eyes and see Duncan standing over me wearing a scowl that would frighten Frankenstein out of his wits.

CHAPTER TWENTY-SEVEN

"I believe we have something to discuss," Duncan growled

He'd waited long enough for Gwendoline to leave the shack before speaking, but not long enough for me to get safely out of the copper tub. I felt incredibly vulnerable all folded up like a rag doll. The once luxurious bath now felt like a sand pit that would swallow me up at any moment. I longed to get out, but I had no idea how to unfold myself to do so.

Can you help me, please?" I asked timidly as I extended my hand. "I'm wedged in here like a sardine and my legs are going numb."

There was no mistaking Duncan's anger. The question that plagued me was whether his anger was due to my infidelity or my murdering his unborn child; or both? My nerves were frazzled and my body shook uncontrollably by the time he'd lifted me from the copper confines and planted me unceremoniously onto the hemp bath mat. After tossing a linen sheeting at me for me to dry myself with, he marched to the nearby stool and sat down with a huff.

I eyed him warily while I dried my slender body and then wrapped the sheeting around it. I wanted to move back to the cot and lay down. I felt weak, shaky, and very, very tired, but I didn't dare. I'd only seen this scowl on Duncan once before and that was the night he battled the vampires who'd interrupted the gang of punks who were mugging me.

"Well?" he said impatiently while he crossed his arms over his chest. "I should like to hear why you have been hiding in this shack for the last fifteen days."

"Fifteen days?" I gasped. I'd had no idea so much time had lapsed.

"Do not change the subject," he growled.

"Lady Helen didn't tell you?" I whined.

"I wish to hear it from your lips," he growled. "All of it."

Oh boy. This wasn't good. I looked around for an escape route, but the only way out of the shack would mean I'd have to get past my angry vampire first. I knew that wasn't going to happen. Panic consumed me for several long and tortuous moments before I finally resigned myself to the inevitable and took a deep breath.

"I do not know where to begin," I began.

"Use modern English please. I cannot seem to get used to you speaking otherwise and I want to focus on the story, not your speech pattern," he commanded.

"Lady Helen said I need to be careful about my spee..." I caught myself before continuing. I had no idea what he did and didn't know.

"I ask you speak normally," he took a deep breath, "please."

"Okay. Where do I begin?" I asked again.

"At the beginning," he blurted, his impatience clearly showing.

"What beginning?" I demanded.

I knew I was stalling for time and I knew he knew it too, but I just couldn't help it. I wanted to be anywhere but there with him and having any conversation other than the one I was being forced to have.

"Jane!" he shouted as he stood up.

I visibly flinched. My fear must have been apparent because he calmed down immediately. Our eyes locked and I began to cry. All of the pent up nervous tension, all of my self-hate, every emotion, opinion, and thought I'd had about myself during this horrendous ordeal were contained in those tears.

When he realized I was in an actual fit, Duncan's whole demeanor softened and he moved close to embrace me. I jumped back before he could wrap his arms around me. I didn't deserve comforting; especially by him. Confused, and a little hurt, he stood with a baffled look and his arms at his side.

"What has happened to you?" he whispered.

"Do you really want to know?" I whimpered between sobs.

"Of course," he replied.

"Even if it means the end of us?" I pressed on.

"I cannot imagine what could possibly mean the end of us," he murmured.

"Oh, believe it. It can and it will," I uttered as I walked to the cot and sat on its edge. When he started toward me I continued, "Stay back."

He stopped in his tracks and stared at me for a moment before nodding and going back to sit on the stool. When I saw he was positioned to listen to what I had to say, I began my story.

Although we'd discussed some of what I had to say, I began at the very beginning of my coming through time. Maybe I hoped that during the time it took to lead up to when I slept with Lord Rufus I'd come up with something to help get me out of this mess. I'm not sure. It just seemed like the place to start. Since Duncan and I had experienced precious little time alone, and when we did we weren't prone to conversing, very little of what I told him was a repeat.

He found my time at the inn fascinating. He'd been born and raised in privilege and never really considered what it would be like to toil as I'd done for weeks while I searched for a way to find his family. A look of genuine admiration and pride covered his face as he praised me for my fortitude. I accepted it with a brisk waive of my hand, knowing full well it would be short lived as my story progressed.

I went into great detail about the countless times I'd been abducted by Lady Vivian and how she'd assured me it wasn't she who'd bound his powers the night he was bitten. I spoke of how I'd been carried off by hawks and how Isabelle used the last of her magic on a locater spell. He closed his eyes with sadness during my tale of how Isabelle died and how I'd narrowly escaped the hangman's noose more often than I cared to admit. My description of the cage I'd been imprisoned in and my companion prisoners was enough to make him visibly shudder.

I openly discussed the venomous encounters I had with

both Lady Lilith and Lady Margaret. I expressed that, although Lilith had made an effort to extend an olive branch my way, Margaret was nothing but ferocious whenever ears weren't around.

I also made sure to point out what I'd learned about the fear and hesitancy the members of the coven had when it came to offending their high priestess. He openly raised an eyebrow at that one.

I was glad for the opportunity to open Duncan's eyes to the true nature of his precious Lady Margaret. She'd been a thorn in my side since she'd appeared out of nowhere and I was tickled to be able to out her to at least one of the Collier men who seemed to feel she walked on water.

It eventually came time to broach the topic I'd been dreading. I still hadn't come up with a way to avoid it so I decided to face it head on. I told him about the friendship that had developed between Elizabeth and me. I explained that, because of this friendship, I trusted her and thought nothing of following her to the remote part of the mansion where her brother waited to meet me.

Up until that point he hadn't spoken, but he stopped me to ask me why Elizabeth's brother wanted to meet me. Surprisingly, it never occurred to me to ask. Why hadn't I thought to ask? I couldn't say.

I still hadn't divulged the name of her brother and he didn't ask. Instead, he shook his head at my foolishness and asked me to continue my story.

Filling my lungs completely, I blurted out the rest of the dreaded story. I spent more time on the fact that he entered my room via the balcony and glamored me than I did on the fact that he'd had sex with me twice, but I left nothing out.

When I'd finished my story with the reason I was lying in recovery under the watchful care of Anna and Lady Helen it was so quiet and still in the shack that, not only would you be able to hear a needle drop on the cot's mattress, I was certain you could feel the breeze of it falling.

"I don't blame you for hating me," I said as I fidgeted with my fingers.

Looking at him would have been too painful.

"Mortal women never survive birthing vampire babies," he said quietly.

"Yes," I replied.

"You were wise to abort it," he murmured.

"I thought it was his seed I was washing away," I hiccupped.

"It was," he replied.

"No it wasn't, Duncan. It was your child I killed," I buried my face in my hands.

"How do you figure that?" he quizzed.

"It was starting to develop. It had a shape," I explained.

"You do not know? Does no one here know?" he looked confused.

"Know?" I copied him.

"A vampire baby is carried no longer than 3 months. It develops rapidly once the seed takes hold. How long after you err... did it... did you abort?" he asked sadly. It was clear he found this conversation difficult.

"Almost a week," I replied.

"It must have been painful. The child must have been close to the size of a mortal baby in the endings of the first trimester," he observed.

"It was a big blob that was starting to take shape," I shuddered.

"'Tis good you aborted," he said again as he stood to leave.

"You're leaving me?" I whimpered.

"Aye," he said softly. "You must rest."

He never turned around as I watched his broad, tense shoulders swagger out of that run down shack. I lay back on the cot and succumbed to the tears that were overwhelmingly crowding my eye sockets. How was I ever going to survive without Duncan?

CHAPTER TWENTY-EIGHT

I have no idea how long I sat staring at the door of the shack before Helen entered. It could have been hours or it could have been only minutes. It really didn't matter. Nothing mattered anymore.

"Come, dear Jane. You must rest," she cooed as she eased me back down on the cot.

I obeyed her willingly. There was no sense in fighting it. Besides, falling back into a blissful abyss was what I longed for anyway.

"You told him, then?" she asked.

Unable to speak, I nodded my head vigorously.

"Splendid, that," she said with a smile.

"He hates me," I managed to moan as I rolled onto my side.

"He loves you, m' lady. Ne'r have I seen such love in man nor vampire. 'Tis a rarity," she mused.

"Why do you say such?" I whined. "He left upon the story's end."

I don't know why I slipped back into her speech pattern. Perhaps it was out of respect for such a good woman as she'd proved to be.

"Aye, that he did," she agreed.

When she offered no more comment, I leaned on my elbow and looked at her.

"Why do you say he loves me?" I pressed.

"He did not tell you?" she asked surprised.

"Tell me what?" I demanded.

"Lord Duncan goes to confront the vampire responsible for your suffering," she said proudly.

"No! No! No! Say 'tis not so!" I screamed as I leapt

from the cot.

"Lady Jane, you must rest!" she wailed as she tried to subdue me.

"Please, Lady Helen, you must help me. You must help me!" I wailed as I paced the floor like a mad woman.

It took some time for her to calm me down enough for me to explain to her that I hadn't been exaggerating when I said Lord Duncan was no match for Lord Rufus. After a long, lengthy explanation about the abnormal power that I felt coming from Lord Rufus, I knew inherently that it was some type of magic from the powerful witch. Lord Duncan had no such witch behind him. If he tried to stand alone he would lose.

"Oh dear, I knew of the strength you claimed he had, but I knew not of these details. 'Tis a problem to be certain," she said as she wrung her hands absent mindedly.

"We must help him!" I commanded.

"I must think," she insisted. "'Twill not do to make haste."

"If only we knew the witch aiding Lord Rufus," I moaned.

Lady Helen played with her hands a bit longer before clapping them together. "I have it! The only coven other than ours is far too advanced in distance to attract Lord Rufus. I believe he works with one of our own. You shall walk amongst us in circle and pick out the culprit."

"How?" I blurted.

Was she kidding me?

"Each witch projects a subtle difference in energy. 'Tis a sort of signature. You shall look for the energy sensation you felt coming from Lord Rufus."

"And Lady Margaret? What shall we say to explain my presence to the high priestess?" I asked.

I had a valid point and Helen knew it. It wasn't like I was on the top of Margaret's popularity list and I doubted I'd be welcome to their new moon circle with open arms. She fretted a bit longer. It was clear the woman was sincere in her desire to help me. She decided to think over a cup of tea. That was one habit I'd yet to get accustomed to. I find nothing finer than a good cup of coffee from a French press, but I joined her.

About ten minutes passed before Isabelle appeared before us. Although I could see her far easier than Lady Helen was able to, there was no denying the woman saw something. Her eyes doubled in size and she choked on her tea. I thought this disturbance would cause my friend to disappear, but she stood firm and waited patiently for Helen to stop coughing and gasping for air.

When all was calm again, Isabelle reminded me of the fact that her mother, Rosalie Johanna Remoras was still alive and not far from our encampment. My heart skipped a beat. I'd forgotten about her. I questioned Isabelle about the reception we might receive from her mother and she assured me that she'd already paid her a visit and warned her. She also smirked as she told us that she'd seen herself being conceived. I scolded her about giving us a little too much information and we laughed. Oh, how I missed my friend.

Lady Helen was only able to hear my side of my conversation with Isabelle, so I filled her in. She was impressed that I would have an "in" with the Queen of Spanish Magic -as Rosalie was often referred to. She was both excited and nervous about meeting her.

We agreed there was no time to lose and set about preparing for our journey deep into the woodland where the Spanish Magical community resided. Isabelle agreed to guide us. As hidden as Lady Helen's encampment was against prying eyes, Rosalie's was even more protected.

I spent the duration of our journey questioning Isabelle and Helen on Rosalie's powers. Helen did her best to decipher my conversation with Isabelle by my responses, but occasionally I had to stop and fill her in. I discovered that Senora Remoras was respected and feared by all covens in the British Isles as well as parts of her native Spain. She'd left her homeland by choice. Her love for an outcast pirate was far greater than her love for her country, so she packed up and followed him; finally settling in the forests of beautiful Essex. Although she left on her own, it didn't take long for loyal followers to find her and settle in. Within a year she was overseeing a community almost as large as the one she'd left.

When we reached the location of the encampment, Lady Helen looked around and sniffed the air. Before us was an empty clearing within the forest. It wasn't as large as the clearing that led to her coven and she was curious how it could house the size community she'd heard existed. Isabelle had us tether our horses to a small lean-to that appeared out of nowhere and then stand on a boulder that rested smack in the middle of the clearing.

We were asked to hold hands, close our eyes, and brace ourselves for rapid movement. Even with the warning, neither of us was prepared for the swirling and twirling that occurred as we rode the boulder from one dimension into the next. By the time the motion stopped, we'd shifted from standing firmly to sitting meekly.

I was dizzy and out of breath. From what I could tell, Helen wasn't much better off. Isabelle chuckled as she led us to the tent belonging to her mother. Helen marveled over the fact that she was able to see my Spanish friend fully and was informed it was because we'd crossed into the fourth dimension where magical beings dwelled alongside earthbound spirits and shadow people. It was a place of adventure, wonders, and danger.

I think what I found most fascinating was the fact that- other than my feeling like I weighed much less- everything looked and felt pretty much the same as on the third dimension. The air had a breeze that hinted of the humidity come inland from the ocean. The trees smelled of fresh earthy pine and rich, ruddy hardwoods. Sunlight kissed the blossoms of wildflowers that scattered the ground. Had I not known better, I would have believed I hadn't traveled dimensions at all.

We reached Rosalie's tent and Isabelle bid us wait outside while she announced our arrival. I heard a baby cry and immediately wondered if that was the younger Isabelle until I remembered that she was not yet born.

When Isabelle popped her head out of the tent to beckon us inside, Helen squeezed my hand so tight I thought she might break a bone while we walked hand in hand into the presence of the most beautiful woman I'd ever laid eyes on. I could clearly see where Isabelle got her looks. It wasn't just Rosalie's features that made her beautiful; it was the energy that radiated from her. She had what I could only call a halo around her entire body. The pull to be in her company and do her bidding was so strong I could easily understand why practically an entire village left their native land to follow her.

As if a slap in the face, it registered with me that I felt the same with Rufus that fateful night. Now, without a shadow of a doubt, I knew there was witchcraft involved with our last encounter. That devious vampire was clearly working with a witch.

Surrounded by members of her court, Rosalie bid us be seated and graciously offered us tea and sandwiches. I was a little hesitant to discuss my situation in front of so many people, but Isabelle assured me it would be fine. I caught Rosalie eyeing Isabelle with a mixture of love and curiosity while I purged my story as quickly as I could. Fortunately, Rosalie already knew quite a bit of it, thanks to Isabelle. I only needed to fill in a few gaps.

Rosalie asked for our empty tea cups so that she could read the leaves. Within minutes she was naming Lady Margaret Jane Chapman, high priestess and scoundrel as the witch attached to the evil vampire, Lord Rufus Elizabeth. I was amazed at how the names came pouring forth, since I hadn't mentioned them and I didn't think Isabelle had either. If anything, this woman was an excellent psychic! That wasn't always the case. Just because someone practiced magic, it didn't mean they had the sight. I wondered if she was as good a magician as she was a seer.

It didn't take me long to find out.

She explained that she'd recently conceived Isabelle as she smiled and beckoned the ghost of her daughter to stand beside her. She took Isabelle's hand and placed it on her abdomen while she whispered something in Spanish to her. Isabelle bent down, placed her ear on her mother's abdomen and then kissed it before rising. Her eyes sparkled with emotional moisture, but I saw no tears flowing. Because she was in a delicate condition, it would be necessary for her to work through me just like Lady Margaret worked through Rufus. Because I was her doppelganger, my genetics would be comparable to Margaret's, which would give me an advantage and which was why I was chosen instead of Lady Helen.

I understood her reasoning, but I won't say I was happy about it. The energy I felt coming from Rufus and the control he had over me was strong. Was I going to be strong enough channel for Rosalie to match it? After all, Rufus was in essence a supernatural being. At best, I was a human who dabbled in magic and- compared to the company I've been in- poorly at that. I would have much preferred to have the Queen of Magic and the wicked High Priestess have a show down and get it over with.

CHAPTER TWENTY-NINE

I was excused to explore the camp while Rosalie sat with Helen and picked her brain of everything she knew about Margaret. It felt good to wander freely without fear of being abducted by crazy Vivian or now... Lord Rufus. I considered petitioning to be able to stay at the camp permanently once the danger for Duncan was removed. Since Duncan and I were no more and I was stuck in the past, it seemed like a great place to live out my days. I'd be able to interact with Isabelle as if she was flesh and not a semi-transparent apparition and I could continue my studies. It seemed like a plan.

I stopped at the center market and chatted with the merchants selling their wares. Many of them came to the camp from nearby farms. Some were alive and traveled back and forth through dimensions, while others were in spirit and this was their home. I lost count of how many times I was warned not to leave the parameter of the encampment where Rosalie's protection was no more. Since I'd had my fill of dealing with the dark at heart, it was easy to comply.

I was strolling about -with no place in particular in mind to go to and no one in particular in mind to visit- when I saw her standing in the thickets along the parameter of the encampment. I could see the life force that was once housed within her clinging to her body like a blanket of light that was slowly dimming to a glow that would eventually either be no more or turn to black, depending on the nature of the person. I called it the glow of the newly dead.

All warnings of staying within the encampment's protective parameter flew to the recesses of my mind as I made my way toward the wicked Lady Vivian.

"You died?" I asked.

She had a confused look on her face.

"What manner of place is this? Do I stand in your home of the future?" she asked.

"'You are dead, m' lady," I said compassionately.

"Jest not," she scoffed. "Tell me true."

"I speak truth," I said as convincingly as I could, "You are dead. Do you know why?"

She scowled at me for a moment and then shook her head.

Do you remember your last moments?" I persisted.

"No," she said sadly.

I spent more time speaking with Vivian until I managed to get her to remember her last moments of life. Obsessed with her hatred for Margaret, she'd been stalking her for several days while she developed a plan to finish her off. Unlike me, Margaret proves far more difficult to get close to for both Vivian and her goons. This didn't surprise me. The wicked are always on the alert where the innocent often get taken unawares.

Vivian followed Margaret to an out of the way cave that was declared off limits to all magical beings of light centuries ago because of its ties to the dark side. Only the darkest of witches ventured there. Even Vivian didn't fall into that category.

She was hiding in the hills when she saw a small patrol of vampire soldiers bringing in a captive. They had his wrists and ankles bound with silver chains and were dragging him on the ground behind a horse as if he was nothing more than a log being dragged off the mountain for firewood. There was a significant trail of blood being left by the near vampire corpse. Vivian knew only the basics about vampirism, but she knew that if the vampire wasn't able to feed soon, he'd disappear into nothingness for sure.

Inching in for a closer look, she realized the vampire captive was Lord Duncan Colliers.

It took her a few moments to process the fact that Duncan was a vampire. She assumed he'd traveled time like he'd warned his family may happen. When she'd been given the credit she didn't deserve for performing the spell to send him into the future, she'd reveled in the notoriety. The thought of torturing Margaret with the concept that she was responsible for her love's disappearance gave her such pleasure, she allowed the rumor to circulate. In truth, she had no idea who'd performed the spell and she certainly didn't realize Duncan was vampire. When did that happen?

I filled her in on the story I'd been told by my former lover. Unlike the pleasure it gave her to have Margaret believe she'd done such a deed as to teleport Duncan into the future, it saddened her to hear Duncan blamed her for his fate for so long. She was guilty only of loving him and hating Margaret; nothing more.

I asked her to reach deep in her being and search for her true emotions. Did she truly love Duncan or was it more the fact that he was the only male who didn't faun over her and drop everyone and everything because she paid him attention. It was time for her to be brutally honest with herself.

She closed her eyes and whispered it was the latter. In truth, she hardly knew Duncan Collier and had barely spoken to him. It was her wounded pride and her long time rivalry with Lady Margaret that spurred her into this spiraling decline from good to evil. She hated the way Margaret managed to camouflage her evil side from the world. More than having Duncan for herself, she wanted to take him from Margaret.

She proceeded to tell me how she snuck into the cave after them to see what they were about. She hid behind a rock and observed Duncan being dragged unceremoniously into a circle of vampires. She wanted to run to help him, but knew she'd be useless, so she watched as long as she could. A tall, handsome vampire she recognized as Lord Rufus Elizabeth entered the circle with Lady Margaret at his side. Since she was unaware that Lord Rufus had become vampire as well, she once again had to absorb the reality of it all. The only thing that didn't shock her was seeing that vile sham of a high priest-ess enter. Vivian knew all along Margaret was evil.

She waited long enough to see Duncan being shoved into a cage that was raised several feet off the ground while the circle of vampires taunted him with snide comments and then scurried out of the cave. She fully intended to get help for Duncan and open people's eyes to Lady Margaret's true self. She was barreling down the path that led to the cave when something struck her on the back of the head and the world went black. When she awoke, she was where I'd found her.

I asked her to turn around so I could see the back of her head and I instantly regretted it. Her skull was bashed in and, since she was so freshly dead, her consciousness still clung to the physical. This meant she still held the shape of her body as it died; bloodied, crushed skull and all.

"A vampire must have hurled a boulder and crushed your skull," I said while doing my best to hold down the bile that was creeping up my throat.

"Truly?" she whined as she felt the back of her head. Gasping at the blood on her fingertips, she turned so I could no longer see her wound and wailed about being ugly forever before darting off into the woods.

I thought briefly about following her, since she never did tell me where the cave was located, but I didn't dare cross the parameter. The threat of being captured by Vivian may have been over but there was other darkness far more sinis-ter to consider beyond the barrier of protection. I headed for Rosalie's tent instead. Duncan's life was in danger and we needed to act immediately.

I breathlessly told my story to Rosalie, Isabelle, and Helen. All were in agreement that time was of the essence. When I lamented about not getting the whereabouts of the cave from Vivian before she'd scurried off into no man's land and cursed myself for not following her, Helen assured me I'd done the right thing. She was fully aware of the location of the cave. All witches knew of it and knew to avoid it. It made sense that Lady Margaret would work her evilness from a location where she was practically guaranteed to go undiscovered.

Helen voiced her disappointment in the discovery of her coven's high priestess' true nature. She regretted being the one to discover it and therefore the one who would have to inform the group. She was also concerned because there were those within the group who already felt she longed to usurp Lady Margaret's role and would more than likely accuse her of falsehood so that she could do just that.

We agreed to work on a plan to help Lady Helen with that dreaded task as soon as Duncan was rescued. Rosalie called her guards to order and selected ten of her finest men to fetch him to her. I looked on in wonderment as they leapt into the air, turned into dragons, and disappeared into the afternoon sky.

By the position of the sun, it was clear we only had a few more hours of daylight left. Vampires were fully functional in the light of day, but without their supernatural powers. This left them far more vulnerable to attack, which was why they either hid the fact they were vampire and mingled with society or remained securely hidden during the light of day. Rosalie was betting these vampires were keeping themselves tucked away not far from the cave where Vivian spotted them with only a skeleton crew to guard Duncan. Sending her dragon guards was an extra precaution, since dragon's fire was the fast way to eliminate a foe; be it mortal or supernatural. She wanted Duncan brought to her with the least amount of delay.

She asked me his eating habits and I quickly explained his diet. After confirming that Duncan's diet may have sufficed in the twenty-first century where vampires kept a lower profile and took advantage of modern technology alongside the rest of the world, in the more primitive eighteenth century it wouldn't do. The vampires of old were far more rugged in constitution and made it a point to remain so by drinking only human blood and drinking a lot of it. Although, only the most sadistic drained their donor dry at a feeding. Because of the amount of blood needed to maintain them, they were required to feed on about ten quarts of blood per week. That's equal to the amount of blood found in two average size adult human bodies. Animal blood didn't have the same properties, so in order to maintain himself at optimum vampire strength, Duncan would have had to drink twice that much.

I knew he wasn't.

Despair raked through me. Duncan didn't stand a chance. Had he realized this when he set out to find Rufus? I wondered. He'd admitted he'd been a loner for most of his vampire existence. Although his love for me spurred him so that he did quite a job on the vampires who'd attacked me in the alley. I mentioned this to Rosalie and she explained that Duncan wasn't a wimp and she was certain he was a fine specimen for a vampire. He just wasn't drinking sufficient animal blood to compensate for the lack of human blood and he didn't have the power of a witch behind him.

I paced the campgrounds like a caged animal while I waited for the dragon guards to return with the vampire that held my heart.

CHAPTER THIRTY

Duncan resembled a waxed doll when they laid him on the cot in the back of Rosalie's enormous tent. I searched for signs of life. His chest showed signs of shallow breaths being taken. Shallow breaths meant he still had life. I'd take that for now.

He needed to feed immediately and it had to be human blood. Knowing how he felt about drinking the blood of humans, I asked if there was another way to save him. There wasn't.

This was my fault. If I hadn't come back into the past, Duncan would be safe in the future, as would Isabelle. My foolish, thoughtless actions caused the death of a dear friend, and possibly the death of the one true love of my life. It didn't matter that he was no longer in love with me. Through him, I'd experienced a love I never thought possible and I would always remember that.

I took a deep breath and looked around. Rosalie had put the word out for volunteers to feed Duncan. A few had arrived, but knowing him the way I did, I doubted he'd be pleased to discover their blood in him. They looked less than desirable. It was interesting to see that even in this realm there were still vagabonds about.

"We must do something soon," Isabelle moaned, "or my friend will be no more. Vampires do not join us in this dimension when they die. They are soul-less. Soul-less creatures simply cease to be."

I spotted a small blade next to an apple on the teacart Rosalie had served us from when we first arrived. Without a moment's hesitation, I grabbed it, slit my wrist and shoved it up against Duncan's pale, wax-like lips. Within seconds he was sucking with a fury I'd never imagined possible.

Isabelle gasped when she saw what I'd done, as did Helen.

"Heavens above," Helen roared, "what are you doing? Do you not know the risk you take?" Helen howled.

"He will not be able to stop," Isabelle said worriedly. "You are still weak from your loss of blood. That was a foolish move."

"I owe him this much," I puffed as I struggled for breath. I could feel the life draining from me as it poured into Duncan. "I owe him so much more than this."

The world began to spin as Duncan reached up and with a vice grip secured my arm against his mouth so there was no chance of my pulling it away. The last thing I remember before the world went black was telling him I how much I loved him and how sorry I was that I'd hurt him.

It was morning when I was roused by the smell of bacon and biscuits being passed beneath my nose. My eyes worked hard to open. The world was blurry and I struggled to focus. Things finally got clear enough for me to see that it was Duncan who was holding the plate so tantalizingly close.

He looked a very healthy Duncan, at that.

I smiled with satisfaction as I murmured, "You're alive."

"As are you," he replied. "Such a foolish thing to risk your life to save mine."

"Not so foolish," I replied. "When you love someone, you do what you can for them."

"You love me?" he asked softly.

I looked into his sea foam eyes, searching for... I don't know what.

"With all my heart," I said softly.

"Good," he huffed and then stood and walked away.

The way that vampire kept walking away from me was damned frustrating.

"Where are you going?" I bellowed.

He picked up the jacket he'd been wearing earlier and pulled a small box from the inner pocket.

"To get this," he said.

My mouth fell open as he fell to his knees by the cot and presented me with the most gorgeous ruby and diamond ring I'd ever seen, while asking me to be his wife. Wow... I hadn't seen that coming at all.

Tears of happiness and confusion rolled down my cheeks while I held my hand out for him to slip the ring on my finger. Of course I'd marry him. Of course I'd be his wife... Of course! Of course! Of course!

We spent the day together walking the encampment and enjoying the many sights and smells of the market place. I'd marveled at how good I felt, but I didn't dare ask why. Admitting that I knew I should be weak as a kitten because I'd forfeited my blood to Duncan made me fearful of changing the wonderful mood of our day. Later that night, when we were in the privacy of our assigned tent and all was quiet and Duncan and I had finished making love for the third time, I got the courage to broach the subject.

"I gave you my blood," he replied matter-of-factly.

I gasped in surprise as I said, "So, I'm vampire now? Is that why you asked me to marry you?"

His chuckle was low and soft as he said, "I asked you to marry me because I love you and it is time to make it clear that you are not on the market."

I knew what he was referring to, but I didn't want to break the mood by discussing it, so I stayed on the topic of his blood being in my body.

"What will your blood do to me?" I asked.

"It will make you feel good for a few weeks," he said with curious hesitation.

"There's something more," I persisted, "please tell me all."

"You have to understand that we had no choice. I was so close to expiration that by the time I'd revived enough to realize I was drinking from you I'd extracted a dangerous amount of blood from your body. A few drops more and your heart would have stopped pumping," he said as he climbed out of bed and paced the floor, mindless of his nakedness. "Rosalie and Isabelle managed to get through to me in time to stop me from killing you." The regret in his eyes when he looked at me was almost overwhelming. "The only way to save you was to give you my blood."

"How much did you give me?" I asked hesitantly.

I didn't know what he was trying to say, but whatever it was, it didn't seem like it was something I'd be happy about.

"Quite a bit," he replied.

"How does that work? I mean... I give you my blood and you give it right back? Wouldn't that make both of us blood deficient?" I wondered aloud.

"That would be a logical conclusion. Fortunately, when I drink blood, I reproduce it almost immediately. By the time they stopped me from draining you, I'd replenished my body nicely," he explained.

"Then, why would you hesitate on telling me whatever you are hesitating about telling me?" I asked firmly.

He took a deep breath and blurted out, "It will take almost a month for my blood to completely leave your body. If you die before it's gone, you'll become a vampire."

I stared at him for some time before calmly asking, "Is that it?"

Shocked, he nodded his head, but said nothing.

I don't know what I expected to hear, but hearing that I could become a vampire if I died wasn't the worst thing I could have heard. After all, I was in love with a vampire. It made sense for me to be a vampire right alongside him; especially since we planned on marrying. I was sure there were worse things he could have said.

We completed the night in each other's arms, alternating between making love and talking about our future together. Vampires had an amazing appetite for sex and it could often times be quite rigorous, but Duncan was considerate of my recent health experience and was incredibly considerate. I couldn't help but compare his treatment of me with the treatment I'd received from Rufus. There was no comparison. In fact, the comparison plagued me in the back of my mind until the following day when the subject was finally addressed.

CHAPTER THIRTY-ONE

I was blissfully displaying my gorgeous engagement ring to anyone with a pair of eyes willing to admire it when Isabelle finally raised the question of what to do about both Lady Margaret and Lord Rufus.

According to vampire law, Lord Rufus was first to impregnate me and therefore was my official husband. Since it was rare for a vampire to find a mortal he or she wanted to mate with, this was a law that was supported and held sacred by every vampire on the planet. Every vampire except Duncan, that is. Duncan stayed away from other vampires as much as possible while integrating with mortals on a daily basis in an attempt to lessen his vampirism. Even so, just because he seldom associated with them, it was still necessary to abide by the laws put forth for vampires; which was why he'd agonized so heavily over what to do about me. My only saving grace was the fact that I'd aborted the child before Rufus learned of his actual success. He only had his assumption to go by.

Duncan was raised to be a man of honor and admitted he'd battled long and hard within himself during my recovery on what to do. He'd actually learned the outline of my story from Lady Helen before he came to visit me. I'd really only filled in the gaps. He was angry about it to begin with, but the information in those gaps sent him into a rage. Although he was raised to honor and respect laws as they have been put forth, this was one time when he would have to go rogue. There was no way he was going to allow a woman abuser possession of the one person who brought him back to life. It took that moment of wresting with right and wrong for Duncan to realize he'd do anything to keep me by his side; including breaking one of the most sacred vampire laws in existence. I'd been tricked by Lord Rufus by the use of magic. In Duncan's opinion, this fact voided out his need to observe their law. He'd battle every vampire on the planet, rather than let me go.

I hoped it wouldn't come to that.

Duncan took the time necessary to update us on who and what we were dealing with. Thinking she was serving Duncan his ultimate demise of a slow and painful death, the prim and proper Lady Margaret had opened up and confided her deepest, darkest secrets to him and shocked him from his head to his toes. The dear ward of his father and his childhood companion turned sweetheart and fiancé had been the one to bind his powers and arrange to have him attacked by a vampire just before their wedding. Duncan flippantly informed her that, rather than going to all that trouble, she need only to say she didn't want to get married. She'd growled at his arrogance and reveled in elaborating about how she hadn't expected him to survive the vampire attack and become vampire. She gloated on how she'd simply passed the time away abroad while keeping his father and everyone else under the impression she was time-traveling to find him after she'd planted the rumor that the wicked Vivian cast a spell to send him there.

Surprisingly, Lady Margaret didn't believe anyone could travel through time until I showed up and proved her wrong. Of course, she couldn't confront me on it without divulging her trickery.

Being a ward of the Earl of Winter Spring and bride to be of his heir had given Lady Margaret a considerable amount of perks. The earl had already provided an enormous settlement as a bridal gift to his ward, which he followed through with allowing the completion of its legalization even upon the disappearance of his son. Being single had given her freedom that she knew would be lost as soon as the vows were said. Her plan was to remain the grieving ward and almost daughter-in-law. She was aware that the earl also provided for her handsomely in his will. The dowry and bequeathing of his estate, along with her inheritance from her own parents, would have left her independent and happy for the remainder of her days. When I showed up on the scene, followed by Duncan, who was clearly enamored with me, her plans were sent askew.

She thought she wouldn't have to do a thing on her own, since that foolish Vivian was doing a good job of trying to get rid of me. Once I was out of the picture, she'd see that Duncan fell in love with her again or at least agreed to marry her and then she'd dispose of him the right way, but somehow I kept escaping.

Recruiting the aid of Lord Rufus was her ingenious idea. Since he was completely and totally enamored with her and I was the image of her, it didn't take much persuasion to get him to go along with the scheme. The fact that he found me delightfully irresistible and far more agreeable than Margaret was an added bonus. Margaret's plan was for Rufus to court me and get Duncan jealous enough to fight him; at which time, she'd use magic to make sure Rufus destroyed Duncan. For that, she would allow him the favor of being with her for a night or two. She hadn't expected Rufus would fall head over heels in love with me after only one meeting and take matters into his own hands. Impregnating me to seal his claim on me under vampire law was his ingenious idea, not Margaret's.

Duncan played right into their hands when he called Rufus out. The duel was fixed from the start. He might as well have just stood there with his arms spread wide and said, "Do with me as you will." Rufus was so protected by witchery that Duncan never stood a chance.

I was so overwhelmed with what I was learning I barely heard Duncan finish his story by relaying the heroic rescue of Senora Rosalie's dragon guards when they swept like lightning speed into the cave and scooped him up, cage and all, before anyone knew what happened. They carried him far away to safely, put the cage down, and released him before continuing on with him on one of their backs. The cage contained Margaret's magic and could easily be traced by her. It wouldn't do to bring such a homing device into Rosalie's parameter of protection.

He praised them highly for their forethought.

The fact that Margaret was the instigator of my being at the mercy of Rufus sent me into a rage equal to any Duncan could muster. I demanded to be given the wherewithal to take her down and it took the better part of an hour for them to convince me to calm down. I don't recall ever being that angry. I wondered, in the back of my mind, if my anger might have been influenced by the fact that a significant amount of Duncan's blood was in me, but I said nothing. I only hoped that if his blood could intensify my mood to that degree it would also intensify other aspects; such as strength and comprehension.

When I finally calmed down enough to be reasonable, we sat together for the remainder of the day discussing what we were up against and the best strategy of attack. There were two separate dynamics to be dealt with. First we had Margaret and her powerful witchcraft to contend with and then we had Rufus and his vampires who felt Rufus had the right to declare I was his eternal wife. Just one of these issues would have been all consuming, but two… well, I don't even have a word to describe it.

It was decided that we we'd tackle getting Margaret out of the way first. Lady Helen was adamant that Margaret should stand before the coven for her crimes. In truth, I would have preferred to just get rid of her completely, but I understood why she wanted it that way.

We discussed our strategy to entrap and capture Margaret. This is where it got tricky. Because we still had to deal with the vampires and needed an 'in' with them, I was to pose as Margaret and get close to Lord Rufus. Rosalie would attach her magic to me and assist me in destroying Rufus and any other vampires necessary. Since Lady Margaret was a powerful witch in her own right, Rosalie's magic moving through me wouldn't be enough to stop her if we faced off. Rosalie herself would have to be there in person for Margaret to be defeated and that was something she wasn't willing to do. I didn't argue the point. I knew the unborn child she was protecting in her womb was my very own Isabelle.

It was a tricky and dangerous assignment that I was actually eager to do. Once again, I attributed it to the vampire blood flowing through me.

I have no idea how Rosalie obtained much of the information she managed to come up with, but she somehow discovered the vampires were holding an emergency meeting to determine how Duncan managed to escape and devise a plan to re-capture him. This meant that Margaret and Rufus would be in attendance.

It was time to strike.

CHAPTER THIRTY-TWO

I did my best to hide my nervousness as I walked into the mouth of the cave that felt more like the lion's den. Elizabeth saw to it that I was dressed from head to toe in Margaret's wardrobe. Her feet were slightly smaller than mine and the shoes pinched, but Rosalie was adamant that every article of clothing on my body have the vibration of the high priestess only. Vampires could smell and hear so much better than people. They had a sense of simply knowing that astounded the witches. Even with the precautions we were taking, there was still a good possibility one of them might discover the ruse for what it was.

Capturing Lady Margaret was a relatively simple task. Duncan's father simply sent her a request to meet in the family's private library. Not realizing he was aware of her true nature, she walked right into the trap. Elizabeth confided that she worried what might happen, should Lady Margaret be exonerated by the coven, but Lady Helen assured her there was no chance of that happening.

No one hoped she was right more than me. I could only imagine the fury unleashed, should Lady Margaret discover what I was up to. Isabelle and Rosalie may have faith in my strength as a magician, but I wasn't so sure and I sure didn't want to test it with her. Besides, they agreed that, although I had the connection and power, I still lacked the wisdom and skill that came with practice. I was no match for Margaret and I knew it.

I couldn't help wonder what was going on at the coven as I entered the cave. They were scheduled to have their meeting at the same time the vampires were having theirs.

My thoughts left the coven and returned to the task at

hand as I passed through the first chamber of the cave and into a long dimly lit tunnel. Another trait of vampirism is their remarkable ability to see in low light. While I was stumbling to and fro as I felt my way forward, vampires were meandering ahead of me as if in broad daylight. I was grateful for Duncan's blood, as it enhanced my sight somewhat. I could only imagine what it would have been like to maneuver without it.

I stopped at the edge of an enormous crystal cavern deep within the hillside. The light from the torches placed sporadically around its parameter danced off the crystals creating a starlit night effect. It took my breath away.

With an effort, I pulled my thoughts away from the beauty of the scene to what was happening before of me. The vampire meeting was already in session. I placed my hand over the onyx stone Rosalie attached to my throat with a ribbon and felt the warmth of its magic. I could feel her presence. It gave me a sense of security I hadn't felt until then. This just might work.

Surprisingly, not one vampire paid me much mind as I worked my way through the thick crowd. I'd be lying if I said I wasn't taken aback by the sheer number come together to devise a plan to recapture my poor Duncan. It seemed incredibly unfair; especially when I still wasn't clear as to the reason they wanted him dead. Surely I wasn't a big enough reason. Was a vampire's claim on his bride that big a deal?

With Duncan's blood inside me, it was easy for me to tell who in the crowd was vampire and who was mortal. The mortals hovered together. I sensed it wasn't in my best interest to stand near them, so I headed off to the far end of the cavern. For the moment, I was only to observe. Rosalie would signal me when it was time for me to take action by sending energy through the hematite I clutched a little too tightly.

I found it amazing and fascinating that she would be able to scry from a distance. I'd heard of the military using people who did what they called remote viewing -which was what Rosalie was doing- but I didn't really put much thought or credence into it. Of course it made sense in the scope of things, but it didn't make it less wondrous.

I placed myself in a small alcove that allowed me a panoramic view of the meeting and phenomenal acoustics for what was being said in the depths of the crowd where Rufus proceeded over the conversation. I could hear him as clearly as if I was standing next to him.

I listened while he instructed two male vampires on the order of events. It was clear he was running the show. After a few moments he held his hand up and the crowd grew so silent I was fearful they'd be able to hear the faint buzzing noise my hematite was making.

One of the humans moaned. I looked at them more closely. It was then that I realized they were hobbled and dazed. There were more than I realized too. I counted about two dozen; eight very heavy women and sixteen large and burley men. The continual moaning of a woman deep within the human huddle sounded like a mixture of misery and ecstasy. It reminded me of the moaning on a stag film I saw at a bachelor party I'd foolishly attended. I found it remarkable how the vocalization of pain and pleasure were so closely related.

What was even more remarkable was the sensation that spread through my body as the moaning continued. My ears focused on it, as if nothing else mattered. My mouth salivated and my body tingled and itched deep under my skin. I rubbed my arms to try to satiate the itch, but it was strong.

Rosalie sent me a telepathic message that the itch and tingling was the vampire blood taking over my body. She ordered me to fight it. I was actually salivating over the prospect of biting into that orgasmic female's flesh and sucking on her like I'd suck soda through a straw. It took every ounce of strength I possessed to restrain myself. It was difficult to concentrate on what I was there to do. I clutched the stone around my neck even tighter as I willed my body to behave. I needed my wits about me in order to accomplish my mission, which was to somehow separate Rufus from the hoard of vampires and kill him. Only then would Duncan and I be free to be together with no risk of repercussions.

Duncan had forcefully insisted he be the one to kill Rufus, but Rosalie, Isabelle and I finally convinced him that he'd only be making matters worse for us. A mortal killing a vampire was far easier to explain than a vampire killing another vampire; especially when the two vampires were in conflict over possession of a mortal.

I realized I'd let my mind wander when the smell of blood sent my body into a frenzy. I gripped the wall to help stabilize myself while I fought the urge to join the others in their feeding frenzy. I could only imagine how strong the desire to feed was for a true vampire if I was fighting the impact of a little vampire blood in my veins. Well, actually it was a lot of vampire blood, but still, I wasn't a vampire so it had to be easier on me than it was on them. It was then that I realized how much self-control it took for a vampire to only drink a certain amount and then stop so as not to kill the donor. The way I felt, I was certain, given the opportunity to have at it with the blood fest, I'd go all the way and not stop until there was nothing left. It must have taken Duncan years of battling for self-control to refrain from drinking human blood and dine on that of mammals instead. My admiration for him increased tenfold.

I spotted Rufus in the hoard of vampires who were feasting on the wailing humans below. He wasn't joining them. Instead, he was staring directly at me. My heart caught in my throat. Did he know it was me? Should I run? Should I stay and continue with my mission? What were my orders again?

Tiny beads of moisture coated my brown and the back of my neck.

My brain felt fuzzy and disoriented.

My throat was constricted and dry.

I longed for just one taste of fresh, warm blood.

I shuddered as he bowed his head in acknowledgement of me and did my best to pull myself together and act casual as I nodded my response. I knew my mission was to separate him from the crowd, but I just wasn't sure I was up to it at that point and time. Perhaps after they'd finished feeding and the scent of blood no longer filled the air? I hoped so.

My knuckles were white while I continued to grip the stone wall and fought for control of my body while I watched Rufus make his way to me. He couldn't see me like this. Something deep inside me warned me that, not only did Margaret not have vampire blood in her veins, she was very familiar to feedings of this nature and wouldn't have reacted in the way I had.

I needed to think of something to take my mind off the blood. Since I'd been warned to keep my mind free of thoughts of Duncan in case a telepathic vampire attended the meeting, I focused on the only thing I believed Margaret would have thought about as I watched Rufus approach; his powerful, masculine physique. I forced the repulsion into the back of my mind as I made note of the thick muscular thighs that that climbed toward me. I watched his shoulders and upper arms strain against the fabric of a waist coat that was unable to disguise their solid strength. As he reached the platform below me and stood erect to adjust his clothing and smooth his queue, I had to admit he was a handsome creature, if not an evil one.

"Hello, my love," he cooed as he approached where I stood, "'Tis unusual to see you standing in the background as such. What manner of behavior is this?"

Phew! His initial greeting had me worried. I was incredibly relieved that I'd allowed him to continue to speak before responding.

"Aye, 'tis an off day for me, I should be attending my coven this very moment. 'Twas a difficult decision to come," I replied with the excuse we'd agreed upon while planning the mission. "I wished to know the plans before I retire for my ceremony."

"Ah, I see," he smiled as he stroked my cheek lightly with

his forefinger.

I struggled to keep from pulling away with repulsion. It figured that he and Margaret would be more than co-conspirators. I hoped I wouldn't be expected to physically interact with him overmuch. I wasn't sure I'd be able to continue with the ruse if that was the case. My last encounter with him was still fresh in my mind.

"How soon until you convene to decide your plan of action?" I asked, hoping my nervousness wasn't obvious.

"We have made that decision," he replied smugly.

"Truly?" I was surprised and I didn't mind showing it.

They'd only just arrived. I'd only just arrived. When did anyone have the opportunity to meet and determine a plan on how to recapture Duncan?

"Aye. 'Twas decided early this morning. This gathering was organized to provide distraction," he whispered as he moved closer, "but then, the true Lady Margaret knew this already since she was in attendance."

I gasped at the realization that my disguise had failed.

"My love, 'tis marvelous to have you returned to me. I thought 'twould be much more difficult a task," he cooed in my ear. I tried to inch away from him, but his arm slipped around my waist and held me close. He placed his broad palm on my abdomen, "I expected to see you large with child by now."

"You expected wrong," I hissed.

He looked at me thoughtfully, "No matter," he sighed, "that can be easily rectified."

"The hell it can!" I roared.

To my dismay and horror, the vampires had finished feeding. Without the moans and wails of the victims, now dead in the center of the chamber, my loud outburst caught most of the attendee's attention. I wanted to shrink away into oblivion.

My hand flew to the hematite as it vibrated at a rate that surprised even me. Rosalie was doing her best to surround me with a shell of protection.

Rufus threw his head back in laughter. He snapped his fingers in the air and the crowd parted to allow at least a dozen vampire witches dressed in black robes and pointed hats to move forward. Had I not realized the century I was in, I would have thought I was at a Halloween convention.

I could feel the magic permeating from their hands as they countered the magic my lone sorceress was diligently working. Rosalie may have been one of the most powerful witches out there, but even she was hard pressed to battle from afar a dozen gifted witches who stood before me.

Within minutes the stone grew still.

I sucked in air while my mind raced on what to do. Clearly it was time for "plan B". The problem was that we never created a "plan B". If we had, I was too terrified to remember it. I searched the room for a possible means of escape, but could see none.

"My fellow nightlings," Rufus bellowed for all the vampires to hear, "I have glad news. Behold, my chosen bride has come to me of her own accord!"

I closed my eyes as tight as I could to push back the tears that threatened to erupt as Rufus held my hand high in the air in a gesture of triumph. The crowd roared their approval. It was then that I realized that the vampire beside me was more than just a member of a vampire lynch mob hot to find Duncan. He was their leader. When I heard him addressed to as "my king" I knew I was right.

CHAPTER THIRTY-THREE

I was angry.

I was angry at Duncan because he hadn't mated with me vampire style to assure I'd be considered his.

I was angry at Rufus because he had mated with me so many times since he'd brought me from the cave to his estate that I'd lost count.

I was angry with Elizabeth because she wandered in and out of the room to tend to my needs, yet didn't believe she could help me escape.

I was angry with Rosalie for not being strong enough to battle and win against a dozen vampire witches by remote.

I was angry with Isabelle for dying.

I was angry with myself for stupidly being the catalyst for all of this by going back in time.

In short, I was just angry.

On top of that, my entire body ached.

I was never as grateful to have Duncan's vampire blood in me as I was when Rufus bedded me with such fury that I wondered if I'd survive. I'm sure, my body having only recently aborted his previously implanted seed, I would not have survived the trauma of his aggressive and abusive sexual acts had I not had vampire blood to help me heal almost as fast as the wounds were inflicted.

My moment of pleasure was when he sunk his fangs into my femoral artery and spat as if he'd been poisoned. Apparently vampires don't drink vampire blood.

I smiled for hours after he stormed from the room and ordered Elizabeth to help me clean up.

Elizabeth ordered a bath to be brought to my room and helped me into it. Even with Duncan's blood to speed up the healing process, my body was a mess. I was bruised both inside and out. If Rufus had impregnated me -and I was fairly sure he had- it would be a wonder if my body retained it after the abuse he'd put it through. Blood oozed from where he'd dug his nails into my flesh while releasing his seed deep into my womb. He'd made it clear that the only reason he hadn't killed me was because I had the blood of another vampire in my veins. Since I wasn't yet pregnant, he couldn't claim me as his wife. If I died, the vampire whose blood I carried would be my protector and we could mate if we chose.

I was fairly certain I was going to end up vampire. I just prayed it was while I still had Duncan's blood in my veins. I couldn't remember how long he said it would remain in me. It was apparently still strong enough for Rufus to taste.

As I lay in the bath, I considered drowning myself in the water, but with Elizabeth so close at hand I doubted I'd succeed. She seemed determined to assist her vile brother in keeping me under lock and key.

"I feel betrayed," I mumbled as I lay back in the copper tub and closed my eyes.

"Forgive me. 'Tis a difficult thing I do, but I know not what to do. He is my brother and," she leaned forward and whispered, "he is vampire."

I opened one eye and looked at her before spitting out, "Really? I hadn't noticed."

Ignoring my sarcasm, she continued, "I would help you, but I know not how. Perchance Lord Duncan shall rescue you?"

"Does he know where I am?" I asked hopefully.

"I think not," she replied wistfully.

"Do you think you could send him word?" I said slowly as I tried to keep my temper in check.

"I dare not. 'Tis a fool's errand. There are eyes and ears everywhere," she whispered.

I sat up so quickly water splashed onto Elizabeth. She jumped back in surprise while I winced from the pain in my groin.

"Please. I beg you. There must be a way to get word to him," I whispered.

I must have sounded as desperate as I felt because Elizabeth reacted with a vengeance that surprised me.

"Where is the Lady Jane come to us?" she said with gusto. "Where is the woman who successfully passed for Lady Margaret? This lady possesses magic. This lady has the ability to communicate without words. I long for this lady once more."

Her words hit me like a slap across the face. She was right, of course. I did know magic. I could communicate telepathically. I may not have been schooled in the spells used in those times, but I was schooled in spells. Surely I could find a way to get in touch with Duncan or Rosalie or maybe Isabelle. Whoever it was, surely I could manage one of them.

I grabbed Elizabeth's hand and kissed it gratefully. I couldn't even be angry with her for being afraid to try to do something to help me out of this. Vampires were highly alert, sensitive, tricky, and vindictive when crossed. I was also afraid, but I knew that if I didn't at least try, I'd be trapped into an eternity with the wrong vampire. If I had to become a vampire, then let it be Duncan who changed me. At least I loved him.

Elizabeth helped me out of the tub and settled me into an oversized chair by the fireplace to dry my hair. As she brushed it free of tangles we whispered about possible methods of getting a message past the vampires. It was decided that, even though I was able to communicate telepathically, there were also quite a few vampires in residence who could do the same. Therefore, telepathy wasn't an option.

We decided that my best bet was to summon Isabelle. I was both surprised and grateful when Elizabeth offered to help. Although terrified, she was also looking for a way to free herself from the bonds her brother had imposed on her. She was afraid of his wrath should she let me kill myself and become a vampire made by Duncan, but, if I escaped, she was sure I'd find a way to help free her as well. Perhaps Isabelle or Rosalie would be able to help her too. I was sure they would.

We felt certain that if I used a few light magic tricks to shield the room long enough to perform the summoning ceremony, we wouldn't be caught. Timing would be vital if I was going to pull this off. We had to make sure we had enough time to ourselves without Rufus or one of his cronies barging in to check on me, as they seemed so fond of doing.

We couldn't do anything until the following day. It would be dark soon and Rufus would be returning to once again claim me as his. He knew, as well as I did, that he'd impregnated me. With the number of times he'd driven his seed deep into my womb, it was practically impossible for him not to. His taking me now was strictly for pleasure. His pleasure, not mine.

I had no choice but to endure it. Perhaps if I was a little more cooperative he'd lessen the amount of wounds left on my body. I wasn't healing as quickly as I had been when first captured. I'm sure all the bloodletting that occurred from the wounds he inflicted was to assist in relieving me of Duncan's blood. At the rate it was happening, it was only a matter of a few days before I'd be free of Duncan's blood and he could turn me into his vampire bride.

I wiped away a tear that escaped at the thought of being lost to Duncan forever and took a deep breath. Now wasn't the time to succumb to despair. I needed to stay focused. I remembered a scene in one of my favorite movies, "The Last of the Mohicans". When Daniel Day Lewis's character was abandoning Madeline Stowe's character at the falls. Knowing full well she'd be captured, he assured her he'd find her and that whatever happened she was to submit and survive.

I kept that scene in mind when Rufus came to me a few hours later. Submitting to him did make it just a little easier on me. Now, I just needed to survive long enough for Duncan to find me and get me out of there.

CHAPTER THIRTY-FOUR

It was so quiet you could hear a pin drop on the grass twenty feet below. I was sure of it. This type of silence was abnormal and concerned me. I'd been locked in my room since Rufus discovered me at the cave, with only the information Elizabeth was able to share with me to tell me what was happening in the outside world. She'd yet to come to my room, so I waited impatiently.

She was late.

It was near noon before a strange serving woman brought my food to me. Since I was ravenous from not eating since the night before, combined with being pregnant with vampire child, I dove into my fare with very little thought as to why Elizabeth still hadn't come to my room or why this strange serving woman was bringing me food.

I failed to monitor my food intake and was soon feeling ill from gorging myself with a trencher made of fresh, crusty bread that was filled with perfectly seasoned mutton stew. I'd left nothing behind. The one thing I had to hand it to Rufus for was his choice of cooks. The food I'd been served had to be the best I'd received since traveling back in time. I ran my hands over my waist. It was still slender, but if I continued to eat as I just did I wouldn't need to be pregnant to lose my figure. I made a mental note to use more restraint in the future, no matter how hungry I might be.

I shook my head at that thought. What future? If all went well, I'd be free of captivity and back in the future with Duncan eating TV dinners from the microwave in my little studio apartment. I checked the time. It was well after one in afternoon. Perhaps Elizabeth had second thoughts about assisting me in reaching out to Isabelle and was hiding in a cowardly fashion? I took a moment to regain control of my emotions as anger threatened to rise. This was not the day to lose control of any kind. The feeding frenzy I'd just had was a warning sign for me. I needed to keep my wits about me. If Elizabeth chickened out, it wasn't the end of the world. I was perfectly capable of summoning Isabelle on my own. I just needed to come up with a different ruse to keep people away from my room long enough for me to perform the spell.

When the old woman returned to collect the tray, she raised an eyebrow at the fact that I'd devoured the trencher, but said nothing. I held my stomach and smiled sheepishly as a new thought came to mind. Rubbing my belly, I admitted to overeating and asked for a few hours of undisturbed rest so that I could sleep it off, after which I wanted someone to come to attend my personal needs. She stared at my stomach as if trying to see inside it and then nodded her agreement before leaving with empty tray in hand.

I listened for the click of the door locking and rushed to the small table next to my bed. Shedding my robe and chemise I scrubbed the vital parts of my body clean as best as I could with the little bit of water left in my wash basin, I quickly dried the areas I'd cared for and pulled the candle from the wall sconce. Setting it carefully on the floor, I lit its wick and dribbled an outline for a wide circle of wax for me to stand inside of. With that done, I set the candle down in the center of the circle and stood in all my naked glory next to it with my arms spread wide. Turning slowing in a counter clockwise direction, I whispered the incantation to call Isabelle from the spirit world. Within a matter of seconds, she was standing in the circle next to me.

"It really wasn't necessary to do that spell naked," she giggled.

I covered my breasts with my arms and replied, "That's embarrassing."

"No matter," she smiled, "at least you are learning. You did well. Your magic is stronger than it was in the future."

"I didn't hang around so many witches in the future. I think it's rubbing off on me," I confessed.

"Good!" she said firmly. "Now that I know where you are we can do something about getting you out of here. Those vampire witches had such a barrier up we lost you as soon as Lord Rufus whisked you from the cave."

"Yes. I'm aware. I can't keep the spell active for too long for fear of being discovered," I explained.

"True. I will leave and inform my mother, Lady Helen and Duncan where you are. We will do our best to get you out quickly," she whispered as she started to fade.

"Elizabeth too," I added, hoping she heard me.

Surprisingly, she solidified again long enough to inform me that Elizabeth was found dead in the woods not far from their encampment early that morning. When I shared with her that Elizabeth had been attending me and was conspiring with me for our escape, she reiterated the need to get me out as quickly as possible and disappeared.

I grabbed a rag from behind the screen and scrubbed the waxed circle away as best I could, put the candle back in the sconce on the wall, and donned my chemise and robe. I'd just finished tying the rope around my waist when the old serving woman returned with a cup of hot tea that she insisted would help with my digestion and aid in sleep. I secretly gave thanks for the speediness in which my interaction with Isabelle took place. A few minutes longer would have meant our discovery.

I accepted the tea cup from her gnarled hand and drank the warm liquid down in front of her while she studied me warily.

I felt an immediate calm flow through my body. If nothing else, it was a good sedative. I was grateful to be standing near the bed when I finished the last drop. I barely had time to hand the cup back before I was sprawled on the bed in deep slumber.

It wasn't until I felt the weight of Rufus as he climbed into bed next to me that I roused from my slumber enough to realize I wasn't alone. The effects of the tea were still strong enough that I did very little to participate in his one sided love making. Although I was warm and supple and breathed, I couldn't keep my foggy mind from equating what was occurring to that of a man screwing a corpse. It struck my funny bone and I giggled. Fortunately, my giggle came out as a moan. So, instead of insulting Mr. Romeo with a giggle while he was climaxing, I gave him the impression that I too found pleasure in the act. No matter. Soon I'd be free of it all. Plus, I had to admit that my subdued condition had earned me very few injuries to heal from. In fact, with the exception of a few gouges from his nails in my back as his passion peaked and a quick bite to my neck to sample the amount of Duncan's blood remaining, I was wound free.

I seemed abnormally wet and sticky from his love making, but I was still too tired to worry about cleaning up. It wasn't like my washing away his seed would prevent a pregnancy. I was already pregnant. I just knew it. Instead of getting out of bed as quickly as he'd allow and stepping behind the screen, I rolled over onto my side and fell back into a blissful slumber.

It was the wee hours of them morning when the tea finally wore off and I was able to maintain a clear head. I felt the bed next to me. Rufus was gone.

Good.

As I sat up I noticed how truly sticky and wet I was. It was far greater than I'd experienced before. It struck me that something was wrong. Grateful that a fire was still lit in my fireplace, I grabbed a lighting stick and lit the small candle at my bedside. Holding it over the bed, I gasped in disgust. There, in the middle of an enormous pool of blood was the remains of my unborn vampire child. Once again I'd shed my body of his unwanted seed. Only, this time, I'd done it without the excruciating ordeal of a magical abortion.

I pressed my hand against my abdomen. It was slightly tender, but no more so than I would be after one of Rufus' sexual invasions. I closed my eyes and gave thanks. The loss of his child meant his claim on me wasn't fixed. Now, if I could just escape before he found out...

The click of a key in my lock caught my attention. I blew out my candle and scooted behind the screen, cursing myself for not covering the bloody mass with a coverlet before I did. I considered trying to do so before whoever it was entered the room, but questioned if I'd do it in time. I decided to remain where I was and take my chances.

The old serving woman entered the room and held her candle over the bed. She passed it over the bloody mess multiple times, as if inspecting it before setting it down on the table next to my bed and lighting the candle I'd just blown out.

"Come out m' lady," she called in a shaky, crone-like voice, "I shant harm you."

I remained where I was and held my breath. If I was lucky, she'd leave in a hurry to get help and forget to lock the door behind her. That was when I'd make my escape, bloody chemise and all.

"Jane," she hissed, "I know you are still here. Come out. 'Tis Rosalie come to fetch you."

The gasp of disbelief that involuntarily escaped my lips gave away my hiding place. I stepped slowly out from behind the screen, keeping a safe distance from the old woman while I watched her warily.

With a wave of her hand she shifted her appearance back to that of Rosalie before returning to the old crone once again.

"We have eliminated his claim on you. Now 'tis time to leave. Hurry, time is short," she urged in a hushed tone.

"I need to clean up," I started to explain.

"There is not time, I fear. You have enough vampire blood in you from Duncan and the babe to prevent the scent of mortal blood being detected. We shall have to risk no one inquiring what vampire is injured. We must leave now," she said adamantly.

Pulling my bloody chemise over my head, I grabbed my robe and wrapped it around my naked body, tying the rope at the waste while I followed her to the balcony. She clicked her tongue several times and a large flapping reptilian with wings appeared.

I hid behind her still gnarled frame as I stared into the eyes of a dragon. I had no idea they actually existed until I'd met Rosalie. Of course, I didn't know vampires were real either until I'd met them in the dark alley of the future.

Pequeño will not harm you. He has been with me since birth," she explained. "Climb onto his back now, hurry!"

She climbed onto the dragon's back and gestured me to do the same. I reluctantly obeyed. With a few flaps of its powerful, broad wings we were in the air and soaring through the night sky.

CHAPTER THIRTY-FIVE

I held tight while her dragon carried us swiftly back to her encampment. During the flight, she filled me in on what happened during my absence.

Duncan went into a rage, declaring his regrets about allowing us to convince him to let me go into the cave in his stead. This information was of no surprise to me. Even so, I was sorry to hear it.

Lady Margaret was brought before the coven and her powers were bound. She was then handed over to the Earl of Winter Spring to do with as he will. The fact that she'd tried to kill his only heir and caused him to become vampire didn't sit well with the earl. Although it was a crime punishable by death, he sent her to the dungeon instead. A kind man by nature, he couldn't bring himself to hang the girl he'd accepted as his ward and helped raise.

I'd lost track of the time and learned they'd been looking for me for the better part of a month. Rosalie actually complemented the vampire witches on their cunning ability to hide me as long as they did. She praised me for the spell I'd cast to summon Isabelle, even if she had already found me by then.

I could see Duncan rushing from the encampment as the dragon lowered us to the ground. He pulled me from its back with lightning speed and held me close. I could feel his panic subsiding as he reassured himself that I was whole and fine. Sniffing the air, he growled slightly, but said nothing. I knew he smelled the blood from the miscarriage, but there was nothing I could do or say to change it, so I avoided the topic.

Sliding his hand through the opening of my robe, he

cupped my breast and smiled. I knew he was preparing to tease me on my attire to lighten the heaviness of the mood and I loved him for it. Unfortunately, we were overtaken by a swarm of cackling witches seeking to assure themselves that their queen had returned safe and secure before he could do much more than give my breast a quick squeeze and pull me close. We inched our way from the mob and held each other close while we made our way to the tent he'd been occupying.

"I am happy to see you dressed for the occasion," he chuckled.

"I missed you too," I teased.

He stopped and pulled my face to his. After kissing me in the most passionate kiss I think I've ever experienced, he assured me that he missed me more than words could express. I was his reason for being. He couldn't imagine life without me.

I believed him.

We were almost to my tent when Rufus stepped out from behind a tree. I screamed and jumped behind Duncan. He held me possessively behind him while we circled to see how many vampires he'd brought with him. I recognized the vampire witches from the cave and my heart sank.

I whispered their identity to Duncan and he nodded. Unlike me, he seemed hardly bothered by their presence. It gave me a sense of wellbeing that I hadn't felt since the nightmare began.

Balls of fire shot past us as Rosalie and her followers rushed to our aid. Duncan picked me up in his arms and swept me off to safety, leaving me in the competent care of Lady Helen, who'd just happened to stop by to check on the progress of my recovery after dealing with Lady Margaret.

I wanted to help, but I didn't dare defy Duncan. I'd done nothing but cause trouble for him and myself since I got it into my head to save the day and return to the past to prevent him becoming vampire. I now realized just how foolish an idea that was. It cost so many people so much.

Lady Helen helped me clean up and provided me with suitable clothing and we crouched near the tent opening to better view the war that raged all around us. Instead of musket balls soaring through the air, fireballs about three inches in diameter whizzed by us. They dissipated almost immediately on contact, but not without leaving a singed circle in their wake. I could only imagine the pain they could inflict if they came in contact with flesh.

While the witches hurled and whirled supernatural ammunition at each other, Duncan and Rufus circled each other in preparation to face off. I wasn't sure I could witness what was to come. When it came to physical build, they were pretty well matched. Each vampire was a fine specimen of hard lean muscle and each was about the same height. That's not what worried me. Although they were both about the same age in vampire years, Duncan spent the centuries dining on animal blood while Rufus followed traditional vampire fare and drank the blood of humans at least three times a week. Animal blood carried different nutrition properties than did human blood. I knew he'd had human blood of late, but I questioned if Duncan's strength was sufficient to defeat the power Rufus maintained.

I'd seen Duncan take on and destroy the vampires who threatened me in the alley. He was pretty impressive. I clung to that memory as I watched them charge each other.

Lady Helen placed a hand on my shoulder reassuringly as she sucked in air to control her own tension.

"He has been drinking the blood of volunteers since you were taken in preparation for this. All shall be well," she whispered, "have faith."

I covered my face with my hands as Rufus lifted Duncan over his head and slammed him onto the hard ground. I was positive the loud crack that permeated the air was his ribs breaking. I poised to rush to his aide, but was stopped by the ever wise Lady Helen.

Once I calmed down, I realized she was right. I would

have been a burdon and a distraction to him at a time when he needed all of his wits about him. I buried my face in her bosom. I wasn't willing to watch my true love be destroyed by the vampire beast who'd forced himself upon me night after night.

The thought of being condemned to live eternity as a vampire mated to Rufus was more than I could bear. I'd rather die with Duncan than continue on without him; with or without being tied to that beast.

I prayed for Duncan to find the strength to defeat him. If not, I was prepared to take my life while there was still a smidgeon of Duncan's blood running through my veins.

A stray fireball entered the tent and we rushed to extinguish the fire it ignited. I was actually grateful for the distraction. Between the war of the witches and that of my lover and my captor, I had barely a nerve left in my body.

Several nerve wracking hours passed before things calmed down. The vampire witches were driven off and the encampment's barrier of protection was intensified. Duncan and Rufus were still going strong when Rosalie entered my tent. I questioned why no one stepped in to assist, but she simply waived her hand and said he had things under control and would never forgive them for interfering.

From where I stood, both vampires looked exhausted and half dead. After closer observation I could see she was right. Duncan did look to be pulling more punches than Rufus, whose movements were drastically slower.

The encampment residents set about to clean up the chaos caused by their battle. If it hadn't been so serious a battle, the way they skirted around and dodged the vampires would a have been comical.

The encampment was almost set aright by the time Duncan finally bested Rufus. My heart swelled with pride as I watched him pull the head of that demon vampire from his body. I know I should have felt bad about it, or even repulsed, but I couldn't. Rufus put me through a tremendous amount of emotional torture and physical pain. Nothing would have satisfied me except his death. I knew that deep inside me. So did Duncan.

I wasn't worried about the condition of my love until he stumbled into my tent and I was able to see the damage Rufus caused up close. He may have killed Rufus, but I questioned whether he was soon to follow. I guided him to my cot and coaxed him to lie down. It was clear he was in need of blood. Without thinking twice about it, I grabbed a small knife off the food preparation table and slit my wrist. Ignoring the sudden horror, I felt as I witnessed more blood gushing forth than I'd expected, I forced my wound against his lips. My semi-conscious vampire sucked greedily.

As I watched the color return to his face, even more so than normal, I felt it drain from mine. The more he sucked, the better he looked and the weaker I felt. I knew I had to stop him, but I was feeling too weak to push him off my arm. His grip was powerful and greedy. Once again I was in danger of Duncan literally draining the life from me.

I looked around the room, frantically searching for someone to help get him off me. We were alone.

Duncan's shocked eyes looking at me when he returned to normal and realized what was happening were the last things I saw before I collapsed in a heap on the floor.

CHAPTER THIRTY-SIX

Isabelle stood next to me while we watched Lady Helen enter the tent and then flee back out of it shouting for help. Duncan cradled my limp body in his arms and rocked me back and forth. He was clearly at a loss of what to do.

Rosalie rushed into the tent with Lady Helen close at her heels. She inspected my eyes and my breathing and announced I was still alive, but just barely. She rambled in outraged Spanish and Isabelle translated it to me. Apparently she was repremanding my almost dead body for being foolish enough to donate blood when the miscarriage took more than it should to begin with. She claimed I had barely enough blood flowing in my veins to support me after such an ordeal, let alone revive a vampire. I'm pretty sure she called me stupid, although Isabelle woundn't own up to it if she did.

I listened while they debated what to do. I was so close to death that if Duncan revived me with his blood they ran the risk of my turning vampire. I wasn't sure how I felt about that. Did I want to spend eternity as a vampire? Was I ready for such a change? I was to marry Duncan, but I'd had it in my head to use a spell to elongate my life, rather than turn vampire. Turning vampire was my last resort, and only if Duncan lost to Rufus. Relief flooded over me when I heard them decide to watch me for a while to see if my body would rebuild my blood supply on its own.

I stayed out of my body for the majority of the time that I lay healing. Duncan never left my side. This was one of the major reasons I remained out of my body. When I was in body, I could hear and see nothing. All I knew was an eerie dark silence. I needed to be out of body in order to be aware of and hear what was going on around me and being said to me.

Duncan looked wonderful. He'd healed completely from the battle with Rufus and my blood had given him Rufus' same healthy, ruddy glow. There was such a major difference in appearance from when he drank animal blood, I wondered if the way he felt was that much different as well.

I listened to Duncan share with me stories of his childhood, stories of his struggle to adapt to being vampire, and finally about how he'd regained a love for living when I came into his life. If I'd had any doubts about the depth of his love, they were dispelled during that time.

My heart went out to him. His pain over the possible loss of me was acute. I watched him stroke my face with his strong fingers and felt all fuzzy inside. I loved him. I loved him deeply. I couldn't bear to see him suffer like he was.

It was at that time that I realized the one thing that would make Duncan truly happy wasn't being mortal again. It was not losing the ones he loved. He'd refrained from falling in love with people over the years, only allowing himself a few choice relationships such as the one he had with Isabelle - who'd managed to keep herself alive for centuries. Being close to a mortal was a heartache waiting to happen. I finally got it.

Once again, my heart sank when I thought of what occurred as a result of my actions. I looked at my dear friend Isabelle standing so near me, yet maintaining the silence I required from her. Even in death she was wise and kind.

"I'm so sorry," I whispered.

"You need not whisper. He cannot hear," she replied, never taking her moist eyes off Duncan.

"You. I'm so sorry for what I did to you," I continued.

"You did nothing to me, my dear. It was just my time," she sighed.

"I don't agree," I persisted, "If I'd stayed in the future, then none of this would have happened and you'd still be alive."

"And you?" she turned to look at me, "Would you still be alive?"

I hesitated, "I... I... of course."

She smiled and said nothing for the longest time.

When the silence was finally broken, she placed her hand on my arm, "In this realm we have the ability to see things that may or will come to be. Follow me now."

I hesitated. I didn't want to leave Duncan and go anywhere, but she persisted, so I finally gave in.

It was an interesting journey at her side. We were walking, yet the world seemed to be flying past us at record speed. When it finally slowed down we were standing in my little studio apartment. Duncan, Doug, Linda, and Chuck were also there. Linda and Doug were crying.

I looked at Isabelle quizzically. She took my hand and once again the world swooshed past us until we stood at the entrance of Moore's Funeral Home. I'd barely had time to register where we were before she pulled me along through the door and down to the preparation room where I saw my still, lifeless body all stretched out with tubes coming and going in my groin and neck. I was clearly dead.

The undertaker was on the phone conversing with someone saying, "I managed to clean her up enough to be suitable for display. Yes, it's tragic. Hit and run victims can be so broken up, it's impossible to make them look good," he smiled as he looked over at my lifeless body, "I'm pretty proud of my accomplishments with this one."

"I'm dead!" I screeched.

"Yes," Isabelle replied.

"When? How?" I continued.

"I discovered a book of records. This book contains all that ever was and all that will be. It isn't what might be. It is what will be." She looked me straight in the eye, "You are supposed to die at the age of twenty-three. It is written in your life plan."

"But... so young," I muttered.

"Yes," she agreed.

I looked at my body closer and could see it had been

broken up in multiple places.

"How does it happen?" I wasn't sure I really wanted to know, but I was unable to resist asking.

"Struck by a bus while crossing the street," she said flatly.

"Are you kidding me?" I screeched. "Struck by a bus? How cliché was that?"

"You felt nothing. Death is quite painless when it happens." She spread her arms wide and tilted her head back, "It can be a marvelous release."

"Duncan," I mused.

"Yes, Duncan will suffer deeply when you die. Whether it is by the bus or another time, he will suffer," she said.

"It's heartbreaking," I cried.

"Yes," she agreed.

I wasn't sure what to do, but I knew I had to do something. If the astral traveling I was experiencing right then resembled death, then Isabelle was completely correct in saying it didn't hurt and wasn't all that bad. I could handle it. What I couldn't handle was watching Duncan suffer over the loss of me. Just listening to his desperate pleas for me to heal and return to him were crushing enough. To watch him adjust to the fact that I was gone and he could never be with me because he was doomed to roam the earth a soul-less creature was more than I could bear.

"I have to do something," I said as I jerked Isabelle around to face me. "We have to do something!"

"There is nothing you can do to change your fate, my dear friend," she said sadly, "I show you this only to help you understand that in a very short time Duncan will lose you anyway. Whether you choose to leave your body now or later matters not."

"So, I could leave my body now? Is that what you're saying?" I asked.

She closed her eyes and nodded slowly.

"Am I that close to death?" I whispered.

She nodded some more.

"I… I thought I was just resting…. healing… not… not dying," I moaned. "I can't accept this! I can't leave Duncan like this!"

The next thing I knew I was looking into Duncan's beautiful sea foam blue eyes. They were wet with tears of fear mixed with joy. He pulled me close and almost crushed me in a smothering hug. I tried to tell him I was suffocating, but all I could do was gasp for air. That was enough to bring him to his senses and release me.

"I am so sorry my love," he half laughed-half cried, "I thought I had lost you. I… I just do not know how I will go on without you."

"Someday you will have to," I whispered. "I will die one day."

Yes, yes I know," he gasped, "but not just yet. Please, not just yet."

I stroked his beautiful cheek with my hand. It felt strong and smooth. I ran my fingers through his silky hair.

"How do you get your hair so soft?" I whispered.

He looked at me in stunned surprise before laughing hysterically and kissing my face.

CHAPTER THIRTY-SEVEN

It was a week since I'd convinced Duncan to speed up my recovery by giving me some of his blood. He'd hesitated for fear of Rosalie's concern of my turning vampire would occur, but he eventually gave in. I really didn't need his blood to heal. I was healing well without it, but I didn't tell him that. When I had Duncan's blood flowing through my veins all of my senses were heightened and my powers more acute. I needed all the advantage I could get for what I was about to do.

I'd managed to connect with Elizabeth's spirit. She wasn't as easy to summon as Isabelle's, but I eventually managed. My heart ached as she told me how Lady Margaret learned of her association with me and arranged to have her killed. She laughed at the irony of how she'd feared losing her life to her vampire brother instead of her human mistress. The danger of being in Rufus' company was so blatantly acute that it never dawned on her to look in other directions.

When Margaret's men approached her, she'd greeted them with warmth and friendship. They'd asked her to accompany them to the dungeon as her ladyship wished to speak with her. She went willingly.

Having lived on the estate for so long, Lady Margaret was well aware of its secret passages. It was one of these passages that her men used to escort Elizabeth into the depths of the dank dungeon where her mistress awaited. Elizabeth's eyes took some time adjusting to the darkness as she walked down the narrow passageway, but by the time she'd reached the dungeon's main chamber that glowed from the low illumination a few small torches propped near the entrance provided, she could see well enough.

They led her past several empty cells until they reached

the one farthest away from the entrance. There, sitting behind bars and with both hands and feet secured in chains was a very bedraggled looking Lady Margaret Chapman. Elizabeth's mind conjured up the image of the women she and I'd been held in the cell with while awaiting the hangman and compared them to Margaret. Margaret looked far worse.

"M' lady," Elizabeth gushed as she peered through the bars, "what have they done to you?"

"Do not feign concern wench!" she hissed. "'Tis well known of your comradeship with Lord Duncan's freak from the future. You cannot have loyalty to me while consorting with the likes!"

"M' lady... I," Elizabeth was at a loss for words.

Margaret spoke truth. She had become my friend, while remaining in her employ. They'd never manifested any type of relationship, other than that of lady's maid and mistress. The fact that Margaret would have expectations of Elizabeth in that direction galled me.

Margaret proceeded to taunt Elizabeth about how she and Rufus had whipped up a plan to destroy Duncan and make me Rufus' wife for eternity. Knowing my love for Duncan was real, she was satisfied that this would be the cruelest sentence she could place on me. Far crueler than death. Then, without a morsel of remorse, she ordered her men to dispose of Elizabeth like she was no more than a bag of trash.

Before she could do anything more than gasp in shock, one of Margaret's men snapped her neck. She never knew what hit her.

Elizabeth rose above her body and watched as one of the guards carried her over his shoulder like a sack of flower, mindless of the many times her head slammed into the wall as a result of the rough gait a poorly healed leg injury created.

When they reached the edge of the witch's encampment, they dumped her body and left without looking back. She was in such shock that all she could do was hover over her lifeless corpse and stare. It was because she hadn't moved on that she was around to witness her murders returning with a scruffy looking third man. They were arguing about how Margaret had insisted they made her death look like it occurred in a manner that could not be tied to them. Margaret had aspirations of convincing the earl to forgive and release her and wanted nothing added to her case to prevent that from happening.

Since Elizabeth had very little to steal, they decided to make it look like a rape. The problem was that neither had the stomach to rape a corpse. She thought she wasn't able to leave the scene of her death because of the shock of it all. She soon learned differently.

The disgusting, dirty man the men had brought with them mounted her lifeless body without a moment's hesitation. To her surprise, she could not only feel the assault, but she could smell the stench of his filth. Apparently the snap of her neck had paralyzed her, but not killed her. Elizabeth was still alive and very much aware of what was occurring.

Tears poured down her ghostly cheeks and my human ones as she proceeded to tell me how the men paid her rapist in coin before tearing at her hair and clothes to make the scene look more like an attack. One of them kicked her hard in the ribs, although she couldn't explain why. It was that kick that took her life. A rib snapped and when they rolled her over to position her face down, the motion drove the rib into her lung. She was dead not long afterward.

Horrified at her story, I vowed to see justice paid for those two murderous thugs and evil Margaret if it was the last thing I did. I summoned Lady Helen to my tent and told Elizabeth's story. Equally horrified, she agreed to help.

Although I'd been freely walked amongst and associated with magical beings, we were actually in a time where witch hunts were all the rage and hangings common place. We decided our best revenge would be to free Margaret from the dungeon and expose her for the evil witch she was to the authorities. The earl may not have the stomach to punish her as she rightfully should be punished, but we were certain the local magistrate and his lynch mob would have no problem with it. As for her thugs, well, accidents happen.

Unfortunately, neither Helen nor I knew the ins and outs of the passageways of Duncan's castle. I was forced to summon Elizabeth to assist us. As painful as it was for her to return to the scene of the crime that ultimately led to her demise, she too was eager to see justice done. Since I was the only one able to see and communicate with her, I acted as the go between for her and Helen.

The smell of the dank dungeon assaulted our noses. Fortunately, we'd been forewarned by Elizabeth and had brought herb infused cloths along to place over our mouths and noses while we moved about. My claustrophobia was acute as we made our way along the and narrow passageway that led to the dungeon. Elizabeth kept telling me we were almost there, but we seemed to go on forever.

When we finally reached the inner chamber, there was only one torch lit to illuminate our way. I grabbed it from the holder it was set in and we moved forward. Elizabeth led us past half a dozen empty cells before she stopped and pointed to the one that housed Margaret. I was surprised at how deep into the bowels of the dungeon they'd locked her, but, then, it obviously wasn't deep enough, since she'd managed to commune with her thugs and order Elizabeth's death.

I peered through the close set bars in the heavy oak door. The moonlight slithering through the tiny window high above her head helped me see her slumped form. Her ankles and wrists were shackled. Her once finely coiffed hair looked like someone had taken an egg beater to it.

"Do you enjoy the view?" she growled from the depths of her throat.

I shuddered. Had I not known better I would have questioned if we were being addressed by a human being.

"Aye, that I do," Lady Helen stated boldly.

"Ah, the fair Lady Helen. I did not see you there. Come

closer so that I might see you in the light," she beckoned.

"'Tis fine where I stand," Helen replied.

"What brings you to my humble abode?" she chided.

I spoke up and said, "I, for one, wanted the satisfaction of seeing for myself how low you've sunk. My only regret is that Duncan isn't at my side."

She laughed the laugh of the wicked. I began to wonder if her time in the dark, dank dungeon had driven her mad. It was highly possible.

"Or Elizabeth. 'Tis a shame she is not here to witness your state," Helen added.

"Balderdash!" she roared, "She stands beside you and you know it."

I looked at Helen and then at Elizabeth. "Can you see her?" I whispered.

"No," Helen whispered back.

"You come too late to satisfy your wicked plans," Margaret hissed, "My men have poisoned me upon my command. I shant see daylight."

"No!" I screeched. "That's not good enough! You can't get out of it that easily!"

"But, I have," she cooed.

She stood and waddled to the bars. The foulness of her breath arrived long before her dirt smudged face pressed against the bars. I pressed my cloth to my nose and looked her in the eye. She had the look of a wild woman. We stared at each other silently for what seemed like eternity before she threw her head back and cackled like the typical witch you'd see in a horror film before waddling away.

I don't know when the mindset of the times with their low regard for human life set into my bones, but, somewhere along the path of time travel, I'd become hardened, vicious, and blood thirsty. I was actually angry about missing the opportunity to be the one responsible for this evil woman's death. True, I had vampire blood coursing through my veins, but it was more than that. I couldn't blame the blood. After all, Duncan was so anti- kill that he practically had to be forced to drink the blood of a human, even though he knew it would make a significant difference in his body's maintenance. No, it was me. Something deep inside me was unleashed. I was no longer the innocent girl who'd traveled through time on a foolish romantic mission to rescue my vampire lover.

What had I done?

"You have done much," Elizabeth said. I gasped at the realization she was able to read my mind. "I harbored the ability to know minds in life. I ignored it. I was fearful of being labeled a witch and hanging. I know no magic, after all," she explained.

There was something about her innocent confession that warmed me all over.

I smiled warmly as I said, "Well, perhaps my dear friend Isabelle can show you a bit of magic?"

"Perhaps," Isabelle said with a grin. She too found Elizabeth delightful.

I raised a brow at the discovery that my dear friend had joined us, but said nothing.

"I shall be happy to show you magic!" Margaret screeched while laughing eerily.

"I shall be happy to show you hell!" Isabelle shouted. She turned to me and looked me in the eye, "The good Lady Margaret is only moments away from death. What will happen at that time is not for you to see. I wish for you to leave now."

"But…" I protested.

She closed her eyes and nodded her head toward the door as she commanded, "Go."

CHAPTER THIRTY-EIGHT

A saddened, yet vindicated, Helen and I parted ways.

I sulked through the woods on my way to the main part of the estate with Elizabeth still in company. I felt let down to have been denied giving Margaret her just desserts. It was clear that when her soul left her body it wouldn't be pretty, which was why Isabelle insisted I leave and take Helen and Elizabeth with me. Even so, it wasn't enough. I wanted her demise to be by my hands, not her own. I really felt cheated.

"Vampire blood works strangely in humans," Elizabeth said softly.

I stopped and stared at her as if for the first time. In truth, I'd been so absorbed with my woeful thoughts that I'd forgotten she was with me.

"How so?" I asked.

"It makes the gentle quite aggressive," she replied knowingly.

I nodded my agreement and continued walking. She was probably right. Even though Duncan was a gentle vampire, it didn't mean that his blood wouldn't react in my body differently. After all, I had the genetic make-up of a human, not a vampire. I excused myself for my barbaric thoughts and forced the gentler side of me to the forefront.

"It looks like I didn't even need the vampire blood. Margaret did the job quite nicely on her own," I said quietly.

"You still need it," Elizabeth said as she pointed to my left.

I looked through the trees at the two men she was pointing to.

"Are they...?" I began.

"Aye, they are my murderers," she said shakily.

Although I'd intended to make sure Elizabeth's murders saw justice, I'd been so focused on Margaret that I hadn't yet devised a plan of action. I certainly hadn't expected to have to deal with them in the middle of a deserted forest with only a newbie ghost at my side. I looked around for a place to hide, but it was too late. They'd spotted me and were heading my way.

"Well, well, what have we here?" the larger one spat.

He clearly knew my identity and just as clearly resented my existence.

"A fine bit of fun, if you ask me," his companion said.

I shuddered as the words slipped past the rotted teeth of his shorter and far uglier companion.

Did they seriously think they were going to rape me? Although I'd been forcibly taken by Rufus, it somehow didn't seem to compare to the dread and outrage I felt at the thought of these two, smelly, disgusting creatures rutting over me. Oh no. That would never happen. I'd die first. Besides, I'd had my fill of being taken by force. Enough was enough.

As those two disgusting and foul smelling, poor excuses for men circled around me, I made ready for combat. I was grateful for the self-defense lessons Duncan made sure I had after that attack in the alley. That knowledge, combined with a healthy dose of vampire blood and some cheering from Elizabeth was all I needed to beat those bullies to the ground in style.

As I stood over their swollen, lifeless bodies, I doubted they were truly dead. I didn't bother to finish the job. It suddenly didn't matter that they still lived. There was some punishment that was even worse than death. In a day where machoism was everything, they'd have to live with the knowledge that they'd had their butts handed to them by a lone, one-hundred-ten pound, five-foot, four-inch woman. That in itself was gratifying. I looked at Elizabeth. She seemed happy with the outcome as well.

Feeling sufficient justice was dished out to Elizabeth's

killers, and knowing that by now Margaret's soul was in the hands of the devil, we walked away from the scene of the battle smug and satisfied. It was time to find Duncan and get back to the future.

I'd walked about a mile or so in comfortable silence. Elizabeth was still with me, but she also seemed to have a lot on her mind. We were okay with just being in each other's company. As I approached a clearing in the woods where I could either go west to the encampment or east to the main road that led to the front gate of Duncan's castle I spotted him coming toward me on horseback. My heart skipped a beat.

I was still too far back amongst the trees for him to see me, but I could see him well enough. He looked so regal and handsome mounted on the back of his huge black gelding. It practically took my breath away. I once again thanked the most high for bringing us together. He may be a soul-less vampire, but he was my soul mate. Of that I was certain.

I hailed his attention. He smiled and kicked his horse into action. I ran through the trees and was almost at the edge of the clearing when I heard Elizabeth scream and the world went temporarily black.

Once again I floated above my body.

Once again I saw Duncan cradling me in his arms, except this time he held me only briefly before darting into the woods. With Elizabeth at my side, we followed him. He moved with the speed of lightning, but remarkably, we were able to keep up. He quickly caught up with the man who'd used lethal aim at the base of my skull with a small rock and a sling shot. I recognized him as the smaller of the two men I'd left beaten in the woods. Perhaps I should have stayed to finish the job. I hadn't realized his desire for revenge would be so acute.

Duncan tore the man to shreds in a fit of rage that shocked even me. Elizabeth and I looked at each other bewilderingly. How badly had I been injured for Duncan to react so violently?

Since I'd left my body before to view the scene around

me and then re-entered it when it was time to regain consciousness, I assumed the same would be the case this time.

I stood next to Elizabeth as we watched Duncan return to my body and cradle me lovingly. He pulled his hand from the back of my head and stare at the deep red blood that coated it. That wasn't a good sign. I was sure that when I awoke I'd have a whopper of a headache. In a time when Excedrin still hadn't been invented, this was not something I was looking forward to.

Something was happening, but I couldn't get a grasp on what it was. Duncan lifted my limp body onto the back of his horse and was now riding slowly toward the castle. He held me close in front of him and my blood was soaking his front.

I remarked to Elizabeth about the abundance of blood flowing from me and was surprised to discover that she was no longer there. I looked around for her, but saw no signs of where she might be.

I considered going off to look for her, but I was unable to move very far away from my body. I assumed it was because I was going to wake up soon. I took a closer look at the wound at the nape of my neck and winced. The rock must have been very sharp. It actually looked to be still in my skull. Ouch. I couldn't even imagine what type of procedure would have to be done to remove it. I was grateful to be unconscious and out of body and certainly not eager to re-enter anytime soon.

With a wound of such a serious nature, I was puzzled as to why Duncan didn't gallop to the castle and call for help. Instead, he was allowing the horse to move at a slow, steady pace while holding me close to his chest and kissing the top of my head.

We were close to the gates of the castle wall when he veered to the left and made his way to a small, secluded hut. I'd never noticed its existence and I doubted very many other people did either, since it was covered from top to bottom with brush and vines. It truly looked like it was part of the hillside.

He slid from the saddle with surprising grace and eased me down into his arms. The door opened before he reached it and Isabelle stood waiting for him. She had a sad smile on her face. To my surprise, he was able to see and communicate with her!

"Isabelle, what's happening?" I said as I rushed through the door before it could be slammed in my face. When she didn't respond, I repeated my question.

Still no answer.

Instead, my deceased friend and my vampire lover tended to my limp and lifeless body as they laid me onto a large wooden table that occupied a good portion of the hut. The rich aromas of herbs and spices filled the interior. Even in my altered state, I was able to enjoy their potency.

Once again I asked Isabelle what was happening and once again I received no notice from her.

With the help of some blacksmith tongs, she pulled the rock from my skull. As I expected, it was almost as sharp as an arrow. She placed the bloody stone in Duncan's hand and he rolled it around for a while before crushing it to dust.

It was amazing how much strength an angry vampire could possess.

Isabelle pulled my body into a sit up position and held me still while Duncan licked the blood from my wound. He reminded me of an animal cleaning its mate. It was somehow intimate, yet protective.

When he'd cleaned the wound and I was able to see it, my stomach lurched. My skull was open wide enough for me to see my brains! I had no idea how they intended to fix that one, but I was very grateful Isabelle had somehow managed to harness the magic from her realm to cast a spell that allowed her to materialize enough to do the job. There was no one in the world I trusted more with my life and wellbeing than Duncan and Isabelle. I was in the best of hands.

I could feel myself being pulled back into my body, but it didn't feel the same as the last time. It felt harsh and painful. Duncan held me tight while my body convulsed in what I can only equate to resembling and epileptic seizure. I burned inside. I wanted to scream from the pain, but nothing came from my lips.

Isabelle was frantically rubbing me down with some sort of herbal solution that brought a bit of relief from the burning sensation on the skin level, but did nothing to relieve the painfully excruciating horror of what was happening inside me. My body was morphing. I could actually feel it morphing. The odd thing was that I could still see me and I looked quite calm, serene and normal. There was virtually no sign of the train wreck that was happening within my core.

It wasn't until I focused on the words Duncan kept repeating in my ear to hang on and it would be over soon, that I realized the truth of the situation. I was becoming a vampire. The creep with the rock had aimed just right and killed me. That's why Duncan took his sweet happy time taking me to the hut. There was no hurry, as I was already dead.

I had a million questions and a whole lot of pain.

True to Duncan's words, the pain eventually subsided and I slid back into a body that felt stronger than I can ever remember feeling in my entire life. I opened my eyes and looked into the loving and very relieved eyes of my lover. He kissed me gently before releasing me to fend for myself.

I swung my legs over the side of the table and slowly lowered myself to the floor. Duncan made move to help me, as did Isabelle, but I waived them away. I was shaky, but certain I could stand alone. It was an odd feeling to be in a body that belonged to me, but in some ways was foreign to me. I'd have to get to know me all over again.

"How do you feel?" Isabelle whispered.

"Strange," I replied. I looked over at Duncan and added, "but happy."

"Happy?" he asked with surprise.

"I'm a vampire now, right?" I said, more than asked.

Both Duncan and Isabelle nodded.

"Good," I said firmly.

"I thought you did not care to become a vampire," Duncan's voice clearly showed the emotions he was battling.

"You thought wrong," I smiled. "True, I didn't want to become the vampire bride of Rufus, but I am thrilled to be the vampire bride of Duncan."

He chuckled and moved forward. Folding his arms around me he whispered, "So, you think I want to marry you and be stuck with you for eternity?"

I threw my head back so that I could look into his eyes and said teasingly, "I do."

He kissed me long and hard before whispering, "I do."

I felt a wave of happiness permeate the room as it lit up like lightning filled it.

Isabelle clapped her hands together with delight as she giggled the words, "I have just witnessed my very first vampire sealing. I now pronounced you married for eternity!"

I smiled with surprise as she giggled and faded away.

"Is that true? Are we married?" I asked hesitantly.

"I hope it is what you truly wanted because yes, we have said the words so it is done. We are bonded by choice for eternity," he replied.

"Good!" I chuckled.

"That settles it then," he smiled. "So, wife. What would you like to do on the first day of the rest of your eternal life at my side?"

I kissed him long and hard before replying, "Why, consummate the marriage, of course."

Eileen Sheehan lives in her native upstate New York where she enjoys the beauty of the New York Countryside.

When she is not sitting at the computer creating a new fantasy, she can be found helping her clients through her holistic business as Lena Sheehan a.k.a. Psychic Lena.

Eileen Sheehan lives in her native upstate New York where she enjoys the beauty of the New York Countryside.

When she is not sitting at the computer creating a new fantasy, she can be found helping her clients through her holistic business as Lena Sheehan a.k.a. Psychic Lena.

She takes advantage of her experiences, wisdom and knowledge of the paranormal and often finds ways to insert them into her writings.

Curl up with your e-reader or paperback and lose yourself in Eileen Sheehan's exciting paranormal/fantasy world of magic, time travel, vampires, shape shifters, werewolves, and more! You'll grab the edge of your seat, befriend -and maybe fall in love with- her heroes and heroines and have a laugh or two as you enjoy her fast paced novels for readers of most ages. Although she strives to create a well-rounded story, Eileen is an incurable romantic so don't expect an abundance of horror. She prefers to make love, not gore.

Visit her online at: http://www.sheehan-author.info
Email: contact@sheehan-author.info

www.earthwisebooks.com

Other Books by Eileen Sheehan

The Vampire, The Handler, and Me
ISBN: 978-0692589311

The Princess and the Vampire King
ISBN: 978-0692598214

Vampire Witch
ISBN: 978-0692594599
Vampire Queen
[A Continuation of Vampire Witch]

Vampire Iniquity
[Book One of the Tugurlan Chronicles]
ISBN: 978-0692619070

The Cure
(Book Two of the Tugurlan Chronicles)
ISBN: 978-0692624692

Vampires and Werewolves
(Book Three of the Tugurlan Chronicles)
ISBN: 978-0692629642

Dark Escape
ISBN: 978-0692629918

The Search for the Crystal Key
[A Continuation of Dark Escape]
ISBN: 978-0692630037

****

Books by Ailene Frances
Love Misunderstood
[Historical Romance]
ISBN: 978-0692590003

Books by E. F. Sheehan
Toast With Jelly
[A Tragedy of a Lesbian Confused]

CHAPTER ONE

The harsh shrill of the quarter hour whistle brought me back to reality like a crisp slap across my face. I was still in that horrid room with those horrid creatures awaiting a fate too horrid to imagine.

Horrid... was that the best I could do? This place was beyond horrid. It was so bad there was no description for how bad it was.

My mind was fuzzy.

I needed to focus.

Those creatures, what were they? They went beyond horrid to look at, horrid to be around, horrid to interact with. My brain would not function properly. I could come up with no word to equal what they were. I gave up. Horrid would have to suffice.

I smiled to myself. What did it matter what word I used to describe what was happening? Was it really that important? In the not too distant future I would become a nothing, a thing of the past. What I thought and the words I enunciated with would mean less than they already did.

"You smile human. Do you take pleasure in this?" said a deep surly voice.

My head shot up and I looked directly into the beady, yellow eyes of my scaly captor.

"Does it matter?" I slurred boldly.

"Not in the least," the lizard beast muttered as it moved away to inspect a woman to my left.

"I thought not," I mumbled as my chin fell back to my chest.

"Silence," a deep masculine voice from the back of the room roared. "I will have silence!"

I could have been defiant and said something else just to irritate them. After all, I was a dead woman soon enough. What could they possibly do to me for breaking their precious code of silence that they weren't already going to do anyway? But, I didn't. My brain thought it, but my tongue stayed immobile. Also, something deep inside my feeble brain shouted for me to shut up and behave myself and I just might get out of this thing alive. Imagine that? I knew it was a fairy tale wish, but I obeyed the command and kept quiet anyway. Maybe somewhere in the recesses of my mind I was holding out for a miracle.

My long, bony arms had been trussed over my head for so long I could barely feel them. The numbness was traveling down my back and into my equally bony legs. I looked around at my fellow captives. They made sense. Each one had enough meat on their bodies to feed these lizard beasts in fine fashion. If they dined on soup then perhaps I could understand their reason for including me in the mix, but from what I'd been able to decipher they only ate meat; and they ate it fresh and un-cooked. My scrawny five-foot three-inch physique barely hit the one-hundred-pound mark on a scale while soaking wet.

I didn't belong here.

But then, did any of us?

Another quarter hour whistle pierced the air. I felt the conveyor belt jolt as it slowly moved me to the left toward the dreaded room. How many were ahead of me? The great hall was long and filled with bodies. Where did they all come from? My eyes were blurred from whatever they'd injected into my neck a few whistles ago. It was a calming agent of some sort. Apparently the lizard beasts preferred their food not fight back. It was working. I reckoned that by the time I reached the end of the line I would be a drooling fool without a care in the world. Do with me what you will creep! I could give a damn!

Rough, scaly, and incredibly powerful hands started poking and pawing at my naked body. I was disgusted by the vile assault, but couldn't even manage a flinch. Yep, the injection was definitely working.

"What is this doing here? Is this a prank?" the owner of the assaulting hands demanded with disgust. "Wumonan, I just asked you a question and I expect an answer. Why is this scrawny female here?"

"I... I ... She was here when I came on duty, boss," replied a very worried lizard-like guard that I assumed was Wumonan.

"It never occurred to you to question her presence?" growled the one he called boss.

"Ahh... no boss, I did not think..." Wumonan began.

"That's right, you did not think!" Boss interjected. "Had you used that tiny worthless brain of yours, you would have realized this female is far too inferior to be presented at our table. In fact, she is an insult to even the lowest Dragos table."

My body swayed in response to his shove of disgust.

"Get her out of here," he ordered.

"Yes boss," Wumonan replied with a mixture of fear and respect in his voice.

Wumonan pulled my drugged body from the hook holding the rope that trussed my wrists together and flung me over his broad, reptilian shoulder as if I was nothing more than a sack of flour. My arms flapped against his thick, scaly back with each step that he took, but he seemed not to notice. I fought back the vomit as my face slammed into his abrasive leathery flesh. Not only was the sensation atrocious, but the stench was overwhelming. I had heard about the Dragos off and on while growing up, but always in a fairy tale. I recalled the stories stated they did not have an elimination system like humans. They eliminated waste through their skin. I now knew this to be true. My conveyor stunk in the worst way. He reeked of dirt, something that resembled sweaty urine, and blood. Having been raised near a farm in Upstate New York, I can tell you that I've been in pig pens that smelled better.

He took me to their garbage dump outside the eatery. I'm pretty sure I felt a rib or two snap when he dumped me unceremoniously onto a raunchy pile of human discard. As I lay amongst bones picked clean of flesh and smelling like blood mixed with vulgar creature saliva, my body purged whatever contents my stomach contained. When it was empty, I continued to heave. It was as if my on/off switch was broken.

By the time the wrenching subsided, I was overwhelmed by the accentuated pain in my ribs. The powerful contracting of my diaphragm as I purged and purged and purged intensified the damage from being tossed onto the pile of bones. I had no doubt at least one rib was broken, possibly two.

As much as I wanted to be free of the pile of human remains, the injection was taking hold full force. I was disoriented with virtually no motivation to move. I could feel the hollow darkness off in a distance calling; waiting to consume me. It was only a matter of time now. Although the substance they injected wasn't lethal, I got the sense I would be out long enough to be buried alive when the next load of remains was dumped on top of me. With my slight frame, my weakened condition, and a broken ribcage, it was a pretty sure bet I would be trapped beneath the rubble. Instead of meeting my death as food for the Dragos, I was going to meet my death from those who had been their food.

How droll.

I decided I'd rather not be aware of my ultimate demise. I closed my eyes and willed the darkness to overtake me.

****

I was warm; cozy, in fact. I kept my eyes closed while I tested my limbs. They were functioning. I felt my rib cage. It was bandaged. Puzzled, I slowly raised my lids to view my surroundings. I found myself in what looked like a cave that was furnished with fairly lavish tapestry of red, green, and gold woven together to create what looked like a coat of arms. The flying dove with an olive branch led me to believe the owner was of a peace loving clan. Thick, lush carpeting from the orient was spread over the hard packed dirt floor. Strategically positioned on top of it were an ornate table and two chairs, one comfy looking overstuffed chair, and the bed I occupied.

Was I dreaming?

Had I died?

I'd heard when you die you select the era and time you'd like to play out eternity in. From what I could see, I'd gone back in time, but I had no clue how far back.

I inhaled deeply. The rich aroma of a thick stew made its way into my nostrils and my stomach reacted with a vengeance. I'd purged its contents in that pile of human remains and it demanded solace. Even the visual remembrance of that horrific place did not deter it from demanding its rightful due.

I looked around the room. Was I alone? Were angels going to come in to serve me?

Spirits maybe? I gasped in trepidation. I was in heaven, wasn't I? My mind raced through my actions prior to my capture. I could think of nothing I had done that would have warranted my going to hell. Surely this was heaven. It just had to be.

The faint rustling outside the cave caught my attention. Since I was uncertain about everything right then, I decided it best to play possum. I had just enough time to close my eyelids far enough to appear asleep -while leaving them cracked open just enough to view the activity in the room from beneath my abnormally long, thick lashes- before he entered. I had all I could do not to gasp with admiration. That settled it! I was in heaven and some sort of god just entered the cave. His six-foot-tall, muscular physique moved with the power, grace, and presence of someone possessing an undeniable abundance of self-confidence. His feet practically glided when he walked. His lean, well-formed muscles rippled with each movement as he fed newly chopped wood to the embers of what had once been a roaring fire. Thick, dark hair framed his pale, aristo-cratic features as he fanned the fire until flames once again danced to his satisfaction. His perfectly formed mouth made me aware of my own thin, overly broad lips. I'd wager his mouth didn't consume his face when he smiled like mine did. His only apparel was a pair of black leather pants that fit like a second skin. The rest of him -including his feet- was bare. I could have admired him all day. I'd never encountered so perfect a man.

But then, he wasn't a man.

He was a god and I was in heaven.

I found heaven very different than what I'd expected it to be. There were no angels playing harps and singing as they floated by on clouds. I struggled to remember my early reli-gious education. If memory served me correctly, heaven con-sisted of various levels. Perhaps I'd entered one that didn't have angels in it. After all, they worked closely with the creator God. My deeds may not have been bad enough to force me into hell, but they were also surely not perfect enough to get me seated next to the creator of all. That was it. I was in one of the lower levels of heaven. It made sense. Didn't I learn that in the lower spiritual realms they ate and drank and felt just like humans? Well, if that was the case, it was perfectly fine with me. That stew that my handsome god was stirring smelled de-licious and my mouth was watering for a taste of it.

"You're awake," he said with his back still turned to me.

I cleared my throat and whispered, "Yes."

"Don't be concerned, your faculties will all return in no time," he assured me as he bent down to fill a bowl with the delicious smelling fare.

His emerald green eyes touched mine and he flashed the most dazzling smile my way.

I was probably hallucinating, but I would have sworn his teeth sparkled like the actors in a gum commercial I'd seen on television. I squeezed my eyes shut briefly and gave him a renewed appraisal. Nope, I wasn't hallucinating. His strong, well defined teeth were a brilliant white and glistening to the point they almost hurt my eyes. Had his flesh been darker, it would have made a hideous sight. As it so happened, his pale complexion blended naturally with his brilliant teeth, creating an alluring, almost irresistible effect.

"Are you a god?" I asked meekly.

His chuckle echoed through the cave as he said, "Hardly. It's a nice thought though."

"I am in heaven, right?" I urged.

"Heaven?" he said with a puzzled look. "You believe this to be heaven?"

He stood up and carried the much anticipated steaming bowl to me. I extended both hands to receive it and almost dropped it. A bit of hot broth spilled onto my leg. It was then that I realized I was still naked.

He watched me with interest as I struggled to maintain control of the precious bowl of stew while pulling a quilt that had been barely covering me over my nakedness as best I could.

"I've already seen everything you have to offer. I see no reason risking a serious burn for non-essential modesty. Please," he gestured toward the stew, "enjoy and relax. If it makes you feel better, I promise I won't look."

With that, he left the cave.

"Are... are you coming back?" I called after him with a scratchy voice that could barely be defined as audible.

I cleared my throat multiple times in hopes of lubricating my vocal chords into working condition.

"Of course," came his faint reply from the distance.

I noted how far away he'd gotten in a very short period of time. He'd moved abnormally fast.

With the stew commanding my attention, I gave my strange rescuer minimal thought as I dove into the most delicious fare I could recall ever eating. My stomach churned and hurt as I stuffed it, but I kept going. When my bowl was empty, I looked around to be sure I was alone before I slowly made my way to the boiling pot for a refill. I would probably regret it in the long run, but I didn't care. The food was delicious and I had no idea when I'd be able to eat again. It was better to stuff my gut as full as I could and hope I was able to keep it all down.

I'd completed my second bowl when he returned wearing a smirk that made me want to slap him and kiss him at the same time. His emerald green eyes twinkled with what I took to be amusement as he stared at my empty bowl, but he said nothing as he extended his hand to take it from me. As he moved to put the bowl on the nearby table, I noticed he carried a small bundle wrapped in cloth. He returned to my side and handed it to me.

I pulled the ties slowly while I puzzled over what he could be giving me. It was a soft bundle. Could I be so bold as to hope it be clothes? The thought hastened my speed of opening the wrap. An enormous smile consumed my face as I looked down at

neatly folded, one on top of the other- black leather leggings, a tan woolen tunic and a beaded belt.   I smiled my thanks and donned the tunic without hesitation. It reached my mid-thigh, which afforded me enough modesty to stand and step into the leggings. Everything fit as if it was specially made for me.

"Thanks," I mumbled, "They fit perfectly."

"I should hope so," he said, with no further explanation

"Where am I?" I asked, deciding I didn't want to know how he managed to present me with leather pants that fit like they were made for me.

"You're safe," he mumbled as he started back out of the cave.

"Safe... where?" I urged.

"Here," he tossed over his shoulder before disappearing.

I waited for what felt like hours for his return, but to no avail. I had no idea who he was, but he was my only contact at the moment and from what I could tell he was also my savior. I didn't want him to leave me. I didn't want to be left alone. I felt tired and abandoned. I longed to leave the cave and look for civilization; at this point I'd settle for anyone to keep me company. I would have at least explored outside my cozy sanctuary, had I trusted my ribs not to shift and puncture a lung.

Somewhere over time, I managed to relax enough to drift off into sleep. The warmth of the fire and a satisfied belly promoted one of the deepest rests I'd had in ages.

CHAPTER TWO

When I finally roused enough to force myself free from the sweetest slumber I can recall in my twenty-four years of life, it took a bit of struggling to remember where I was. I sat up on the bed and swung my feet over its edge. They barely touched the floor. I didn't recall being so small in it before, but then, I'd been pretty messed up with drugs and injuries.

Injuries.

I remembered my ribs and felt for the bandage beneath my tunic. It was gone. I pulled the tunic up to inspect more closely. Searching the cave interior with my eyes, I was disappointed to find no mirror. I checked myself out as best I could without it. There was no sign of any damage that I could see, nor was there any pain! How had I managed to heal so quickly? It had been quickly, hadn't it? I couldn't tell, since I'd lost all concept of time.

I made note that my rescue was the second miracle to happen since I'd been captured by those grotesque creatures; the first being my rejection in the food line. I said a small silent prayer of thanks. I was pretty sure I'd already done so, but I wanted to thank my god-like savior again with a clear head. I sensed his presence and that he'd been coming and going, but I saw no signs of him at the moment.

I hopped off the bed with more vitality than I'd felt in a long time. What was in that wonderfully delicious stew? I wondered as I padded over to the fire. It was still going strong with signs of recently being tended. I looked around. I was alone.

Feeling energized and curious, I decided to brave the outer limits of the cave. I needed to know where I was so I could make plans on getting home. I really hoped those beasts hadn't teleported me to some obscure location, or worse...planet! Although I knew it could be done, I had no experience with teleporting. It would be difficult for me to get back on my own. Would my altruist be willing to continue his aid and help me get back? Did he even have the ability?

The air felt crisp and cool against my exposed flesh as I stepped out into the moonlight. I estimated it was after midnight. I listened for sounds of life around me, but all was quiet. It looked like the whole world was sleeping. All except me, that is.

I noted the fullness of the brilliant moon. This meant that I'd been in the cave healing and sleeping heavily for about two weeks. I really owed my benefactor a debt of gratitude.

The cave was on the edge of a forest. Tall pines mingled with gnarly oaks and maples. It was a perfectly normal looking forest that gave me no hint at all as to where I was or what era I was in. An owl screeched its presence and startled a small squeal out of me.

"Be careful. We don't want to give away our hiding place," said a rich, sultry voice through the night.

I jumped to look behind me to find my handsome savior with a load of firewood balanced in his arms as if it weighed no more than a sack of feathers.

"Where are we?" I asked.

"Safe for now," he replied as he turned to enter the cave, "unless you keep that howling up."

"It was a little squeal," I muttered as I followed him back inside.

"Haven't you ever heard the saying 'the forest has eyes?'" he chided.

"Is that the same as the hills have eyes?" I said sarcastically.

I was referring to the movie, of course. It was a way of testing things. If I'd gone back in time, he wouldn't have a clue what I was speaking about.

"I saw that film," he said as he dropped the wood next to the fire. "I didn't much care for it."

Okay, so I was still in my own era. That was excellent, but I still had questions such as what was a Dragos? I remembered that word from my nightmare as if it'd been branded on my brain.

"Can I know your name?" I said with more self-confidence than I really possessed. I felt it best to be polite rather than burst into a line of questions about my whereabouts and the creatures that abducted me and then left me for dead.

"Jack," he said, matter-of-factly.

"Nice to meet you Jack," I said as sweetly as I could.

"Is it?" he chuckled with a tone that could only be de-scribed as sarcastic and walked back out of the cave.

I was really growing tired of the way he just up and left as the mood struck him.

"Wait," I commanded with more intensity than I'd intended. It left me a little shaken. I did my best to hide it from him.

He stopped in his tracks, but didn't turn around. I watched his shoulders tense and then loosen again. It was as if he was struggling with what to do while he remained with his back to me.

"Please don't go yet," I said in a gentler tone that I was only able to accomplish after some serious breathing exercises. "I... I'm very confused and lonely and... well I'm a little frightened. I was captured by..."

"By the Dragos," he interjected. "I pulled you from their refuse pile."

The tone of his voice left me uncomfortable. I'd angered him. I wasn't sure what I should say. 'I'm sorry for barking at you and thank you for all you've done' was the most obvious, yet it didn't seem appropriate for the mood, so I said, "I owe you my life," instead.

"You think so?" he almost growled.

Although I was taken aback by his aggressive tone, I refused to be deterred. I was determined to smooth things over. I needed to show him my gratitude; for my sake, if not for his. There was no doubt in my mind that I would have died had he not pulled me from that abhorrent pile of human remains.

"Yes," I said steadily.

"Be careful.... I just might take it," he half whispered before bounding out of the entrance.

Suddenly my legs refused to hold me. I collapsed in a heap.

The thick carpet acted as a barrier between me and the cold earthen ground. I could smell the earth in its fibers, yet it looked fairly new and fresh. I would have pondered on how long the cave served as Jack's plush sanctuary had I not been overwhelmed with his parting comment.

Did I hear him correctly? Did he threaten to take my life? Had he saved me from certain death at the hands of the Dragos only to kill me himself? If I hadn't heard his words with my own ears, I would never have entertained such a thought. He seemed like a perfectly normal man. True, he was a little uncommunicative, but, considering where he'd found me, I assumed he'd seen some trauma of his own. Maybe he also narrowly escaped being food for those beasts. Or... horror of horrors... he was a cannibal and scavenged the remains off the bones of the refuse!

I shook my head. Now I was being ridiculous. If he was a cannibal, he'd have surely eaten me over the course of the last few weeks; not feed me. I forced myself to giggle. It was amazing how the mind could dream up such ridiculous stuff and make it seem real in a flash.

I took a closer look around the interior of the cave that was now my sanctuary. This was clearly someone's home or -at the very least- place of refuge. If Jack hadn't set it up, I was sure he'd used this place for his own. Yet he'd barely spent any time there since I'd arrived. Did he have another dwelling nearby? That didn't seem logical, but then, nothing about what had happened so far seemed logical. Dragos weren't real. They were creatures from fairy tales told around campfires for the purpose of scaring your fellow campers. Since when did creatures in fairy tales come to life?

Several days passed with no words spoken between Jack and me. When I saw or sensed him coming, I feigned sleep in order to avoid speaking with him. I needed time to process the fear his comment instilled in me. It had to be the better part of a week gone by before I started to get restless. I'd completely lost track of time. I had no idea how long I'd actually been in that cave. When did I arrive? I estimated I'd been there a total of three weeks, but was I correct? I kept falling in and out of sleep; staying awake only long enough to fill my stomach with the ever present stew -that I never grew tired of and couldn't seem to get enough of- and then right back into slumber land I went.

"You've been here for six weeks, not three," said a feminine voice from a distance.

Startled, I jumped and quickly looked around, but saw no one.

"Over here dearie," the voice cooed.

I couldn't decide if it was a friendly coo or not.

"You're rather rude, aren't you?" I stated bluntly.

"You're an expert on rudeness?" the owner of the voice spat, clearly annoyed.

"It doesn't take an expert to recognize rude," I replied bravely.

It didn't matter that this was my first and only visitor

other than Jack. Sneaking into the cave and remaining in the shadows was rude and I intended to make that clear.

"You're an ungrateful bitch, aren't you?" the voice said.

"To whom am I being ungrateful and for what? I thanked my rescuer. I see no need to be polite to someone who sneaks in here, reads my mind, and then speaks from the dark recesses of the cave instead of showing himself," I spat.

"Herself, you twit," the voice spat back.

"You sound like a man," I lied.

I'd actually meant to say 'her', but, in my nervousness, I got confused.

"You look like you just escaped Auschwitz!" the voice blurted out.

I had no response for that because I was sure it was true. I stood in stunned silence for a while and then burst out laughing. I mean, seriously...I was arguing with a bodiless voice.

"Touché," I breathed between peals of laughter, "You've got me there."

Before my startled eyes, a glowing translucent ball emerged out of the shadows and slowly grew to enormous size. The larger it got, the opaquer it became. When it reached a size large enough to accommodate a body, a tall, slender, but shapely brunette stepped out and stood not five feet away from me.

I stood mesmerized by the overlarge almond shaped eyes that were perfectly positioned on her small, creamy bronze, oval shaped face. Her pixie type nose looked at home between her smooth, arched brows and full, ruby lips. Had it not been for the pointed ears on the sides of her head, I would have labeled her perfect.

"I'm not perfect either," she chuckled good-naturedly while pulling on her ears and lifting her chiffon gown to display grotesque and hairy feet.

"It's an odd combination," I mused as I slowly admired her slender curves and perfect complexion.

"Not where I come from," she smiled, seemingly unaffected by my comment that most would consider rude.

"I'm from New York. The state, not the city. That's on earth," I replied without thinking.

Between the lizard beasts and this odd looking person, I'd come to the conclusion that I'd left earth for some other planet, but I was surprised to hear myself say it aloud.

"Me too," she chimed. "Earth, that is."

"How can that be?" I asked with genuine surprise.

"Now that's typical," she snorted as she walked to the large, comfortable looking chair by the fire. "You humans are all the same."

"I'm sorry," I said and then chastised myself silently. What in heaven's name was I apologizing for? "It's just that I've never seen anyone from earth that looked like you, so I don't understand how you can claim your look is not an odd combination."

"You can't help it, I suppose," she sighed. "It's just that I hoped you would be different. I mean, it's not like Jack to take in just any stray human." A sparkle of amusement tinted her large eyes as she continued, "It's especially not like him to let them live. You must be too skinny for him too."

"He eats people?" I gasped as my hand flew to my throat. My fears were being confirmed.

"Ha, ha, ha, you're so funny," she chortled, but offered nothing else.

My visitor seemed to know her way around the cave quite well. She produced some herbal tea and two cups from a cupboard I hadn't even thought to investigate. We spent the next few hours sipping tea and getting to know each other. She told me her name was L'oana, a name quite common to her kind. She equated it to Jane or Ann in my language. When I asked her what her kind was, she spat, "Earthling" as if I'd insulted her. I let the topic go for a while and just enjoyed her bubbly conversation. It'd been what seemed like an eternity since I'd had the luxury of enjoying light hearted conversation over a cup of herbal tea. I wasn't in a hurry to give it up.

At some point over the course of our discussions, L'oana grew more comfortable with me. I discovered that my new female friend was well over a century old. She took great pains to explain to me that she belonged to a raced called Squachula. Although they lived upon the planet earth, they lived in an alternate dimension than that of humans.

I learned that, like the Dragos, Squachula had a life expectancy of approximately two-hundred years. This meant she was what we would consider middle aged. I compared her youthful, light hearted actions and appearance to that of a middle aged human and smiled. No wonder we were considered an inferior species.

L'oana enlightened me on the variances of Squachula around the planet. Apparently they differed in race just like humans differed. Some were of highly superior intelligence and skills while others bordered on primitive. She confided that, over the centuries, there were times when they interbred with other species, including the humans, which added to the variances in race. Her race was a product of such interbreeding.

L'oana was not only light hearted, intelligent, and beautiful. She was also highly skilled in the art of teleporting from one dimension to another. She often made trips from inner earth to outer earth; which was how she met Jack.

I learned she was a missionary of sorts. Like humans, Squachula were prey for the Dragos and, therefore, like humans, they wanted them eliminated from their planet. L'oana traveled between planets, by way of teleportation, to assist in the task of weakening the Dragos until the time came that they could be fully driven out. This was a dangerous mission that only a few were allowed to participate in. Although she made light of it, I knew she was more than she was letting on to be.

I mentioned to L'oana the fact that, for centuries, there were sightings on earth of a large, man-like, ape-like beast in various locations of earth. Some called the beast Big Foot. Some called him the Abominable Snow Man. Some called him Sasquatch. All were basically names for the same type of being. She nodded, smiled, and proceeded to tell me that they were of the Squachula breed, but significantly removed from her clan. She equated it to the Chinese of the human race verses the humans from the continent of Africa. They were human, but significantly different in size, shape, coloring, and features. One thing that was similar was their ability to move from one dimension of the earth's etheric layer to the other.

I learned that earth was made up of four vibrational dimensions that housed physical inhabitants. For the most part, the planet looked and behaved the same in each one. They even housed similar, if not identical, plant and animal life. The truest difference was the variance of species of intelligent beings in each level.

The dimensions eventually melded into one within the core of the planet where the vibrations were denser. It was in this area that the Dragos who teleported to earth from other planets dwelled. Their location allowed them to travel into any outer level with ease to capture and accumulate the life they depended upon for sustenance. They were an evil, lizard type humanoid that migrated from another part of the galaxy some millennia past when their own planet got so overpopulated that food became a scarcity. Earth and Kurr weren't the only planets they dispersed their pioneers to, but they proved to be one of the more desirable for the Dragos to inhabit.

I'd had the misfortune of being abducted while walking down a remote section of road in the wee hours of the morning. It turned out that road was one of their favorite locations for acquiring food since it was fairly isolated and easy to remain undetected. I heard discussions during the early hours of my capture that the mountains of Arizona and the Arkansas hot springs were other prime locations. L'oana gave me a detailed list of earth's hot spots for abduction. I burned it into my memory bank and vowed to heed it when and if I ever got back home.

I questioned her method of dealing with the Dragos. Did she fight them head on or was it a sneak attack? To my disappointment, she refused to discuss the topic. I'd gotten all I was going to get about the Dragos out of her for the moment.

I noticed her energy level was fading. She was no longer as bubbly and vivacious when speaking. It was clear she needed a rest. Since I was feeling a bit weary myself, I suggested we take a brief rest. When she acted offended at the concept of my thinking her weak, I emphasized that I was still in the stage of recovery and would appreciate a little down time. This appeased her wounded pride and she eagerly obliged by leaving the cave, stating she'd return in a few hours to continue our conversations.

As I stretched out onto the mattress, that I assumed Jack abandoned in order to accommodate me, I thought of my new found acquaintance. I'd never met someone who wasn't human before. It was an odd experience, but a pleasant one. I sensed she hadn't been completely honest with me. I didn't believe she was from earth and was probably a native of the planet she said I was on at the moment; Kurr. Even so, I liked L'oana. I had very few female friends back home; mainly because we lived in such a remote area and people were not in abundance. I was looking forward to L'oana and I becoming good friends.

As I lay on my back, with my arm resting over my eyes, my mind wandered to thoughts of Jack. I'd seen very little of him since he'd brought me there. He'd entered a few times to deposit firewood, stoke the fire, and stir or freshen my ever present stew with fresh herbs or meat. He said minimal words to me. In fact, I didn't recall him saying much of anything to me since he'd frightened me into thinking him a cannibal.

Of course it was still questionable what he was. After all, didn't L'oana make that odd comment about him leaving me alive? Had I survived the clutches of the Dragos only to die at the hands of Jack? If that was the case, if he truly planned on killing me, what was he waiting for? Was his dragging things out as a sick form of torture? L'oana said I'd been in the cave for six weeks or so. Why would he forfeit his home, monitor the fire, and keep my food well stocked if he planned on killing me?

I slid my hands to over my stomach and hips. Had I gained a little weight? The tunic and pants he'd presented when I'd first arrived allowed room for it. It sure felt like I had. I cupped my tiny breasts. They felt like they too had increased in size, if only a little. Was that it? Was he fattening me up for the kill? My heart reacted to the thought so powerfully, I thought it was going to escape my chest on its own and run away. The pain in my ribcage was excruciating. I was having a heart attack! I didn't need to worry about being killed and eaten by anyone. I'd be dead in a matter of minutes from a failed heart.

The raspy sound of my gasping for air that echoed off the tapestry covered stone pounded at me like a hammer against a dull, rusty nail. It brought back memories of my aunt's mini-farm and her incessant attempts to recycle the old barn wood; pulling and prying at century old nails while doing her best to keep the wood from splitting under the nail's screeching resistance.

"What's wrong?" said a deep male whisper from seemingly nowhere.

The voice sounded more in my head than in my ear. It was familiar, yet I couldn't quite place it.

I sat up in a panic and looked around for the source of the voice but saw no one.

"Come out!" I demanded.

"I'm right here," Jack said calmly from the cave entrance. "What's wrong?"

"How did you know?" I whispered.

His ability to come and go so quickly and silently was unsettling.

"What's wrong?" he insisted.

I backed up as far as I could on the narrow mattress while I searched for an escape route. There was none. The only way out was the entrance and Jack was blocking it.

"I don't like to keep repeating myself," he growled. "I asked you a question and I expect an answer."

"Nothing!" I burst out, "I'm fine."

"Your heart is ready to explode. What frightened you?" he persisted.

I held his gaze for a few seconds that felt like an eternity, while I debated what to do. I fought the urge to fall into his serious emerald eyes. There was something about them that pulled me in, hugged me, and then debated about letting me go. Or at least that's how it felt.

I shook my head and decided to tell him the truth.

"You frighten me," I said in a voice that was barely above a whisper.

"I don't understand. Haven't I been good to you? Why would I frighten you?" he asked.

He looked genuinely puzzled.

"You made a comment about taking my life a while back and then L'oana said...," I began.

"L'oana!" he bellowed. "When was that she-wolf here?"

"Not long ago," I winced.

"I should have known," he hissed as he stomped back out of the cave.

I wasn't sure if I should still be frightened for myself or perhaps transfer that concern toward my new found friend. She seemed like such a fun and agreeable sort. I couldn't imagine why Jack would be so unhappy to discover she'd paid me a visit.

He'd called her a she-wolf. I thought it odd, but it wasn't long before it was made clear.

L'oana dashed past me with lightning speed; followed by Jack who was traveling equally as fast. I had to rub my eyes to make sure I'd seen correctly. When I was in focus again, I gasped in horror at the sight of L'oana pinned against the thick tapestry wall. She was hanging onto dear life with Jack's hand clamped around her throat. Her head was tipped to the side and his teeth were elongated, ready to sink into her tender flesh.

He was a vampire! That couldn't be, could it? I thought vampires were products of folk lore. Of course, I didn't believe in life on other planets and lizard people either, until I was kidnapped by them and brought to a planet called Kurr. I wondered what else in fairy tales was not really a tale, but fact.

I screamed for Jack to stop with every bit of air my lungs contained, filled them back up, and did it again. Eventually –and thankfully before he'd sank his teeth into her beautiful, perfect flesh- my screams penetrated his thick skull and he looked over at me. Seeing my terrified expression must have brought him back to his senses because he retracted his fangs with surprising speed and released his captive.

She raced to my side and huddled behind me as best she could while breathing heavily. I patted her arm reassuringly while I glared at him defiantly. It was clear to me he was not human. Real or not, from what I could see he was a vampire. Surprisingly, I wasn't frightened. In fact, I was relieved. At least he wasn't fattening me up to eat my flesh.

"What's your problem?" L'oana spat from behind me.

"You stay away from her!" Jack bellowed.

"Why is she so special? Why haven't you killed her?" L'oana hissed.

I didn't like the tone L'oana was using. It seemed far too hostile when referring to me and my possible demise. It actually sounded as if she resented the fact that Jack had nursed me back to health instead of draining me of my blood. This was a twist in personality that I didn't like.

"I warned you," Jack hissed.

"I don't understand," I interjected. I was shocked when I looked at L'oana to see the fiery red that glowed in her eyes. Her lovely face was distorted to the point it was borderline unrecognizable. The animal in her was coming through loud and clear. "What are you?" I gasped.

"She's trouble," Jack said.

He reached for my arm and pulled me off the bed with such force that I propelled into his chest. My muscles tensed with apprehension about being held so closely by a blood sucking creature. When I could finally move past my fear, I noted he felt surprisingly warm and supple. Whenever I'd read or watched shows about vampires, or listened to the tales of them from the neighborhood story tellers, they were always described as being cold, hard, and corpse-like. Had I not witnessed his fangs with my own eyes, I would have never believed Jack to be anything but a human.

"You're warm," I thought aloud.

He chuckled and wrapped his arms around me protectively while saying, "You've been listening to the story tellers."

"Did they tell you he's of the devil?" L'oana shouted. "He's evil. Don't be fooled by his warmth. It's the fire of hell that burns in his body. That's what you're feeling!"

Jack's body stiffened.

"How did you find us?" he demanded.

"Ha! Do you really think you can hide from me? Do you really think you can hide from them? You fool!" she said in a tone that sounded almost animal.

"What are you?" I asked again.

"You are looking into the face of the demon's woman," Jack explained. "She neglected to camouflage her grotesqueness. Usually she appears in human form to humans." He jutted his chin in her direction, "You surprise me, L'oana. Can it be you're slipping?"

"The demon's woman?" I gasped.

My confusion was clearly apparent.

"His queen if you please," she hissed. "And he's no more a demon than you are, Jack. You're just jealous because you and I didn't work out."

"Watch what you say, L'oana," he spat.

I watched L'oana coil her body in a snakelike fashion as she transformed from the beautiful woman with odd ears and feet to a reptilian androgynous creature with an incredibly long forked tongue that darted in and out with lightning speed. I threw my hands over my mouth to stifle the scream that I couldn't help emitting and buried my face as best I could into Jack's chest. I'd spent hours talking to this creature and actually considered her a new found friend and ally.

"Be gone with you or feel my wrath!" Jack said between clenched teeth.

"Who is she to you?" L'oana hissed. "She's a scrawny thing and a poor excuse for a woman in any species. Why do you protect her so?"

Peeking through my fingers, I was mesmerized by the sight of this snake like creature moving its mouth and tongue in a manner that formed clearly understandable –if not lispy- words. In fact, I was so engrossed in the scene before me that

I almost missed his response.

"She's not your concern," he bellowed with an authoritative tone.

"But, she's yours?" L'oana hissed.

"She's my ward," he said defiantly.

"Your what?" I wailed as I pushed my head back to look up at him. How preposterous was that statement? I'd never set eyes on him before in my life. How could he claim that I was his ward?

My mother and father were killed in a car crash when I was still in diapers. I was raised by my mother's sister, Jenny. Three years my senior, her son, James, acted as my protector throughout the years. How could he possibly claim me as his ward? It just didn't make sense.

Jack rested his chin on the top of my head as he hugged me close. Even in my distress, I couldn't help noticing how natural it felt. I found myself breathing in unison with the rhythm of the beating of his heart. It was an odd realization. It was like we were an extension of each other. How could that be? I barely knew him, yet I felt like I'd known him forever. It was unsettling.

I pushed myself away from him with a force I didn't know I possessed.

"Let go of me," I said with surprising bravado.

I spared a quick glance at L'oana -who had returned to human form and was now laughing hysterically at the situation- before my focus returned to Jack. He seemed undisturbed by my refusal to be held. Instead, he also looked amused. I would have been annoyed at the smirk on his beautiful mouth, had I not been held captivated by his deep, alluring eyes.

After what seemed like an eternity, I managed to regain control and pulled myself to full height before stating as firmly as I could, "You have some explaining to do."

The Princess and the Vampire King
ISBN: 978-0692598214